"The narrator of Sartori's hilarious, insightful novel, his first to be published in English, is none other than God, a proper monotheistic deity stirred in a very human way by one of his own creations. . . . On page after laugh-out-loud page, this articulate God—and author—cover just about every cynical and lofty concept concerning one's own existence that humans ever pondered. This is an immensely satisfying feat of imagination."

PUBLISHERS WEEKLY,
STARRED REVIEW

"Who better to reflect on the state of the planet than its creator? *I Am God* is by turns funny, sad, outrageous, and tender—a cosmic romp."

ELIZABETH KOLBERT, PULITZER PRIZE-WINNING
AUTHOR OF *THE SIXTH EXTINCTION*

"A highly original novel, showing that there is, thankfully, more to Italian fiction than Elena Ferrante."

HOWARD DAVIES, *FINANCIAL TIMES*
BEST BOOKS OF 2019: CRITICS' PICKS

"This novel is an utterly serious and wildly comic test of the strange idea we take for granted in reading prose fiction—the pretense of the omniscient narrator. . . . By speaking in the voice of God, Sartori has simplified the premise and complicated the result of writing as such. . . . This God [is] the brilliant, hilarious, and utterly believable creation of Sartori."

JAMES LIVINGSTON, *THE NEW REPUBLIC*

"*I Am God* is like a mirthful dream made real by the ingenuity of Sartori's prose and Randall's splendidly pointed and sly translation."

"In this riotous philosophical romp, Sartori has invented an omniscient narrator like no other and an identity crisis with truly cosmic implications. Poignant, hilarious, and serious by turns, this is a jeu d'esprit with both heart and mind."

"Delightful, strikingly current, infectiously readable. . . . The irrational pull of erotic love has never had a funnier incarnation than the one in *I Am God*. . . . Sartori pulls out all the stops in a long tradition of first-person confessions by the Creator, beginning with the Ten Commandments . . . Transcending mere blasphemy, Sartori refuses to take the Lord's name in vain. Every little chapter of *I Am God* forces the reader to decide whether laughter or outrage is the proper response. There's a grand tradition of Italian artists (Dante, Michelangelo, Verdi) who shock us with their new and unsettling images of God. In his modest and profound way, Sartori belongs in this terrific company."

"What a funny, smart book that tweaks a kind of philosophical view of 'God's' work against the quandary of said God falling in love with an odd young woman scientist, which throws him off his game. You've got to love both his problem and his surprise at his compulsion to drift back into it regularly while he discourses on the waywardness of humans in general. Giacomo Sartori is a wizard here with the way his light touch in fact is anything but, providing readers with a most entertaining read full of necessary, shall we say, unexamined hubris on the part of all characters within our author's focus. What a refreshing delight."

SHERYL COTLEUR,
COPPERFIELD'S BOOKS (SEBASTOPOL, CA)

"A playful, exciting, mockingly modern voice, translated, what's more, by one of the few translators who can really make the Italian vernacular sing truly and fluently in English."

TIM PARKS, AUTHOR OF *ITALIAN WAYS*
AND *ITALIAN NEIGHBORS*

"*I Am God* is compulsively readable, with passages so crisp and funny that readers will want to read them aloud. Sartori, an Italian scientist, has written a book that, beyond its philosophical wit, draws attention to hypocrisy in all forms."

CINDY PAULDINE, THE RIVER'S END
BOOKSTORE (OSWEGO, NY)

"God, famously upstaged by Satan in Milton's Paradise Lost, gives a livelier performance in Giacomo Sartori's *I Am God* (Restless, Feb.), his first novel to be translated from Italian into English."

MATT SEIDEL, *PUBLISHERS WEEKLY*
WRITERS TO WATCH: SPRING 2019

BUG

ALSO BY
GIACOMO SARTORI

I Am God

AVAILABLE IN ITALIAN

Tritolo (TNT)

Sacrificio (Sacrifice)

Rogo (At the Stake)

Anatomia della battaglia (The Anatomy of the Battle)

Cielo nero (Black Heavens)

Autismi (Autisms)

GIACOMO SARTORI

BUG

· *A Novel* ·

Translated from the Italian
by Frederika Randall

RESTLESS BOOKS
BROOKLYN, NEW YORK

Copyright © 2019 Giacomo Sartori
Published by arrangement with The Italian Literary Agency
Translation copyright © 2021 Frederika Randall

First published as *BACO* by Exòrma Edizioni, Rome, 2019

First Restless Books paperback edition February 2021

Paperback ISBN: 9781632062741
Library of Congress Control Number: 2020948972

This book is supported in part by an award from the National Endowment for the Arts.

This book has been published with a translation grant awarded by the Italian Ministry of Foreign Affairs and International Cooperation.

Cover design by Matt Dorfman
Set in Garibaldi by Tetragon, London
Printed in the United States of America

1 3 5 7 9 10 8 6 4 2

Restless Books, Inc.
232 3rd Street, Suite A101
Brooklyn, NY 11215

www.restlessbooks.org
publisher@restlessbooks.org

CONTENTS

SUMMER

BUG

WINTER

LIKE A BANK SHOT CAROMING
OFF THE RAIL

THE RUSSIAN SEMI didn't brake because that Sunday, every-thing had gone haywire right from the start. Haywire on high and down below: sky spinning like an angry sea, floodwaters making mud whirlpools on the road, beehives thrumming under the rickety awning, even our pellet stove stubbornly refusing to light. Imagine what it was like inside Mamma's head, brimming with worries and words she was getting ready to say.

You couldn't see a thing in that downpour, and the Ukrainian driving the Russian semi didn't even try to brake. *Like I look through the porthole of a washing machine*, he said, in his language that nobody understood.

Earlier, inside the former chicken coop where we live, it felt like a waterfall had been loosed, like icy rain might drill straight through the corrugated steel roof. There weren't any gutters, but even if there had been, even if it had been a real house, a wall of water still would have been coming down in front of the bayonet windows. The wet knives were stabbing hard; even though I can't hear high-pitched sounds, the racket they made shot up my legs and backbone into my brain. Nobody was talking, it was all shouting.

There at home, what we call home, you could see your breath, it was so cold. With a normal stove, all you need is a match and some paper, but ours is a smart stove: it will light only when the mini-sensors give the go-ahead and the regulation and machine-learning programs are all in accord. IQ tapped and re-tapped the keys on the control panel, the way an astronaut who's become isolated from the rest of humanity will try something merely to try it. But the wood pellets just sat there, glum and immobile.

Mamma was in a hurry to leave for her monthly meeting. Last summer, seventeen families died and another five in the autumn because the bees that had survived the neonicotinoids were then hit with the varroa. But even in the other colonies, the apiculturists were sweeping up the cold, dead bees with shovels. So the meeting was extremely important, they had to do battle with death. And the president of the regional bee-keepers' association is Mamma, not one of the big boys who rely on government handouts and cut their honey with some inferior Chinese product. The weight of those dead bees, and even the ones that were just suffering, was on her shoulders.

In her head, she'd already left home; she was going over what she was planning to say. Their assemblies are terribly stormy; there's always someone who disagrees with this or that point, who wants the total opposite of what everyone else does. It's always up to her to fend off the worst attacks and convince the stubbornest ones. However, she couldn't of course leave home until Papa got here. She was a bull ready to charge at any handkerchief she saw waving.

Even under cover from the rain the atoms in the air were fizzing uneasily and my red blood cells were dancing along with them. The artificial neurons of the stove's control system had gone on strike, and as for Mamma's neurons, the sparks were flying.

Only my father could have made the pellet stove come to life. He's the one who wrote the program that tracks the number of times the front door opens, and for how long. IQ just added a machine-learning element. But Papa hadn't arrived yet because he had to do some urgent thing for Nutella. Mamma had smoke coming out of her ears, even though she's a Buddhist and Buddhists generally remain cool. She detests Nutella, and the way she sees it, if my father's involved, it's not going to work.

Grandfather might have been able to calm the waters. But he'd been classifying transparent worms all night long, so we absolutely couldn't call him. And then there's his famous asthma that's always getting in the way. Anyway, Mamma had already asked Papa, and you can't brush the positive wire against the negative or you'll get a short circuit. You have to keep them well apart.

At a certain point the clouds parted in front of the mountainside, the way when you make a wild move your clothes gap to expose some skin, and the snow was right there where the woods begin, it looked like you could touch it. But then the grayness closed over a new wall of water. If the snow had really arrived it would have buried all that wet and turmoil because snow is seraphic, it pacifies the molecules of things and people. It actually comes to keep us warm, but prefers to appear chilly and indifferent.

Ever more impressive walls of water were preparing to carry off the chicken coop, my bones were humming, and Papa still hadn't come. Mamma says when you want him to beat it, he doesn't budge, and when you're waiting for him to arrive, he's off somewhere up to no good. He'd promised—he's a wonder at promises—but in actual fact he hadn't even sent a message saying he'd be late. And he wasn't answering his phone.

I'm gonna kill the guy, Mamma said.

She was also irked at my grandfather because whenever some glitch occurs she suspects he's equally to blame; he's only concerned about his great tome on worms, she thinks. Once in a while she looked out toward the parking area at the other end of this tumbledown house of ours, as if staring deep into a tunnel, and thought of him. I can see what her synapses are imparting, although some people say I'm making it up.

My brother says there must be some kind of programming bug in the system that runs the stove, or else some malware. He thinks that's the problem, not the neural networks he installed to promote machine learning. The segments of the program Papa wrote are competing with one another, he thinks. I was surprised to see him puzzled, he's usually on top of everything and makes certain you know it.

My mother wasn't listening because she can't stand micro-electronics, never could. For her, real life is cabbages and radishes and, of course, bees. She was staring at the time on

8

her phone and struggling to breathe, thinking about my father. *When you need him that idiot always gives you a kick in the ass*, she was thinking.

Actually she was nervous because her bank account was deep in the red. This year the honey had earned nothing but she still had to pay off those ominous stacks of invoices, and then she got wiped out by the homeopathic remedies for the varroa mites. Useless homeopathic remedies.

The thing about the television had been weighing on her too. We've never had a TV because she's opposed to them, like she's opposed to Nutella, but two days ago one arrived. A very nice 28" model with an internet connection, an excellent brand. A jewel of a TV, anyone would agree. Remove the packaging and install, easy. She, however, told the Albanian driving the van that she hadn't ordered it and she didn't want it. He replied, with his foreign hand signals, that her name was on the order slip, as well as our address.

After careful study, the order slip divulged that the TV had indeed been bought using her name and paid for, too. With her credit card. Mamma nearly fainted when it emerged that I had ordered it and used her card. She couldn't believe I would do such a thing—after all my promises, she said. More than enraged, she was dejected, which was even worse. *You're out of your mind, kiddo*, she said, her curls swinging this way and that.

I myself had trouble believing I had done something of the kind, after solemnly swearing to be good. I certainly hadn't counted on how she would react, sinking into this swamp of despair, her sad, sad eyes. But what has been done cannot be undone. Words can cover up many atrocities, but they can't reboot the past, the way you do with a video game when you begin again. *I shouldn't have*, I said to myself. *I'm a moron, a stone-deaf moron.*

The rain sounded like applause. Applause is something I can't hear, but when the whole room begins to vibrate I sense it perfectly, it reverberates in my chest and sets off visions in red. Those hands were clapping to celebrate the rising tension of this perfect family tableau. The grand finale, it seemed, was on the way.

My father still hadn't appeared, and our breath continued to make white globes in the waiting room. In the kitchen Grandmother was hunched over, looking terrorized. Poor thing, she loves the sun and cicadas; we have a plan to move her to the South.

Mamma didn't want to leave me without an adult, she says that every time she's not around they have to take me bleeding to the hospital. Or I might commit one of my doozies and risk attracting the carabinieri. IQ, rather than keep an eye on me, has his head glued to his supercomputer, she says. And God knows how much she trusts me after the bombshell about the TV she had to send back.

My brother had spent the previous evening going through the electronic waste bin at the recycling center, a flashlight on his forehead. He came back with a shopping cart full of junk and sat right down again to his encrypted chat with the other hackers. The discussion about Bayer hadn't calmed down at all; if anything, it was even more fiery.

IQ is a statue, he never loses his cool, but when it comes to hacking, he really throws himself into it. I mean, he chose the handle Robin Hood, not Peter Pan. He thinks they should carry out a major attack, defacing the Bayer website and disabling their computer system. An action in grand style, undertaken by many militants and using all the resources at their disposal, with the aim of extracting their secret files about the bees. He thinks that's the only way the Bayer bosses can be nailed to their responsibilities and forced to reverse their policies.

On the other hand, a German guy considered by all to be a real guru maintains that the best strategy would be to slip in unnoticed, calling no attention to themselves. Because he's German, he assumes he knows more about Bayer's defense systems than the others do, a fact that annoys my brother. The American famous for various incursions into US government systems was pretty much in agreement with the German, however he insisted it was extremely important to be sure some kid didn't do something stupid that could put him in jeopardy, and so they must be cautious.

Now twenty tons of steel riding on a tsunami of water cannot be stopped by anyone, and that's a fact. Even supposing that between the crazy curtains of rain, the Ukrainian truck driver without a regular job contract had spotted the little Nissan Micra coming onto the motorway about to cut him off. Mamma was driving slowly, all Buddhists do, and that morning she was going even more slowly than usual because you couldn't see much with that rain. And what was more, the fight with Papa had upset her.

Her right hand was hurting pretty badly because before my father arrived, she'd gotten furious with me. She'd bandaged the hand herself, using her left, and it wasn't at all professional-looking. The problem was that she'd found a one-kilo tub of Nutella hidden behind Grandmother in the kitchen, and she had immediately stomped into my cell to get an explanation. She was enraged, the dark curls on her head were going up and down like threatening door knockers. *You promised me!* she shouted. *You swore you would never stuff yourself with Nutella again!*

In sign language I told her that I knew nothing about that half empty tub of Nutella, but even I could see that my line of defense was extremely weak. She knew very well that Papa had given it to me, and when I said nothing, she grew more and more irritated. Too much is too much even for the most Buddhist of Buddhists, especially when they are very tired and hassled. *You're going to pay for this*, she said, her jaw locked in rage.

You're a liar, she said. *You're unbelievably full of it.* And then I had the brilliant idea of biting her, biting her until I could taste the blood between my teeth, which was probably the very least good thing to do on a morning like that. Also because it had been quite a while since it had happened, and we had all figured it would never happen again.

The Russian semi slammed into the Micra like a bank shot caroming off the rail, and Mamma's little old car darted forward, looking for a place to hide. But there was no place to hide, just galvanized steel guardrails on each side, and it bounced back and forth from left to right like a drunk. Then the little car calmed down, as if it had decided to be wise and consider the pros and cons of this dramatic situation.

At that moment the semi, its twenty tons not even trying to brake, caught up with the Micra and hit it front on—headed the wrong way as it was. After that second blow the car flew backward, the way you would if you were regretting your strategy up to now. It slammed into something on the right and something on the left and finally ended up crushed between the behemoth and the guardrail, a tiny pebble blocking a giant set of gears.

Papa thinks that with driverless technology, a disaster like this would never have happened. The Micra would have sensed the truck, and the truck the Micra, and the two would have come to an agreement on what to do next. He thinks you have to be crazy to go on using manual controls on motor vehicles like they did a century ago, endangering yourself and others. By now autonomous systems can handle automobiles very safely; the technology is mature, he says. The human brain can make a whole bunch of mistakes while an integrated circuit never errs, he says. Best of all would be to hook up human neurons with artificial ones, that way there wouldn't be any more problems.

When he comes out with this stuff, Grandpa just stares at him as if he were a Martian who's just landed and is already brainwashing the first child he meets. Grandpa thinks he shouldn't say things like that, things that risk harming my nervous system that's already so "dot dot dot." Papa just laughs and says there's no way it could get any worse.

I was spying on what IQ was up to via my own computer when they telephoned asking to speak to Mamma's husband. Papa said there was no husband, they were divorced. *If you want, I can even tell you why*, he said. He always likes to make it clear that he wasn't the one who filed for divorce. And he likes to joke around. He even joked around with Mamma when, that awful morning, he finally arrived home dripping wet on his smart scooter, and the poor thing went into hysterics. And that's why what happened, happened—you can't just accuse me of making things up and ignore the evidence. So anyway, it was the highway police on the phone informing us that there had been a very serious accident. And although Mamma was in critical condition, they'd taken her to the hospital in an ambulance, because the helicopter couldn't take off. At which point Papa called a taxi, because he doesn't have a driver's license.

AN AMPHORA BURIED IN
A SUNKEN SHIP

DEAR MAMMA, this is a message that I won't send you, because certain things shouldn't travel by fiber optics, they're too damaging. They're like those bombs that are better off existing only in the movies, so they don't hurt any real people. Logo and I discussed this until we were both exhausted, and this is the compromise we reached.

She insisted and insisted, she said that writing you a full report was exactly what I needed. And so forth and so on. But I stood firm, I felt very sure of myself. Certain things that happen can only be captured in words if the thing is to remain locked up in an encrypted electronic archive, never to be looked at and not getting out and about online or anywhere else.

So we agreed that she would write down what I told her in sign language, but then these letters would be parked in my computer and remain on file there until the end of time. Like an ancient amphora buried in a sunken ship in some deep ocean trench. She's not very happy about it, I can tell from the face she's making right now, but you know what, she'll get over it.

The thing is, yesterday was a load of caca right from the minute school began. First we had a lesson on the Sumerians. I like the Egyptians, not the Sumerians, end of story. Everybody has their favorite team and hopes the others will lose. And even if I was interested I wouldn't have understood much, because the teacher with his piggy cartoon head was facing the other way as he spoke. The vibrations of his lowest-pitched remarks came up my femur bones through my feet, but from there to really being able to follow him was a stretch. It's not that he doesn't pay attention to me, but he thinks the reason I don't keep the stupid hearing aids on is so I don't have to listen to him, and therefore it's pointless to make sure I can always see his lips.

And then we had a lesson on irregular verbs, and I wasn't too involved in that either. I already have a lot of trouble with the regular ones. Still, it's an exaggeration to say I was slapping my hand on the desk like someone trying to kill flies, and making faces to get my classmates to laugh, as the piggy with the round glasses claimed. It's not pleasant to be publicly slandered, it's really very unfair.

Just to make things worse, this was followed by an hour of the nasty English teacher who looks like a coat hanger with clothes hanging off it. My legs were so wound up that I couldn't even sit down, maybe because I'm always being told off for supposedly moving around too much. I told myself that it was very important to resist, to limit my pacing around to the absolute minimum. *Once you step onto the path of progress, you'll keep going forward out of sheer momentum*, I said to myself, thinking of all the promises I'd made.

The English teacher was toggling between the rows of desks, talking and asking surprise questions. I could see her bony back, her switchblade shoulders, her shrunken behind, but her carp's mouth only appeared from time to time, as if playing hide-and-seek. I certainly couldn't make out anything she said in that high-pitched voice. The support teacher with the tufts of fur above his knuckles was supposed to be there to help me, but as usual he'd called in sick.

The Shakespearean skeleton continued to shamble around, convinced of course that the shambler was me. My synapses were getting very irritable. And just then, the coat hanger in the flowery blouse materialized in front of me. She asked me a question in English and I didn't understand. She repeated the question with a look that said I was less than dog dung in her eyes, and once again, I was floating in a thick white fog.

The hamster with the orange gym shoes who sits on my left began to laugh. Without even thinking about it, I leaned over and bit him on the ear. I'm not sure why I chose the ear, some things just happen.

Now that I had the ear of the orange-shoed rodent between my teeth, I wasn't letting go. This was no hit-and-run nip, it was the canine grip of a very angry dog that doesn't give up quickly. My incisors squeezed his earlobe and he was screaming like an eagle. In my sternum, I could feel that he was using the full power of his lungs. Maybe it was the fact he was shrieking that kept me from letting go and actually made me bite harder. The top part of his ear reminded me of the beef medallions with the chewy edges they used to serve for lunch in elementary school.

The English teacher began to pull on my arm. Or rather, I felt something yanking at me and when I swiveled my eyes around to look, I saw it was her. This made me lose it; she wasn't supposed to interfere between me and my classmate. She kept on tugging as if she wanted to pull my forearm right off, like a chicken wing.

For that nitwit to lay hands on me was just the thing to irritate my red blood cells and send them to my head. The more she squeezed my arm with that comic-book skeleton claw of hers, the more I bore down with my teeth. Obviously. My mouth tasted iron, and my arm hurt, but I didn't let go.

Then she had the brilliant idea of grabbing my hair with her other claw. She pulled hard, like she intended to pull it out. At this point, I let the ear go. My mouth snapped around the other way, and I bit the side of her hand, the way you bite into a sandwich when you're very hungry. Only for a second, because the bony consistency was quite repellent.

The ugly little rat with the phosphorescent shoes was now very puzzled, and sniveling with his mouth wide open. His hand was clapped to his ear in case it fell off, his eyes were squeezed tight, and his nose was wrinkled up like a real two-year-old.

It made me laugh to see him like that, and I showed him the finger. He jumped back, hand on the other ear in case I decided to bite that one too. I couldn't help but smirk at that; a rodent's not supposed to be afraid of being gnawed at. There was a math book on my desk and I tossed it at him. The way he fell backward, you'd think I'd thrown a sack of cement at him. As he was falling, he hit his head on the window frame.

The uproar in the classroom was incredible, I've never seen such chaos. Everyone was on their feet, some knocked their chairs over, books and pencil cases fell to the floor. They were screaming like it was a terrorist attack. I could feel the screaming in my lungs and my temples; the floor shook with something like seismic tremors.

The English teacher was now leaning against the blackboard, one hand pressed against her pointy chin, to keep her jaw closed, I guess, and the other arm behind her body. My unfortunate classmate seemed to have started a fad. She was as red and shiny as a hot pepper, and seemed to be having trouble breathing.

I gestured with my arms to signal it was nothing serious, and suggested she start the lesson again. My words probably weren't perfectly clear; I myself wasn't all that calm. So I repeated what I'd said, trying to shape those resistant blobs of air in my mouth as nicely as I could. *Shall we go on with the English thing?* I said, waving my arms. Often when I say something everyone giggles, but no one was laughing now. They were looking at me like I was an extraterrestrial carrying an alien weapon, an automatic electro-ray shooter.

I signaled to my classmates to be seated again. The comedy was over, we should now resume the lesson, even if it was boring. The excitement was over. *Hey guys, it was nothing serious*, I said.

The teacher, rather than take the situation in hand, was creeping backward with her eyes on me all the time, like a lion tamer in trouble. Crab-walking backward to the door, she slipped out faster than an eel.

I kept waving my arms trying again to get the kids to calm down, but nobody was listening. And they were all keeping their distance from me, you'd think I had a contagious disease. They acted like orange-shoes was dead, when it had only been a little blow. I didn't know what to do now, they were so weird. I wished I could come up with one of those numbers of mine that makes everybody die laughing, but nothing at all came to mind.

I would have liked to explain my perspective on all this, but I didn't have many words in my head, and above all, I lacked the calm to put them in the proper order. Sometimes the words spring up like monkeys and start crawling all over the place, they won't be mollified. With sign language it wouldn't have been a problem, but nobody at school understands it.

Two custodians appeared in a great hurry and grabbed me like pincers: the one on the right had my arm in a clamp, the one on the left, who's as big as an armoire and usually very friendly to me, had his huge arm firmly twisted around mine.

It wasn't easy to walk, with a giant lifting me off the ground on one side and a crazy man pulling me the other way. But it didn't seem to matter. They dragged me to the vestibule outside the principal's office. When we got there, they knocked, but nothing happened. They knocked again, but the door stayed shut and the great man didn't come out. So we stood there waiting, statues, on foot.

My infallible intuition told me that the English teacher was in the principal's office, that her reverse motion had brought her here. If I weren't deaf, I might have had the proof, but my condition made scientific certainty impossible. I tried to inch backward and sit on one of the yellow chairs against the wall, but the two custodians held me tight. Apparently we three imbeciles had to remain standing there until the door opened, even if we had to wait ten years.

Finally the big boss came out, and in fact the cranky teacher was lurking behind him in his office. She looked like the Virgin Mary at a funeral for anorexics, but proud of her injured hand. To add to the drama she was wearing a sling made out of a scarf knotted at the neck. How she got organized so quickly I have no idea. I smiled at her to break the ice, but she just leaned her head back further and widened her eyes. You'd think I was an Islamist wearing an explosives belt.

The sumo wrestler of a principal told me to sit down and announced I had done something very serious. Very, very serious. He enunciated his words quite clearly; I might still be dangerous. I tried to explain that what had happened wasn't anything special, it was they who were making a big deal of it. But first, I don't handle spoken language very well, and then I was dealing with a know-it-all blowhard who never stops talking for a second. And of course, my support teacher was nowhere to be seen.

One hand on his belly, the principal told me I was suspended and they would have to evaluate whether the conditions existed for me to be readmitted. As if being readmitted was a very unlikely possibility, pretty much impossible. I said I was quite happy to get out of there, and he stared at me as if I was speaking a foreign tongue.

Your teachers are not very good, I added, indicating the skeleton with her arm in a sling. Once again, he didn't seem to catch what I said.

Just then Grandpa showed up in his Cuban guerrilla jacket. I was mighty pleased to finally see someone who qualified as a human being and wanted to run over and give him a hug. But he, too, seemed to think a tragedy had taken place, and he was keeping his distance. Which surprised me because he says you must always rebel against authority, whether it's those bullies of the police or our present masters of the universe, the engineers my father idolizes. He was very pale and looked older than usual.

Logo says I shouldn't think I'm always right. I have to be more objective. Pretend to be a TV camera recording the scene. She insists on this and makes me repeat it, she wants me to say it, in sign language or in my own twisted way so she can write it down.

Often I don't fully recognize the consequences of my actions, that's the problem: those are the words she wants me to dictate to her. It's worrying when a person bites a teacher, or even just a classmate, she thinks. And so I say, or rather I sign, the words—but I'm not convinced, there's no use pretending I am.

Massaging her blond baby-doll cheeks, she says we'll have to go over it again. She thinks my father is wrong not to be around more, he should be spending more time with me. I object that

I'm not a printed circuit board; I say the only things that thrill him are complex integrated circuits.

All the more reason he should be looking after you, she says and I can't tell from her face whether she thinks I'm kidding or not. I have to admit, I like it that she's not sure.

On the way home from school Grandpa didn't mention the usual worms, he told me that my father had cut short his business trip to the Nutella headquarters in Alba and would be back tonight. He didn't say anything about the principal's crazy threats, but I'm pretty sure he was thinking about them. I guessed he wasn't completely convinced by my version of the facts. *Now don't bite your arm*, he said.

A DOG RUNNING OUT
OF THINGS TO DO

WHEN IQ CAME IN from the weekly hacker meeting yesterday, he, too, figured out that we'd be waiting for the evening pizza until the next climate shift took place. *Just finishing something and then I'm coming*, Papa's message had said. Some words are like those butterflies that have huge eyespots on their wings that aren't really eyes, they can make you think whatever they want.

Idly scratching his head (which always looks two sizes too big), IQ asked me how I was doing. He said it out loud, because Logo has convinced him I need to train at speaking. As usual the pellet stove wasn't working and I could see the sentences break away from his lips and float on the air. I feel like a queen bee, I told him; not going to school definitely has enormous advantages. My breath clouds were smaller, I don't speak very well.

Then IQ went to his cell and started doing what he does with his supercomputer, the one that looks like a powerful chest of drawers with no drawers. I passed by the kitchen to grab the tub of Nutella that was parked behind Grandmother, check-ing how much was left with scientific attention. I followed IQ somewhat listlessly, a dog running out of things to do. Seating myself on a pile of old electronics magazines, I studied him while I scraped the spoon around the jar in slow motion to make the soothing sensation last. He hadn't yet taken off the Hun's helmet he wears when he rides his super souped-up electric scooter, but he was stripped to his T-shirt because the superPC gives off a lot of heat. He looked like a praying Hun on his knees in front of the keyboard. He's really very different from me, no surprise that everyone says so.

And yet the ingredients are the same, and so is the recipe. Same spermatozoa, same belly, same chicken coop converted into a house, same child-rearing doctrines. The only difference lies in the number of parents, because in my case there is only one. But I came forth deaf, my red blood cells hysterical, while he's as pacific as a dead calm sea, highly gifted, and wins all the prizes.

Actually, I was feeling a little sad that Mamma's always in the hospital and never, ever here. *Because when you're home, it's all different*, I said, talking to her like I sometimes do. *When you're here there are smells of things to eat, and signs of activity, of fun*, I said.

It's like comparing a beach in the middle of winter when the sea is raging and the few hardy souls outside are battling with the beach umbrellas, with the light-hearted charm of a summer's day, I told her.

Maybe you'll even return this very evening, and tomorrow you'll make one of your unforgettable vegan lunches, I said.

25

My neurons were picturing Saturday, and I watched her prepare a big casserole of pasta al forno for lunch. I hadn't precipitated any catastrophes, and she was calm and smiling. And in the afternoon we'd play Wherever It Lands: lying next to each other on the bed, she holds her arm straight up and lets it fall, and if it falls on me it falls on me—and scares me. Otherwise, it just falls the other way. And then we'd go to see one of those films that makes me laugh. In short, my imagination was flying high, as it always does when things are difficult. My mood, though, was down at the level of my socks. Sometimes it's tough to feed yourself a line; no matter how willing you are, you just don't swallow it.

Seeing that I was turning gloomy, IQ asked me to come have a look at something on his extra-large monitor. And this time he signed to me, because he knows I prefer sign language a million times over. On the monitor you could see inside the smart beehive where he's installed more sensors than you can count. He knows how I adore the bees, but still, he never does things for no reason.

The bees, visible via the infrared webcam, seemed to be sleeping. They were a little scary, with those huge sad eyes. As if they were waiting to break into someone's dream and frighten them.

IQ showed me the honeycomb cells with the pupae in them, and then, flicking through last week's images, he pointed out that the winter cluster was 220.16" larger than a week ago, an increase of 21.19%. Which meant that the temperature had risen and the bees were clinging to each other less, he said. In the center of that nascent colony the temperature was in fact 97.11° F, while at the periphery it was 42.04° F. IQ adores the nonnegotiable precision of numbers.

Maybe because he saw that watching bees survive the winter didn't thrill me, he then told me to look out the window and pay attention to what happened. This time he stroked his chin with the promising look of an Asian mystic.

Open, gate! he commanded, raising one arm like a traffic cop. And the light on top of the neighbor's gate began flashing, and then the gate began to open. I couldn't believe it. And neither could the neighbor's stupid dog believe his stupid eyes. He sauntered over to the exit, as if for some reason a ghost was about to arrive.

Then IQ said *Close, gate!* Like the traffic cop on the corner by the university building that resembles a giant cake, he was giving orders left and right. The two halves of the gate began to swing shut.

Seeing how much I liked his little game, IQ said *Open, gate, and stay open*, and in fact the gate did open and remained open wide. The idiot dog hesitated for a moment, considering the pros and cons, and then made up his mind to head out for the provincial highway. Now IQ ordered the gate to close.

But that wasn't all, as I could see from IQ's Buddhist eyes that were sparkling with laughter. *Open, garage!* he ordered, and the high-tech garage began to open and the backside of our neighbor's super-duper late-model automobile appeared. I was laughing, knowing how much of a fuss Imidacloprid makes about his wheels and picturing his face if he saw this.

Close, garage! said my brother, like someone who wants to show he's cool with speaking English. The garage closed and the car disappeared.

IQ was extremely pleased with his show. He scratched his stomach, his belly button delighted, then put a finger to his lips to let me know this was a state secret. I made it clear there wouldn't be any problems, but he raised his index finger and his nostrils flared threateningly. It's true, sometimes the secrets burst out of me like uninvited belches.

We were still laughing when Papa came in all cheerful, frozen pizzas poking out of the supermarket bag. He's always in an excellent mood when his Silicon Valley colleague comes to visit. The guy has a Santa Claus beard and always wears a red hat, and he's amazing at mining the social networks, he can tell you what color jockey shorts different people wear, and their political preferences, past, present, and future. I watched him on IQ's PC, which is synchronized with Papa's to keep an eye on what he's up to.

When he'd put the pizzas in the oven, Papa took a small plastic box out of his pocket, made a Japanese bow in IQ's direction, and handed it to him. My brother's mouth was hanging open; he looked like he was about to cry (think high-tension pylon that starts to dance and do splits). Even Grandmother, dolled up in her best with the white flowers, was paying attention.

At first my neurons were just fibrillating helplessly, but then they grasped what it was. The box contained the integrated circuit IQ had been working on like a crazy person for the last year. An extremely complex gem that's capable of magic. Papa had been able to get it produced by sneaking it into the job he was doing for the Americans. It was his way of repaying IQ for his work on the algorithm that flushes out terrorists, which Papa had passed off as his own work.

IQ was holding the little box in the palm of his hand, not daring to close his fingers, like it contained a precious butterfly. He looked almost like a normal brother, not the little genius he's always been. He was still wearing his Hun's smart helmet with the webcam that captures a 360° view; he had forgotten to take it off, and he was rocking back and forth from one foot to the other the way a two-year-old does. His face was a little red, to tell the truth.

In the meantime, Papa sat down at the table, in real life an old telephone cable spool. He was having trouble making sense of how different IQ seemed today, and so he was badgering him a little, an activity that made the small portable he always has on his knees bounce up and down. It drives Mamma nuts that he's always got that portable on his lap when he comes to visit, like a woman with a lapdog. But now she's in the hospital, and he's here and does what he pleases. As I do with the Nutella.

He was barely looking at his computer, he was smirking. *Maybe you're not that happy with it, maybe I'd better take it back*, he said to my brother, holding out a knobby hand in his direction. IQ slapped the palm of his hand in the crook of his elbow, and did the *eff off* thing; I'd never seen him do that before. It had been ages since we'd enjoyed this kind of class-trip atmosphere at home—to be precise, since before Mamma's accident.

You're my favorite gangster, Papa said to me, grabbing my head as if it were a soccer ball.

Papa knows very well that the fatal neuromorphic chip is for the robot that my brother has been plotting forever. He spent his whole childhood talking about it. Even the bees know. But Papa believes that the robot IQ has in mind is one of the usual ones, with antiquated blinking lights and pincers for hands. He thinks my brother is still miles from the finish line. Instead, IQ's not the least bit interested in making a waltzing vacuum cleaner that says stupid crap in the voice of a train-station announcer. He's way ahead of that, and Papa doesn't know it.

He's decided that he can live with a robot without a body, what matters is that it's as intelligent as a very intelligent person and can do even more intelligent things. He'll deal with giving it a body when he has the necessary means. I know these things because I scout around regularly in his PC, logging on through mine. I don't understand everything, but I get the general outlines.

You have to thank Nutella and their profiling operations, said Papa, indicating the little package with his gnarly, tendony arm. IQ nodded his grown-up-kid's head and stared at me without moving his eyes, as if you could communicate with just the pupils. Papa's main job is to profile terrorists, not people who can't resist Nutella, we all know that. Only Grandmother believes the Nutella story, because she always believes everything.

You have to process mountains and mountains of data before you find even the shadow of a terrorist, it's the classic needle in a haystack. Papa's the outgoing type, but in this case it's a delicate matter; he can't shout about what he's doing from the rooftops, and not even from the balcony. I probably shouldn't be writing about it here, you never know who might see it. Even Logo can't figure out whether it's a good idea to write down what I've told her; you can see it on her pensive Virgin Mary face.

Hey, it's chilly in here tonight, said Papa, tightening his arms across his chest. The cloud of vapor that contained his words hovered a moment in front of his four-day beard. IQ said he hadn't even tried to get the stove going, he worried it might make things worse. His cloud was longer and narrower than Papa's because his words are always pointed and right on target.

Better if you don't touch anything, it generally starts up again by itself, said Papa, being agreeable and pushing his lips forward, as if to show that the more he thinks about it, the more he agrees.

Under normal circumstances he would have said it was all IQ's fault for splicing a complicated neural network that, among other things, feeds data from the weather forecasts of three different services into his stove program. IQ's idea is that it makes no sense to put the heat up when you know the following day will be warmer, also because when you know it's going to warm up you feel less cold. IQ admitted he'd fiddled with the program, but insisted he wasn't to blame for the fact that it wasn't working.

Hmm, gotta figure out what's wrong with that program, Papa said, sounding as if it was not at all urgent. Then he pulled the zipper on his down jacket all the way up so it covered most of his skinny turkey neck.

Halfway through his pizza, seeing something on the computer screen on his lap, he slammed a hand down in the old phone cable spool, our table. *And we have to live in this shithole?* he said.

Even a camel knows that the only solution would be a really efficient interface hooked up to the neurons of the cerebral cortex, he went on, holding up the portable to show us an image of a girl with a ponytail in a space suit. They must be the neurons, those twisted, mouse-colored coils that lead from her hair to a computer, I figured.

The human brain must be rendered more performative, he said, putting a hand on his head to be sure it was still in place.

Meanwhile, the digital illiterates who run this city didn't approve the financing, he announced.

IQ listened and said nothing. He had taken off his sensor-studded Hun's helmet and returned to being the impatient statue he always is. He was now in a hurry to get back to his cell beside the feed silo and begin trying out the new deep-learning chip. Breathing though his nose and pressing his lips together, he was preparing for a long, hard job. He knew that the time for fun was now over and trusted that Providence would make things come out right.

IQ himself had told me more than once that a chip that seems to have been beautifully designed often doesn't work at all when tested. Even the tiniest little hitch, and all your work was for nothing, he explained. *Like a cake that's burnt*, he said, figuring, as always, that I understand nothing about AI.

He's the kind of guy who's not used to making mistakes, and he doesn't expect he will make any. But this time, he's not completely cool; he knows it's very unlikely that he'll have another occasion or get a second chip, if the cake comes out flat. In short, he knows that the life of his robot, the thing he cares about more than anything else, is hanging by a thread.

We need to empty out their cranial vaults and fill them with artificial neural networks, then they might begin to understand something, said Papa, touching his head again. *And some happy memories*, he added, chewing on a fingernail.

LIKE A SHEET OF TURQUOISE PASTED
THERE FOR ADVERTISING PURPOSES

LOGO TOOK ME OUT climbing again today. On a path as smooth as a concrete dam this time, because I'm very good at it, she says. Papa is convinced that a kid as twitchy as I am can only end up a heap of shattered bones, that my real specialty from early childhood has been cutting myself and accumulating holes in my head. But Logo insisted, she says it's very good for me.

He needs to vent the tensions he has inside, she told him, twisting her bread-colored curls around her index finger.

I don't think he deserves a reward outing, said Papa, short of better arguments.

It will help him move forward, she replied.

Let's hope so, he needs to, said Papa in return. People always think he's my brother. And when he gets testy about something, he seems even less like a father.

A magnificent sun was blazing on the pale gray rock face, and the sky was as blue as the deep blue sea. It seemed like summer, but it was the end of winter. As we climbed, the huge lake beneath us became more and more beautiful. It looked like a sheet of turquoise pasted there for advertising purposes. I was happy to be on that skyscraper of clean rock, far from the arbiters of who's allowed to go to school and who's not.

Pay attention to what you're doing, said Logo, who seemed a little worried. *You seem more distracted than usual today*, she said.

Far from blackboards and quizzes, I thought, and I felt the gratitude tickle my ribs from inside. The hours this angel devotes to me—Logo burst into my life right after Mamma's accident—are countless grains of sand, far beyond her two contractual lessons a week.

She was climbing ahead of me in her red helmet with grissini-colored curls poking out, and now she stopped and turned to look down, smiling to let me know I should follow. I'm swift as a cat; for me climbing is easier than talking, even though climbing, too, demands you find something to grasp onto and pay attention so as not to plunge into the void. Rock is solid; it doesn't play dirty tricks on you the way words do, and if anything bad should happen, the rope keeps you from crashing. It's so nice when things come easy and are actually pleasurable.

Don't get distracted, it takes an instant to fall, wild man, Logo said again. I usually don't put on the helmet with the smart hearing aids that IQ designed and built because it sends my red blood cells into orbit, but I have it on today to make her happy.

I have a long way to go, I know that, but in spite of school, I've learned a lot of new words with her, I thought. It had taken some heavy hammering, but they made it into my head, like nails in hardwood. The name of this, the name of that, the name of this other thing. It's hard to believe how many names there are, each one different from the other but also similar enough to foment every sort of error and misunderstanding. And that's not all, because those naughty fellows then have to be linked up to one another, with all niceties and the intricacies that apply, otherwise no one will understand anything.

Logo says if I keep going like this I'll be able to say whatever I want whenever I want, the way she can. People won't think I'm retarded, they'll realize I'm anything but stupid. *Life isn't all that easy for us hearing-impaired, but it's not impossible*, she says. *We have to show them what we're worth.*

You're going to wake up soon and you'll see how much progress I've made, I said to myself, and to my precious Mamma.

I told you, pay attention and stop daydreaming, Logo said again. She knows me inside out. *You mustn't rely too much on automatic reflexes*, she said, sometimes taking her usual care to let me see her lips, sometimes not. She thinks my fundamentalist refusal to wear the helmet with the non-invasive cortical interface is wrong, I have to get used to putting it on all the time. I reply that with smart hearing aids, all I can hear is bothersome neuron noise, but she said I was talking bull, it was a brilliant invention, and I do hear something.

Sure, once in a while some small incident gets blown up into a Greek tragedy, I said to myself, but let's not despair, there's always a solution. Even the crazy ones back down and everything is as it was before.

Yep, I was imagining the principal calling home to say that what had happened was now water under the bridge, and it was pointless to keep dredging up the past. *Anyway, he's a good kid*, he said.

I said, take it slowly and think about what you're doing, Logo warned. So for a while I paid attention only to my hands and my feet, in charge of every nuance like an orchestra conductor. But then my neurons would lead me off to you again, as I climbed lightly, like a spider. I wished that you, too, could drown in that ocean of inky blue, that you could stroke this rock that winter has cleaned, this rock with the dry smell, and here and there a fearless weed struggling to grow.

Pretty soon you'll begin to move and talk, it can't be much longer, I said, floating in the sky-blue sky. You were listening and answering me back. *Sure*, you said.

The doctors don't hold out much hope, they think the chances are slim if all the noises they made in your room didn't budge you. They even tried to sweet-talk you with classical music, I tell you. But they don't know you, they don't know that you're used to deciding for yourself when you do things and how, you don't like being spoon-fed. Papa's most aware of it, but even IQ and I have noticed. Not to mention Grandpa, who knew it when you were too small to reach his knees.

One morning you'll have had enough of lying around, and you'll get up, I said. Like when a person's in that lovely warmth under the sheet and they decide it's time to get moving. *You can't spend the whole day flat on your back like some deadbeat.*

Everything must come to an end, you say to yourself. And maybe you have to repeat that a few times, but you finally screw up your courage and rip off the sheets and blankets, a fearless samurai unsheathing his sword. Your heroism is soaring, you push yourself out of bed and aim your feet at the floor.

There we go, now I'm almost up, you think, even though to tell the truth, the hard work is still to come and the temptation to lie down again is strong. Your eyelids weigh a ton, they want to come crashing down like old shutter blinds. Life is like that, sometimes even the smallest things become difficult and you need a lot of determination and cool.

Now concentrate, Logo broke in, so that I nearly freaked. *This is the most difficult point*, she added. Her words traveled lightly through my head, like the shrieks of the buzzards wheeling in circles beneath us.

What are you doing, put that phone away, she said, seeing I'd dug it out to read the message that had just arrived.

It'll be great when you're back home again, I told you, my fingertips stroking the rock warmed by the sun, reviving after a harsh winter. When everything is going well, it's natural to be happy, I thought. The bees will make a ton of honey, and you won't have to worry about money anymore. Logo will have taken off for her trip to Australia and we'll send her messages to keep her up-to-date.

38

It happened in a millisecond, a millisecond that lasted about a quarter of an hour. My foot slipped off the minuscule ledge it was resting on, and I lost my foothold. My chest banged against the rock face. For an instant the fingers of my left hand clutched the protrusion like a piece of wooden fluting, and then they didn't anymore, and they let go. There was nothing at all holding me up now and no time to react. It was too late to try to protect myself, I was plummeting. Slowly, with all the time in the world to think, but also very fast. In far less than a second I was going to be smashed to pieces.

The jerk of the rope arrived just above a ledge; if the rope had been a meter longer, the impact wouldn't have been pleasant. My head was now very clear, and I could see I had screwed up. And that I always fooled myself thinking I had everything under control, and then reality would deliver one of its mighty slaps in the face.

I was hanging in midair like a salami, wondering if the rope was going to hold. Below me, the rock face was dour, and the lake didn't look at all friendly either. Fear had worked its way under my skin, and it felt cold. I thrashed around for a while, then grabbed onto the rock again.

Logo was terrified. She was at my side in two seconds, prodding me all over the way you poke a doll to see whether it's still in one piece after falling from the third floor. Just when I needed someone to shout at me, all she did was say, *Don't let go, don't move.*

Now we'll go down slowly, she said, after adjusting my ropes and my helmet. She was terribly nervous, and with each step she paid out only a tiny stretch of rope. But I knew nothing bad was going to happen now. Fear had turned my legs to jelly, but I wasn't worried.

Sure, there's still a ways to go, but you'll be proud of me when you see me, I told you, looking down at the lake, which had turned very dark. I know I haven't given you great satisfaction up to now, but just as soon as your eyes start up again following people's faces and flies when they move, you'll understand at first glance that the picture has changed. *Hey, this smart and positively seraphic kid is my son*, you'll say.

Move slowly, and watch where you put your feet, Logo cautioned, her blue eyes nailed on me constantly.

You won't have those worry lines on your forehead, the ones I don't like one bit, and you won't live in terror that I'll crack my skull again, or hurt someone, I said to you silently. You won't get discouraged, as sometimes used to happen. In short, we'll be able to live in peace.

Put that phone away instantly, Logo screamed, pretty exasperated.

When we got down to the bottom of the rock face, the sun was in pajamas, a fiery red getup with lighter stripes. And suddenly it was very cold, because winter hadn't really gone away yet. The lake had become a well of pitch, deep in nocturnal musings.

You were fabulous, Logo said. The way she told it, I hadn't taken a false step all day, apart from that little fall; I'd been magnificent. Climbing did me a world of good; it would teach me to keep my legs still and not bother other people. She didn't actually say that Papa was dead wrong, but the silences between her words screamed it.

Certainly, having to sit still at a desk is tougher than a climb ranked Very Hard–Severe, she said with a smile. She didn't specify that no one would hear of my plunge, but for certain purposes there's no need to traffic in words. In short, I slept like a stone in the car, full of emotions and sensations, my head on her jacket smelling of violets and wind.

When IQ got home he came to my cell, flash drive in hand, his Adam's apple bobbing up and down like it does when, under his taciturn titanium armor, he's dying to surprise you. Waggling it like a pendulum in front of my face, he told me he'd finished the voice translation program.

I can't believe it, I said, playing the Kid Who's Completely Blown Away.

It hasn't dawned on him that from my portable I can see everything he does on his supercomputer. As far as he's concerned, I'm an IT loser, just like I'm a loser at school. Which is true, but I do have some memory because when he was using my PC and needed to bypass his own gargantuan defense system, I copied everything.

And even though I knew the translation program was just about finished, I was actually very pleased, and I threw my arms around his neck. *You're the world champion of brothers*, I told him. He made a sick face and wiped his cheek with the back of his hand. He hates smooching.

41

Now he uploaded the deep-learning translation program to my PC and we tried it out with a TV series. This new version works with fifty-six different languages, including Malaysian and Kyrgyz, even if maybe there aren't very many Kyrgyz TV series. In any case you don't need to identify the language, the translator takes care of that. And there are many fewer errors because the complex-valued neural networks use advanced systems like those Papa can tap into to find terrorists. He doesn't know they've been borrowed, and if he even suspected it, he would pass out, but that's how it is.

If you miss something, you can rewind, or you can slow the actors down if that allows you to read the translation better. And of course, you can do all this with vocal commands; you just say *slow down a little* and the program slows down. I know these marvelous tricks were actually invented for the robot IQ is working on, but for now it's the undersigned who gets to take advantage.

We tried it out and found it also works well when it's me speaking. Which is fabulous, considering that when I speak, people listening usually look puzzled. IQ was puffed up like a rooster to see that his supersmart trickster already understood me without any problem. We put on a soccer game, and the written translation was perfect there too.

You're some brother, I said.

SOME STICKIER-THAN-FLYPAPER QUESTIONS

WHEN I CAME TO SEE YOU today you were looking really well, there in the white silence. What other people call silence is not to my ears real silence; it's a jangling noise I harbor in my body, or better yet a sublime explosion of colors, but you adore it. You could never bear any kind of commotion, and you've always had a thing for white. Not by chance in all your photographs from India you're in pure white, an angel. And when you handle the beehives you dress up like a very stern swan, hiding your hair which reminds me of the sun gleaming on petroleum. The bees, too, adore white, it pacifies them, you say.

At the moment your hair is very short, but only because of the operations on your head. It's always flowed down to your shoulder blades. You're not a young girl anymore but your hair is thick and rebellious, like the mane of some energetic filly. As soon as you can you'll let it grow again, that's for sure. And you can put on the nice straw hat I just brought you as a present. You adore summer hats.

So I sit down on the metal chair with the stuffing that smells of hospital and begin to talk to you, like always. Talk to you in sign, because when I say words out loud they're never right, they come out all screwy. While I'm an ace when I sign, even though I learned it late, by then I was considered retarded. Your eyes seem to move mechanically, like the hands of a watch, but you do see what I'm saying, I'm sure of it. I sense it from the pressure on your chest, as if someone was pushing down with a hand, and also on your cheeks. Whenever I suspect you're not following me, I repeat.

I give you all the news from home, because I know you like to be informed about everything, even tiny things, happening to us. Nobody tells you anything, they come in here and stare at you the way they might look at the facade of a building, or a traffic light. They think that merely because you're in the hospital, you're uninterested in anything that's going on. But you need to know, all the more so now that you're a prisoner. Not long ago it was you at the helm, you decided the balance of power, and knowing that soon you'll take that role again, you don't want to miss anything. You lose your cool if somebody doesn't take the trouble to include you, although Buddhists are never supposed to lose their tempers.

I tell you that IQ has finished the automatic learning algorithm and it really does seem to be infallible: it minces data mined in all four corners of the globe and from the most powerful organisms, and the more it kneads it all together, the more it's capable of picking up even the most minimal suspect traces. And by drawing connections between those traces it gets

44

better and better at finding other even more hidden traces, that in turn point to other traces, and so forth until finally it finds the actual terrorist, photo and all. Nobody really understands what it does or how it works, and the deeper it goes, the less anyone understands, but the results are visible to all. Papa's bosses are super happy, they don't know that the person who wrote the algorithm is thirteen years old.

They think he's a retard at his new school because he's always asleep with his head on his desk. He conks out soon after he gets there: who wouldn't sleep after having spent the entire night perfecting those miniature cyber-gems that drive the world's top IT experts crazy? And apparently it happens to other kids with Himalayan intelligence quotients, even those who don't match his 185. In any case, he finished reading his school texts the first week.

I also told you that Grandmother's in great shape; she's made some lovely flowers because she has great taste. White flowers that smell delicious when you smell them. And she doesn't have lice anymore: that all-natural spray worked.

I also told you that there were some minor issues at school, without going into detail. *It's pointless to fuss over minor problems*, I said, spinning one hand in the air as one does in these cases. *You yourself always say one must think positively and act confident*, I added. At this point you yawned, which I took as a yes.

I didn't say that they'd told Papa they would have to think about whether I was qualified now to attend their magnificent school (the implication: no). Not only do I have attention deficit disorder, I'm violent and dangerous. They mentioned an institute called something not very appealing, where they say I'd be treated like a king. My bet is that it will all end up like the inside of a soap bubble that's burst, but right now they're making a real mountain out of a mole, as the saying goes.

It was good chatting away in your little room, nice and peaceful. The blades of sunlight flashing on the white sheets were so bright they hurt our eyes, like virgin snow. In its way, the sun seemed to be doing everything in its power to make the moment special. Once in a while a nurse, also very white, would appear, then fly off like a seagull in a hurry when she saw I was there. No one bothered us, no one made any fuss. Even a stone-deaf kid like myself could appreciate the deep silence.

They made me go see a guy in colored glasses, the kind that kids wear. He started asking me sticky questions, like those traps made to capture flies. He seemed to take it for granted that I was microcephalic, like in the old days, not realizing that if there was one of us who didn't understand what the other was saying it was him. As soon as he opened his mouth his neck would begin to shrink and his eyes would blink, and he'd smile, with a smile you couldn't understand.

He assumed he knew me inside out: he knew how many times I scratch my head during one particular lesson, how I spin my legs, where I keep my phone, what games I play, what the marks of my teeth look like on skin. It seems he had discussed me inside out with the Italian teacher, that piggy who always seems to be willing to go out of his way to help and is probably a first-class traitor. On the wall behind him hung various diplomas; apparently he'd applied himself to his studies and was super proud of it.

He blew his big, beaky nose and asked why I kept on standing up and sitting down, but I couldn't confess that his questions made my ankles nervous, and to tell the truth, his face, like a fox circling the henhouse, did too. So I told him I needed to stretch my legs, but pretty soon it would pass, I knew it. He asked if that often happened to me, and I said less often than it happens to many others, but from the wrinkles on his "Athenian philosopher's brow"—Logo's words—I understood that I'd pissed on the toilet seat; I should have just said no.

As for myself, I asked him if his job was a good one, but not only did he not reply, but he acted quite astonished that I would ask him anything. He had the exclusive right to pose questions, it seemed. It made me think of those people with a dog who take it for granted that only one of them is a genius— and it's certainly not the dog who holds the leash and opens the cans for supper.

He paused as if to think, then asked me whether I liked my classmates. By now I'd learned, and so I said, *Yep, all of them, very much*. So why did I punch and kick some of them, and even bite them, he asked. I said I didn't know, although when I think about it now, I do know, absolutely. He was really making me irritable with those crappy trick questions of his, and those notes he tickticktacked in his notebook, so satisfied with himself.

He even wanted the most squalid details about life at home, and he simply couldn't believe that we live in a chicken coop, he thought I was joking. He asked me if we had hens inside, and I said once in a while, yes: when my father buys a roast chicken at the food truck outside his office. But my mother doesn't like us to eat the cadavers of animals, the most we're allowed is some frozen fish in a square or rectangular shape. He wanted to know what time Papa came home from work, and I said it varied a great deal; sometimes he has some stuff to do for Nutella. When IQ was born, Papa was only sixteen, which is why everyone thinks he's our brother.

When I fell off the chair, he looked mighty satisfied. Actually, it was the first time I'd ever fallen off a chair I was sitting on. I mean, it hadn't happened in a long time. It's awful when someone's looking down on you. You have to do what they want you to. I wanted to grab his nosy-kid glasses and crush them, pound them first with one ski boot and then the other.

IQ was waiting in the hallway because Papa, as usual, hadn't been able to come. My brother was so deep in thought he didn't realize I'd emerged from the interrogation room. Busy on his encrypted-reencrypted channel with the hackers, still discussing Bayer. The hack was on now for sure; they just had to agree on the details.

Theoretically the group doesn't have a boss, but in reality there are three or four generals, and Robin Hood is one of them. He always has a slight advantage. He had already begun, very, very quietly, to scout around in the Bayer system, the company that makes, along with other delicacies, that imidacloprid so beloved of our neighbor, the pesticide that's responsible for his nickname, Imida. Breaking through invincible firewalls and such has been one of IQ's passions since he was a kid; he's been pretty much everywhere, including the Vatican and NASA. Of course, I pretend not to notice.

Now that I think about it, I'd rather redact that paragraph about Robin Hood; it might make you nervous, I mean you would probably have preferred a son who adored butterflies and yoga; smart algorithms and information insubordination drive you crazy. I said so just now to Logo and we agreed that these facts shouldn't go beyond this room. However, the road to hell, etc. etc; as I was writing this, I played a friendly game of chess with a Russian guy while scanning Imida's email on the side.

Otherwise, there's nothing new, I tell you. Our pellet stove is still doing whatever it pleases, but we're used to it by now; you just put a sweater on or take one off, and if things get really rough, you put on a down jacket too. It's one of those issues no one wants to talk about, because it can only lead to arguments. IQ thinks there's some cracker playing dirty tricks, that's why it doesn't work. When he hears that, Papa raises his tomcat's eyes to the heavens: in his view, it's all the fault of the neural networks that are supposed to learn stuff on their own but never learn anything. I have to say that IQ sees hackers and crackers everywhere, because when a person's—say, for example—stone deaf, that person tends to think everybody's stone deaf.

He's gotta be Chinese, because he hasn't left any traces, he says. *The guy's a pro, he could get into the Pentagon in five minutes.* It's a little strange to see him put on that admiring face, because he usually behaves like a statue looking down from a pedestal, convinced he's superior. In any case, winter will soon be over and then we'll all feel better.

What's making Papa antsy, as I said, is the TV he brought over from his own apartment, the studio with the expressway view. It's playing tricks on him: whenever the stove starts going great guns, the TV drops dead, but as soon as the stove slows down the TV comes to life again. IQ says there's no connection between the two things. The stove doesn't work because Papa's software is shit, and the TV malfunctions because it's a shit brand. But I'm convinced there's a link, that the saboteur shifts from one to the other. *Kiddo, you don't understand anything*, IQ says, a hint of weary amusement lurking at the sides of his stoical nose.

Papa howls like a wolf every time it happens. *Ooooooohh*, he goes. *Oooooooohh*. When it's the news, war, earthquakes, etc. it doesn't matter so much, but it's a tremendous drag when the TV blacks out at the crucial moment of a thrilling soccer game. Papa loves to lie on the sofa and watch sports when he's finished his algorithms for the evening. Even when he used to come over to visit us on Sundays it was the same thing, and it used to infuriate Mamma; he's like a baby who needs his bottle, she says.

Papa says this too is IQ's fault because he fiddles with everything. IQ reacts like an archangel on the curlicued rooftop of a church oozing pity for passing pedestrians: he denies he ever touched the TV. If there's one thing that doesn't interest him it's TV.

But Papa's convinced. *There are unmistakable clues pointing to your supercomputer*, he says. IQ raises his shoulders, like he thinks it's not worth wasting any more time on this. That makes Papa even more nervous because he considers himself a world champion microelectronics expert. The truth is, the two of them have been bickering like an old couple since the days when IQ started cracking video games and reassembling them.

But then I change the subject, because this stuff has always driven you crazy, in fact Grandpa says it's part of the reason you kicked Papa out of the house, not just because he didn't want me to learn sign language. He's only interested in algorithms; to his way of thinking they're much more important than hardware. When you're not talking about algorithms he yawns and looks at his phone. *I love you, kid*, he's always telling me, but you can see he's thinking about something else.

And then, after relating a few more bits of news, I say nothing at all, because I know that in your view, there isn't anything that can beat floating in a void of silence. You hunker down in a yoga posture under the pear tree that doesn't produce pears, and let yourself be inebriated by that silence of the abyss that hydrogen atoms have carried with them since the dawn of time. You often tell me I'm very lucky to be deaf, that you would be delighted not to be tortured by the noises stressed-out people and modern gadgets make. You don't believe it when I tell you that for me, silence is very noisy.

You know, I understand why you always refuse to wear the hearing aids, you once said. You were teasing, but deep in your eyes as green as new grass, I could see you were serious too.

As far as you're concerned, even the bees sometimes make too much noise. In particular, when they're preparing to swarm and start buzzing like nutcases, glomming together and dive-bombing the hives. And on very hot days when they beat their wings like crazy to ventilate the young. You love them, but once in a while you can't take it anymore, just as you can't take me sometimes.

Believe me, I understand, because words have always seemed pointless crutches to me. Unlike signs, they're never really precise, never truly sincere, even in the best case they lean to one side or another, concealing intentions that never correspond exactly to what they'd have you think. If only we could rein them in, but the fact is, they always win.

TREES LINED UP AS ORDERLY
AS SOLDIERS ON PARADE

TODAY WE WENT OUT to take samples of the earthworms. When we left home the sky had just begun to lighten, and we got onto the ring road right where you, Mamma, bursting with things to say, didn't respect the right of way. Even the trucks were passing us on the highway; Grandpa says we have to reduce our emissions. His car doesn't have air-conditioning or GPS: it's really primitive, but I like to ride with him because he always has good stories to tell. He lets go of the steering wheel sometimes and instead of keeping an eye on the probable accidents up ahead, he looks at me: it's a little scary. But he listens to what I have to say, not like those people who ask *how are you?* when they're thinking about what they had for lunch.

He asked whether it wasn't boring to stay at home. *A couple of days is fine, but then I start to get as bored as a hippopotamus*, I acknowledged. *But soon they're gonna take me back; it shouldn't be long now*, I said.

Shaking his big shiny head and anarchic beard back and forth, he told me that things were not so simple. The principal

53

wanted me out and even the Italian teacher wasn't defending me like he once did; it seemed I'd become unmanageable. And the psychologist who'd seen me didn't think I should be readmitted. He says I might hurt someone really badly.

That guy's a total idiot, I said, still signing, and Grandpa signaled he agreed by lowering his eyelids slightly, but without saying anything.

Don't hit your knee on the car door, you'll hurt yourself, he said.

From what Logo says, the place they want to put me is a real concentration camp, and the kids are in training to become sociopaths, I said. Grandpa didn't say anything; he doesn't want to take sides openly. On paper my father is still my father, even though we all know that's just his title. And he's in favor of the concentration camp.

They'll keep an eye on you there, kiddo, and if there's some bug in your software, they can repair it, he said to me yesterday, laying a hand on my head.

Let's first do everything we can to keep you in school, and then we'll see, said my grandfather in his usual encouraging way. Judging by the way he screws up his mouth like an old camel, he's not convinced by his own words, but now that you're in the hospital he's determined that I shouldn't feel low, and he tries to make everything sound easy and complication-free. I guess he pities me.

The important thing is that you don't fall behind in your studies, he said, using the very same words as Logo. That was my confirmation the two were colluding, and that he's the one who asked her to come by every morning. An idea like that would

54

never occur to Papa. Right now, as she transcribes what I'm dictating, she pretends to be another person, someone who has nothing to do with any of this, but that's merely the proof that I'm right.

Watch out for that knee, you're going to get a bad bruise if you don't stop banging it on the door.

When we got to the first field it was like pink snow had drifted down from the heavens because the peach trees were at the height of their flowering. It was truly beautiful, a panorama dressed for the ball.

This is where we have to get the worms, Grandpa said out loud, stowing his jackknife in one of the many pockets of his pacifist pants, faded from hundreds of cycles in the washing machine. He started getting his equipment out. *If we find any*, he said. *Stop looking at your phone*, he added.

He wasn't in a good mood because he can't stand fields where the trees are lined up as orderly as soldiers on parade. It's terrible that farmers are allowed to commit such crimes against humanity, he says. He belongs to the same school as you, although you two never agree on anything when you argue.

We had the usual plastic jerrican full of irritant liquid to bring out the worms, and Grandpa had me sprinkle it over the ground. *Be very careful not to spill it on you*, he signed to me; he's always worried I'll do something stupid. But no earthworms appeared. We waited, and I sprinkled more liquid, but we didn't see even the shadow of a worm. Grandpa heaved a sigh and marked No Macroannelids Present on his form. *We're not only exterminating the bees, but the earthworms too*, he said.

Having finished there, we moved with the jerrican and all the equipment to the neighboring field and did another test. *Now pay attention*, he repeated once again, sticking close to my side. As a joke, I pretended to spill the jerrican on me, and in spite of his age Grandpa made a heroic leap and pushed me out of the way of the liquid.

Just kidding, I signed, but I could see he didn't appreciate my humor. He ran a hand over that bald head of his, relieved to have avoided disaster.

There were no earthworms here either. Well actually, when I looked very carefully I discovered one *Lumbricus rubellus* scuttling all alone through the decomposing leaves. Grandpa was pleased, he loves it when I find some little thing he hasn't seen. He says I have eyes like a hawk because my brain compensates for the hearing deficit.

The ones that live in organic matter that collects on the surface are less vulnerable to insecticides, he told me, tossing the worm into a bottle of pure alcohol. He looked like an apostle, with that shiny cranium of his and the big white beard, and behind him the background of pink flowers that made you think of paradise.

While I checked my phone messages he was whacking a steel cylinder into the ground with a milky plastic hammer head designed for that purpose, in order to collect a perfect sample. The soil was very hard; some purple spots popped out on his neck, and he was wheezing. But then he succeeded, and collapsed with one of his weary asthmatic smiles.

Among my messages were two advertisements for automatic gates. I have no idea why, but for a few days now the algorithms seem to think I'm in the market for an electric gate, and they're persecuting me. I'd talk to IQ about it.

While Grandpa wrote out the label I transferred the soil in the sample cylinder into a hermetically sealable bag, taking care not to lose even a tiny clod of it. I could feel that my arms wanted to do their own thing, but I managed to keep them under control. I put the bag in the cooler with the ice packs.

I've tagged along with Grandpa a million times, so we don't need to talk. I just have to resist getting too caught up in my internal movies, as Logo calls them. It's not always easy, when you have a subscription to that streaming service.

We got lost a couple of times on our way to the next place because Grandpa doesn't know how to use the new GPS to find his way. We ended up in an illegal dump that was full of old washing machines and a PC that looked practically new. But then we found the right road, and it took us to a farm with muddy geese and flourishing green weeds. There were peach trees here too, but not all the same variety and with fewer blossoms.

There were as many earthworms as you could wish for, however. As soon as I sprinkled on the liquid they came leaping out like March hares. We had a hard time collecting them before they ran off in all directions. A lot of *Lumbricus terrestris* but also a few *Aporrectodea caliginosa*, which are pretty rare. Grandpa was really happy; he said everybody should plant like these people.

And now we've earned some rest, he signed after we finished our sandwiches and he rolled a cigarette, exceptionally, of tobacco only. I've been watching him smoke an afternoon joint and an evening joint since I was born, but Papa always says it's dangerous to set such a bad example.

All we need is for you to turn into a drug addict, he says. It's another of the rules that came when he invaded our house, like eating meat. He thinks that if I don't eat animal cadavers I'll never learn to speak well.

On the way home we talked about you. Grandpa told me that they're going to try to wake you up again soon, this time following a method developed in Switzerland. *Let's hope it works*, he said, but he looked like a man who'd just missed the train. I replied that they had to give you time, that was best.

Mamma detests being told what to do, and if someone insists, she'll do the exact opposite, I said. He said I was absolutely right, and he even looked like he might start laughing. The fact is, if there's anybody you don't like to hear advice from, it's him.

However, we have to be prepared for the possibility that she won't emerge from the vegetative state, he said after a pause, in a voice that seemed to be having trouble putting the words together. I told him I could never imagine that you wouldn't wake up.

In any case, don't bite your arm, he said, still speaking aloud.

Mamma knows we need her; she's not the kind of person to leave us stewing in our own juices, I signed.

Grandpa said nothing for a moment, as if he was trying to focus his mind. Then, his face all toothachy, he told me I was right to be optimistic, that was the best way.

The only thing I shouldn't think was that everything I desired was bound to happen, he said after pausing a while to study a truck decorated with pictures of giant biscotti. It was very important not to confuse one's fantasies—although this happens to everybody—with facts, reality. And this also sounded to me like Logo's words; it wasn't something he'd say.

Watch out, if you bite your arm like that you'll really hurt yourself, he said.

What's that smell? he asked suddenly. I realized I could hardly breathe. When he stopped at the first rest area, we found that the trunk of the car was soaked in that irritant liquid. All his equipment was dripping. Including the prehistoric German field manual and his windbreaker. I hadn't closed the jerrican properly.

With some old newspapers from under the seat he began blotting up the worst, wheezing like when he's down with asthma. *Now don't you move*, he said. *And above all, don't you touch anything, because you could get a bad burn*, he went on, struggling to contain the spill.

I was feeling like a very stupid microannelid. *I still have a ways to go*, I thought, like someone doing one step forward and two steps back.

He didn't yell at me, though; he never yells. *Don't bite your hand like that or I'll have to take you to the emergency room*, was all he said.

When we got back to our chicken coop, Papa hadn't arrived, nor was there even the first of his funny messages to tell us that he'd be late. So he wasn't imminent. Grandpa, who was already stressed out over the ecological catastrophe in his car trunk, was getting fretful. He was in a hurry to get home and take the transparent worms out of the soil samples and then spend the night looking at the things under his binocular microscope and classifying them. I've helped him a bunch of times; I can do the job with my eyes closed.

The pellet stove was working great; if anything it was too hot. *A person could suffocate in here*, said Grandpa. I pretended not to understand.

Then he went to have a look in the refrigerator, but that made him even more irritated. Lately, it resembles the polar ice pack, where apart from the remains of a few failed expeditions it's a total food desert. Finally he ran a finger along the shelf of photos from India that sits under the feed hopper, and when he saw his fingertip, he made a lemon-eating face. But he doesn't like to criticize Papa; it's not educational, he thinks.

You can't expect a wolf to guard the sheep, I said to defuse the situation.

Actually, he loves you, and insofar as the school goes, it is up to him to decide, said Grandpa, as if in a hurry to be done with the subject.

We went into IQ's cell, something we hadn't done for a while. As soon as my brother saw Grandpa he held up a hand to signal him to wait. He opened the bayonet window and stuck his arm out, pointing his phone at an airplane high up ahead of its vapor trail.

See, this is the departure airport, here's the arrival, here's the route, and the model, he said, pulling his arm inside to show the display on his phone. I already knew about this app, because he'd showed it to me, and also because my classmate with the lisp has it. But Grandpa just scratched his big head like a hot-air balloon.

And you can see what flight it is and where it's going? he asked.

Sure, and if you want, much, much more, IQ said. *So let's see if we can find out who's on this flight,* he continued, sitting down at his PC, which as it happens looks very much like the cockpit of a commercial airliner. He tapped a couple of keys and the various processors all working in tandem began to chew on some data. After a short pause a list of names appeared on his screen, divided according to nationality.

So, these are the passengers, said IQ, massaging his sternum with the palm of one of his angelic hands. Which is always a sign he's very pleased with himself.

The names and surnames of the passengers? Grandpa had that shriveled-up look around the mouth of someone who's having an attack of diarrhea.

If we want we can also get dates of birth and other stuff, the neural networks are pretty smart and learn on their own, my brother confirmed, patting the list of names on the screen.

And it's okay to do this? asked Grandpa, darting back and forth between IQ's face and the computer screen, one hand on his neck. He shook his oversize head left and right, not saying yes or no.

Hey, I'm not fishing for credit card numbers, said my brother, with that telling look of a very clever statue.

You watch out now, nothing illegal, said Grandpa. His face looked even more creased than usual.

Look who's talking. You went to prison! said IQ.

That was different. We were fighting to abolish military service, said Grandpa, stretching his already long neck even further.

And we're fighting to keep the internet free, said IQ. I'd never seen him so gassed up.

Airplanes actually have little to do with it. He's in a good mood because he got a job in a start-up. With my brother, you always have to scrape away the top layer to find out what's going on.

The boss of a start-up with the wind in its sails noticed him in a forum—IQ is the guy who always finds solutions to impossible problems, so it's hard not to notice him. He asked to meet him, and when they did, he was shocked to find he was only thirteen. *You're Robin Hood?* he asked, involuntarily shaking his head.

IQ told him he'd been thirteen for two months, so he was really going on fourteen. He told him what he can do and showed him a few things. The start-up man hired him on the spot to design a bot for a very demanding client. An interactive robot that replies appropriately to a client's questions, without melting down or making a fool of anybody.

He can't pay him because my brother's under the legal hiring age, so they agreed that the start-up will finance all the integrated circuits IQ desires. The guy made him the offer, having understood immediately that that's what he was interested in. But he thinks IQ is into entertainment; he knows nothing of the robot my brother's working on.

He'll provide IQ all the processors, video cards, memory, sensors, smart videocams, and 3D printers he wants, he only has to ask. For my brother, this is heaven-sent, because he's used to procuring his electronic components from the recycling bin on the way out of town, at the risk of being attacked by local vigilantes, or else buying stuff thirdhand on the Web. Now he can have all the expensive goodies he wants, no problem.

Papa is super proud he has a son who belongs to that tribe he values so much, the ones who invent gadgets fundamental to human existence in their garages. At the same time, something seems to be bothering him. He says it remains to be seen whether those self-learning algorithms really are going to contribute to pushing the human brain's limits of understanding and memory, whether they'll compensate for present delays in interfacing processors and the human nervous system. It's too soon to say, he says, chewing his fingernails already consumed right down to the roots. IQ looks at him as if he were maintaining that the Earth isn't actually round but maybe square.

The struggle is sacrosanct, Grandpa now intoned. *The important thing is not to play into the games of the new oligopolistic technocrats*. He was wearing that fearless warrior face he dons on great occasions. IQ was just about to tell him too about his new job, but just then Papa called to say he was bringing the best hamburgers in the world, only he was a little late.

Okay, I'm off, see you tomorrow, said Grandpa, shouldering his medieval postman's leather bag. *Hey, be sure to keep an eye on your brother,* he said to IQ, eyes trained on the bite marks on my arm.

TOO MANY HAPPY ENDINGS IN
MY INNER SOAP OPERAS

TOMORROW THEY'RE GOING to try out the Swiss professor's new method and you will certainly fling open those eyes of yours, greener than emeralds. You'll flip them from right to left like seagulls when they let themselves fall into the void, searching for the people you love. You've been here a good while, you're sick of seeing without seeing, aching to walk on your hands, you're so good at it, aching to plant coriander, to scrape off the propolis that's gumming up the frames in the hives. You do so many things and you're constantly in motion, you learned it from the bees. It's only when you're seated in a yoga position that you stop whipping up the air molecules with your eyes. And you can't wait to start lining up the words again, making those word-chains that sound harmonious but are also fiercely meaningful; you're a true virtuoso. You've had enough of that silent den of yours.

You don't say so, but I know you're thinking about the bees. You know that soon they'll begin to come out and run around, and that they'll need you. They're waiting for you to take them to the quivering-in-the-wind green of the acacia woods, far from our jesting neighbor and his poisons, object of your nasty looks. They're waiting for you to clean their houses; they know they can't do it on their own. Without you, they'd begin to cry. The experts don't know it yet, but bees cry: I've seen them. We'll cry too if you don't come back. We can't bear to be without you either.

Logo also warned me that I shouldn't be so sure that you'll wake up. She thinks I put too many happy endings in my inner soap operas, so that what's really happening gets distorted. *And even if she does wake up it'll be a very slow process*, she told me; I shouldn't expect someone who leaps to her feet one morning and runs to the bathroom to pee. We'll have to wait and see, supposing that she does wake up, whether she's able to think like she did before, and speak.

I said that you've always done things nobody expected, and that those doctors trussed up like salamis in their white coats will be amazed by your feats that seem to spring forth of their own accord. You're made in your own way and you like to do what others consider impossible—and then burst out laughing to show your dazzling teeth.

Yes, yes, said Logo, twirling her bread-colored curls on her index finger like she wasn't totally convinced, and even now she looks like someone who's just swallowed an unripe plum. Our deal is that she writes down whatever I say—whatever—but if it were up to her, I expect she'd be tip-tapping out a different message.

66

Papa on the other hand is convinced that this is our lucky day, for once we're in agreement. He talked on Skype to the big shot who's coming down from the milk-producing pastures of Switzerland, and reports that there are already various cases where this new technique has worked wonders. *You need courage to challenge the religious timidity of the present science*, he says, spreading his knotty arms like when he does his morning gymnastics in his striped sweatshirt.

As soon as you're awake we'll celebrate, although at first we'll advise people not to sound their horns or take off in helicopters because your ears are no longer used to the din of daily life. Human existence is very rowdy and boisterous, you need training for it. And your eyes, too, will have to accustom themselves again to speeding motorbikes and all that other stuff that used to bother you: they've gotten used to staring at motionless white, what Eskimos see.

Later on we'll raise a glass to you, because despite your Buddhism you love to dance, with your elbows tight against your chest and the face of someone sucking a tasty cough drop. You'll return to your bee meetings, and words will flow from your mouth like blades of water from a powerful waterfall, but you won't be moved, like rocks that can't be budged by furious whirlpools. The dozing elderly will wake up and even the most cataleptic eyes will shine when you speak. You always find arguments to draw in the ones who are doubtful: you're a battling Buddhist, as Grandpa likes to say. Other people seek compromise, but you stand tall like a revolutionary on your barricade, your rebellious hair rippling in the breeze, calling for demonstrations against the politicians, raids of the warehouses where they store the bee-killing toxins.

Now that I know you'll soon be back, I'm feeling better. Logo works hard to encourage me, but when you get expelled from school it's like you're a banana peel tossed in the garbage. I never dreamed I would miss the smell of dust mixed with armpit sweat and feet. Papa says that in the concentration camp school they have a lot of experience treating manic deaf kids like me. The optimal solution would be if I also boarded there; I'd make better progress. That's why Logo talks as if I already have one foot in a mass grave. *I'll write to you from Australia*, she says, her eyes puffy and sad.

The only one who assures me I don't need to worry is IQ. He said so again today, confident as an archangel who knows what's going on and immensely bored at always having to explain everything. And then he repeated the whole thing signing, just to be sure there were no misunderstandings. He's great at sign language, he doesn't just improvise like the rest of the family.

I can already picture your principal changing his mind, he said, puckering up his nostrils.

Everything there is to know about our neighbor he also knows, my brother with his Indian guru eyes. But this time it wasn't me going hunting, following the arduous path he had revealed without meaning to. His superPC came to me instead, and one day a window opened up on my screen. *It's gonna be those basketball shoes nobody will buy me*, I said to myself: the usual personalized ad crap.

Instead a guy who said he was a friend appeared and proposed he show me something that I'd certainly find interesting. I only had to click where he indicated. *Go for it*, he said. *Don't be afraid!*

So I clicked and found myself in a locked vault of IQ's superPC containing a long chain of emails between our neighbor and his builder. I could see the traitor's big ugly sideburns and smell his ashtray smell as I read his messages, the two of them discussing how they were going to transform the chicken coop we live in—it's owned by him—into a bunch of new town houses.

There he goes pulling my leg again, that crazy genius, my brother, I said to myself, thinking IQ was teasing me. When I was small he loved making me think he could move a salami sandwich around a chat room, or that processors could mate and give birth to microprocessors, stuff like that.

But my assumption soon evaporated like an ice cream cone in the sun. It simply made no sense that he would try to draw me into the hidden recesses of his supercomputer. He has no idea that I'm already able to get into some of his secret compartments.

The plans of those town houses—to be plopped down on a stretch of land that has never seen a *town*—were fully drawn up and approved, I learned from those emails. Which meant we were about to be evicted. The con artist who plays Casanova when you're around now wants to take advantage of your absence to toss us out.

And there was some other pretty disturbing stuff in there, beginning with my school principal's email account. And also the English teacher's. These are topped up whenever a new message arrives and all those that have my name in them, and even those that simply deal with my class, are transferred into a special folder.

IQ's secret vault also had the key to get into the hospital's IT system, and your medical records. The notations and messages from the various doctors on your case, and all your lab results go there.

It was becoming absolutely, mathematically clear that it wasn't IQ who had led me to all this. The fox doesn't invite you for tea in his secret den hidden away in the woods. In fact, I was getting nervous that he would show up and find me here where I wasn't supposed to be, in this place guarded as it were by security cameras. *You're such a snoop*, he'd say.

In my opinion it's better that you know nothing of the eviction plan, and I'd also like to move this information into the wastebasket of my own brain, so let's pretend I know nothing, and deal with more pressing problems. Anyway, Logo thinks I'm making it all up; I can see that from looking at her bucolic shepherdess's face while she's writing down what I say. Which to her is full of crackpot comparisons and inelegant similes. She thinks I suffer from galloping flights of fancy and will make her gallop until her spleen explodes.

Tomorrow you'll be smiling again, and that's what matters. Your smile is like a full tank of gas, it fuels many miles. First you'll look after the bees and the fridge, then you'll be off to school, where you'll tell the principal he can enroll in that institute for cretins himself if he likes. You've never been a fan of euphemisms, and pleasantries even less.

We'll return to life as it was, with all the problems that once seemed insurmountable but when expressed in words suddenly become normal administration, even quite entertaining. Grandpa will come to lunch on Saturday, slinking around like a cat that's committed some crime, and he'll bring us organic vanilla ice cream. Papa will come over on Sunday and we'll have a ball with the PlayStation, and you'll get nervous. I won't use your credit card again, and I won't bite you—I promise.

A MIRACLE OF HIGH
ARCTIC JEWELWORK

MY DREAM CAME TO AN END, ripping me cruelly from the soothing cotton wool of sleep the way it does sometimes. It was a reassuring one in which Mamma moved the air with her long hands and said what she thought without mincing words or watering down her opinions. She was so matter-of-fact and so heartbreaking, and I tried to hold onto her the way you clutch a hot-water bottle, praying the warmth will last as long as possible.

It was certainly a great relief to see her up and about, rather than lying on her back, her eyes roaming all over the place. In the cave of night my fears and worries receded, now that she had the situation in hand. Everything was still possible, everything could be repaired. Maybe because of that reassuring note it took me a while to notice that the house was all lit up. I couldn't hear if there were any unusual noises, but the lights were definitely on.

I got up and dragged myself to the waiting room (what we call the living room), where I saw what I thought must be a second dream. There was my father in his pajamas with the fishes—nothing special about that—next to our neighbor dressed like the perfect ranchero. The ranchero was waving a hand at the window and ranting, then pointing again at the filthy glass and scratching his maxi-muttonchops with the other hand. My father had an arm thrust against his forehead and was also looking at the window, plugged up by night's blackness. He was shaking his skinny head, which sits atop a body as lithe and flexible as a feline's.

When I approached the windowsill myself, I saw that Imida's apple trees were draped in icy stalactites of every shape and size, all of them blazing and sparkling with lights. It was right out of *A Thousand and One Nights*: ice crystals and their shimmering reflections as far as the eye could see. The moon was gigantic and as bright as a photograph that had been retouched. I've never seen it looking better.

I really was sorry that Mamma, who'd been with me just then while I was streaming my neurons, couldn't be there to see this marvel. She goes crazy over stuff like that. She would have been sighing and squeezing her hands together like a kid who didn't want a fly she'd caught to escape, and pointing out a thousand details I hadn't noticed. If she can give an entire lecture on a dried-up leaf that's glued to the asphalt, just think what she could do with that miracle of high arctic jewelwork.

And she would certainly have invented one of those stories of hers, like, it was the Martians who did it, because it's their Christmas Eve. They wanted everything to look very beautiful, the way we do when we decorate our trees and bell towers with lights. We should help them out, so we must turn on all the lights. All this so she could crush me in her strong arms and cover me with kisses, like I'd won a contest or something.

The unhappy one was our neighbor Imida. Actually he seemed less unhappy than well on his way to stark raving. His hair—salt mostly, a little pepper—had totally ceased to obey the force of gravity and his cheeks were redder than a maraschino cherry.

The reason for all that ice was that the sprinkler system had suddenly come on. All by itself. And it couldn't be stopped; it just kept spraying water that froze into pretty popsicles and sleek stalactites. These were weighing down more and more branches and fragile twiglets, and soon they'd start to snap.

One must never wish for bad things to happen to other people, says Mamma, she and her Thursday night Buddhist friends. Fine, but still, this seemed fair punishment for a moron who intended to take advantage of our terrible troubles to evict us. Someone in the cosmos had taken the case file in hand and issued the appropriate opinion. Some divinity with good taste, because the retribution was truly elegant.

My father smoothed his piscine pajamas with the palm of his hand, making that disgusted face he wears on great occasions. He thinks the irrigation system—Imida's pride and joy—lacks even a gleam of intelligence, it's just plain stupid. Even in the darkest Dark Ages they didn't make things like that. And further, he thinks the Mac—and the computer controlling the irrigation system is a Mac—was dreamed up to appeal to suckers; the amazing thing is that something much worse didn't happen.

Knowing him, he was deep in a fantasy about a supersmart system based on algorithms that also took into account the crude psychology of farmers and the hormonal balance of trees, and that could teach itself to improve its functioning. Ever since he saw the results IQ's been achieving he's become a fan of deep learning. Once it was patented, a system like that could be sold around the world, beginning in California, with his name featured prominently on it.

His harsh opinions notwithstanding, he didn't actually detest our wiseass, lecherous neighbor. He really kind of liked him, the way you like certain animals that don't have a clue but are appealing and make you smile. And obviously he adores anyone who takes it for granted he's a world IT genius. I should add he still knew nothing of the eviction notice.

But Imida was tugging at Papa's pajama sleeve, which was annoying. *You'll be able to repair it, I know*, he kept repeating, meaning his Mac, which controlled not only the sprinklers but the gate, the garage door, and the dog's electronic collar. My father patted his tablet in a fishy pocket; he'd have been delighted to go back to bed. He loves snoring, maybe because he's so much younger than a normal parent. But he had no choice, the best he could do between one yawn and another was to cross his arms and squeeze his chest tight like he feared someone was going to steal it.

In the meantime IQ appeared in his nighttime garb, something like a Formula 1 driver's fireproof gear, loaded with sensors. He stared at the two of them the way he looks at people who get excited or talk too loudly, asking himself what kind of design flaw causes behavior like that. Then he glanced at the ice show, scanning it and pursing his lips like someone trying to determine what flavor of cough drops he's sucking.

He was probably thinking about whether moonlight could be converted into BTU-ready energy, or whether it wouldn't be better to equip the countryside with a heating system connected to the nearby volcano. He's forever asking himself questions that pass normal people right by. He didn't seem very shocked by the stalactites either, or, even less, unhappy about them.

At this point an idea shot through my head like a guided missile: *He's the one who did it.* Sometimes a missile hits the target and settles down in the middle of your brain and you just can't dislodge it.

But then IQ's scientific eyes fell on the open gate, and the garage door at half-mast, and his eyebrows puckered up. Like when an investigator stumbles on something that rouses his sleepy brain lobes. He looked astonished, although he rarely finds anything astonishing. Now he was listening intently to what the two so-called adults were saying.

After some more tug-of-war, Papa went off trailing the rockabilly farmer. The defeated warrior, he had no other choice. IQ put on that show of indifference he wears when he has some specific plan in mind, and he and his smart sleepwear retired to his overheated ops center. I played the weary one and retired to my cell.

As you might guess, I immediately hooked up to his superPC to see what he was up to. I needed to know if he was the one who had opened the sprinklers, the way you sometimes feel an irresistible need to scratch yourself. I took it for granted that the gate and the garage were his work; he'd even shown me the debut performance.

First, IQ tried to get into our neighbor's late-model Mac, which appeared dead. His efforts to connect directly with the irrigation system also failed. It was like a space engineer trying to contact a satellite that's gone AWOL. But IQ is not at all accustomed to losing satellites, or failing in other ways. I figured he was getting more and more nervous.

I didn't know what to think anymore. A terrorist does not return to the scene of the crime to check what kind of bomb he used. Still, Macs don't lose their minds all by themselves, and if there's anyone who adores driving them crazy, it's IQ.

Papa reappeared with our neighbor, whose muttonchops were now pointing toward his rubber boots. No one had anticipated that the entire electronic security system—right down to the security guarding security—would go bust. We were left with nothing to stop water falling on the trees but a prehistoric sluice valve. He tried to open it, to no avail, and now he was covered in rust. He was beside himself, he couldn't believe that the man he considered a world IT expert could only repeat that the programmer responsible for this mess should be sent to Guantanamo, and that Macs should be outlawed. He was smoking one cigarette after another, and my father can't stand cigarettes.

It was beginning to get light, and the pinwheels were still sending out fine ribbons of water that morphed into ornate jewels on the trees. The first branches began to snap, with a popping sound like bottles being opened, and the ground underfoot had become one big glossy skating rink. It was a fairy-tale landscape; a pumpkin-shaped sleigh driven by golden reindeer wouldn't have been out of place. The Supreme Vindicator, or whoever was his agent, had decided to do things right.

Logo appeared just as the sun began to show its shy, chilly rounded back. Now she comes in the morning too, before IQ goes to school, and supervises the toothbrushing, chides me about this or that, and takes care of other mamma tasks. She seems to think I can't do without this. She speaks to my father the way you speak to colleagues at work you'd be just as happy never to see again, she's been doing that for a while now.

She didn't peer out the window through the filthy glass to admire the immense lace curtain of ice as everybody else did, she inspected my feet, as if they were the mind-boggling spectacle. She pointed them out to Papa, all but convicting him with her indignant policewoman look. My bare feet were an appalling breach of the rules. My summer pajamas with the short pants could maybe be overlooked, although the point was debatable, but bare feet on icy cement, no. He pretended not to understand, because he hates being criticized, and above all by her. He thinks she's a busybody, not to mention a digital illiterate.

Logo balks at writing down what I've just said, because she thinks these are piddling problems that can very well be overlooked. My father's basically a good guy, and he loves me; I'm the one who's twisted here, for whatever reason, she insists. I've got this bee in my bonnet that he's to blame for Mamma's accident, but he wasn't involved in any way. To me, though, these are important details and I insist she continue tapping out what I'm signing and my aborted pyrotechnic phrases. Language exists to arrange your thoughts in good order, not to bury them in your brain. I'm never going to learn to speak well unless I cram in all the right words for what I want to say. On the other hand, she was right about the cold; when I had noticed it my feet were two colorless blocks of ice.

Now Logo whipped into my cell like a pissed-off electron and came out with the heaviest pair of socks I own, the ones I was wearing when, while skating, I split my skull on the pole holding up the No Skating sign. She put them on me, yanking my feet hard to teach me some kind of lesson. Pointless, no one was paying any attention to her performance. Imida, stuffed into his boots, was wheezing like a cyclist about to fall over dead on an Alpine hill, while my father scratched his unruly hair, like anyone dead tired and wondering how he can escape the situation in which he is entangled.

After studying his fingernails for a long time he looked at IQ—a cry for help disguised as a casual glance. IQ meanwhile looked the other way, pretending to be deep in thought. He didn't have any idea what to do either, as unlikely as that seemed. Actually, he was gazing at the garage door, just now opening, as if he were watching a dead man rise from his coffin and walk away.

Who's freakin' doing that? he muttered, looking at the tablet he had in hand.

The garage was now wide open and you could just see the SUV that looks like a hearse. Our neighbor revived a bit and said he was going to hunt up the plumber, who wasn't answering his phone. *That's the only solution*, he said, massaging his rock-and-roll walrus mustache.

Then I gotta go look for the dog, he added; it was clear that the frozen apples came first. He was somewhat disappointed that Papa hadn't been able to fix his Mac, but it had been nice to talk with him as equals.

The second he was out of there my father let out a sigh only a bit less explosive than a volcanic eruption, and opened the window.

Never seen anyone more ignorant; he's never even heard of neuro-engineering, he said, hoisting his PC onto his knees.

Someone's jerking us around, muttered IQ as if he were talking to himself, his lips pursed like he was sucking a mint. Except his lips are so thin you almost can't see them.

Just then Grandpa showed up; he and IQ had agreed my brother would help him translate earthworm excrement into mathematical formulas. His face looked gray, and we all knew it wasn't just because he had been up all night classifying transparent worms. Since Mamma's been in the hospital, he seems to have aged twenty years, poor guy. And his asthma has gotten much worse, the air just won't enter his lungs.

While we were having breakfast, Papa spoke up to say that farmers were stuck in the Neolithic period, when they first appeared. *Tomorrow's farming will be done by engineers sitting comfortably in their offices*, he went on, staring at the screen of his PC as if it was agreeing with him.

Lettuce, cabbages, strawberries, all managed by robots that will be constantly learning, he said, his hand sketching out rows of cabbages in the air. *The fact is we already have the technical skills, we only need the will to apply them on a large scale*, he said. Once upon a time he'd been quite skeptical about autodidactic neuromorphic programs, and he used to quarrel with IQ about them, but now he's decided they can resolve everything.

Grandpa was staring at him like he was a lunatic who says he's going to take a stroll on water and then multiply some fishes. He thinks farms like the neighbor's apple orchards are crimes of technocratic capitalism; they're the ones that cause world hunger. The only solution is to go back to farming the way they do in Africa, growing fruits full of blemishes and insect bites.

So you can guess what he thought when he heard that Papa intends to stock the fields with androids and processors. But in the interests of us boys he didn't want to seem contrary, so he merely contemplated his words with sad, gray eyes, like when you watch rain that won't stop falling.

OUR THROATS WERE FULL
OF POINTY STONES

DEAR MAMMA, I wanted to tell you that I'm not mad because you didn't wake up. Sure, I wish you'd blasted your green marbles at me, but if you didn't, it means you have your reasons to keep circling slowly and surely, the way the arms on an alarm clock go around. You must have thought about it and decided to wait a little longer.

I don't feel like running around again just yet, another couple of weeks in bed and I'll be properly rested, you thought to yourself.

I'm fine with talking as we did before, no worries. I'm young and you're not old; a month more or less doesn't mean anything. My legs are going to resign themselves to behaving. Like all legs do.

Sure, we all felt pointy stones in our throats when we saw that even with those hundreds of electrodes they screwed into your head, you didn't move. Papa never stopped talking; some people can't tolerate the vacuum between air molecules, they have to fill it up with words. He thinks the Swiss guy's device that fires stimuli resembles those contraptions you see at the

Lombroso Museum. *Medicine is never going to make progress if it doesn't combine forces with artificial intelligence*, he said. He said pretty much the same thing when they found out that because I had a malformation, they couldn't install a cochlear implant. He wanted them to connect the digital sound processor directly to my cerebral cortex.

Poor Grandpa had palpitating purple spots on his neck; a whale of an asthma attack had closed up his throat and he looked like he was about to cry. With all his sage advice about not entertaining illusions, he'd been counting on the Swiss magic. Even IQ sucked his cheeks, a great upheaval for someone as immovable as he is.

Maybe the dapper, famous Swiss doctor didn't inspire you, we should have known you wouldn't believe in him. You've never liked people who look like they just came out of an elegant clothing shop, whose skin is all relaxed. You prefer farmers, big hands dirty with the soil and honest wrinkles, even illegal immigrants begging on the street. You were raised in a forest full of wild boar and ideals, without electricity and without rules, and like Papa says, you're half-wild.

Dinner that evening was like a wake. Grandpa wanted to wait for Papa, but he could no longer breathe at all, so he returned to his hole in the wall in the people's hive down by the factories to fill himself up with cortisone. In the meantime Logo, by now one of the family, turned up and said she'd stay for dinner. Her smile, though, was that of a hostess whose shoes are too tight.

Papa rode in on the scooter he'd borrowed from IQ and began bending our ears about the interface between human neurons and neural networks.

At this point some good news rained down, sweet as a ray of sunlight on a bombed-out city. My elementary school teacher, the one who'd insisted I learn to sign because he'd decided I wasn't a moron, always said life is a roller coaster, you've got to be ready for the ups and downs. At dinner time the principal called, the man himself. Logo answered the phone: Logo, so serious but also so relaxed and breezy. He told her that from the following day, that is today, I could return to school. I'd been readmitted.

Stop making that moron face, Logo signed to me, but this time her topaz eyes were shining. Even she was stunned at first, but she recovered. *It means you deserve it, knucklehead*, she said, rubbing those slightly rough cheeks that blonds have. My father scratched his feline beard and IQ's perfect cool grew even more rarefied, more sidereal, more in tune with the immensity of the cosmos.

I wagged my head *yes*, but honestly, this thing made no sense. To the principal, I'm a mosquito specialized in vexing the teaching corps' nervous system. The English teacher would like to put me in an oven like they did with the Jews, mix my ashes in concrete, and pour it in the foundations of the overpass. And even that piggy of an Italian teacher, who started out so nice and said I was making great progress, now thinks I'm a wreck in the middle of the road blocking traffic. At first he thought I could be fixed, but he doesn't anymore, whatever he says to Logo.

They took me back, I say, repeating the words slowly so they have time to lodge in my brain, perhaps even build a nest in some far-flung corner of it. *This time it's not just me imagining it*, I think, although it certainly feels like a thrilling dream.

If it was up to me to choose, I wouldn't hesitate a second: I'd have you awake and me expelled. Especially since my passion for school has never been extreme. But as Logo says, reality is reality and wishes are wishes, and there's no toggle key to convert one to the other.

This morning Grandpa and IQ and I made our appearance with great pomp and ceremony. It was my second first day of school. I might have been an athlete coming home after winning three golds at the Olympics. Everyone was staring, everyone was amazed. I'd been kicked out the back door and was now returning by the main entrance, every bit the triumphant gladiator. The hairs on my skin stood up as I caught a whiff of the stale smells of school, the dirty, jaded walls, and all the other details I know so well. Grandpa was touched; he looked sweet, his shoes too large and his pants too short.

Before going to my classroom we passed by the principal's office, as agreed. *Certainly you have learning gaps in many subjects, enormous gaps, but I'm sure you'll close them*, said the overripe tub of lard, resting a flabby hand on my shoulder.

I'm fully confident that certain episodes won't repeat themselves, he added after studying his feet, half concealed by his large pregnant woman's belly. Grandpa gazed at him as he might inspect a worm of some species he's not familiar with, unhappy at this gap in his knowledge. He couldn't figure out how this metamorphosis had come about. No one could.

That letter about disabled students that's going around is false, the principal explained, making a triangle with his two hands as if to protect a disabled fledgling. *I feel it's very important that the school should help disabled children*, he went on. A long pause. His eyes were slightly sad, as if he was watching a lame duckling limp away.

I won't hesitate to go to court to stop this slander. His triple chin was quivering with waves of indignation. A further pause.

That parrot nose of his would be strange to bite, surrounded by all those blobs of fat, the thought passed through my mind for some reason. *Noses don't get fat*, I said to myself, thinking I shouldn't do something stupid.

Grandpa was fiddling with the buttons on his neorealist wedding jacket, his hands trembling. The spots on his cheeks and his neck were as purple as bilberries, shading nearly to black around the edges, and his shiny bald head was dewy with sweat. He'd been picturing me locked up in a gruesome insane asylum, and here we were being received like the delegation of an important foreign country. His broad benevolent forehead shone with the conviction there'd been a misunderstanding, and now things had been cleared up. IQ was silent, a cat enjoying the warmth from the radiator after finishing his bowl and licking it.

The myth of the good principal held up until three in the afternoon, when I got home and took a look at IQ's PC, specifically the strongbox full of emails that the mysterious guy who called himself a friend showed me.

Now I knew what "letter about disabled students" the Paunch was referring to: it had been sent out via IQ's supercomputer to numerous associations representing disabled persons, and to newspapers and journals dealing with pedagogy and psychology. When my brother does these things he does a superb job, and so it went out to a ton of recipients. It was an email the principal had originally sent to the school administrator; my brother hadn't changed a word, but it looked like this present copy had been sent out by the principal himself, by mistake.

The gist of this ill-famed email was that the principal didn't want too many "losers and retards" in his school. They would hurt the school's prestige and prejudice funding from the regional government. Now as we know, these aren't sentiments that go down well with associations of parents of blind children or kids with Down's. So in order to show that the letter was a gigantic fake, the principal had readmitted me, jazzing up his obese language to make him seem to say the opposite of what he thinks.

So it was Robin Hood who got me readmitted. Him and him alone. I probably shouldn't tell you this, Mamma, but you know better than anyone that my chest risks exploding, and probably my head too, when I try to keep certain things to myself. First my red blood cells start fizzing, then my heart and my eyelids start thumping, and the more megatons of explosives there are, the greater the risk.

But you shouldn't be mad at IQ. All's well that ends well, as your friend says: the one who went to live in Canada but came back because she said even the fish in the freezer suffer from the cold in Canada. What matters is that I'm back in school, I didn't have to go to the concentration camp with the bars on the windows. Okay, IQ's a hacker, but it was a good cause.

Just my luck, my first class today was English. I was in a foul mood, as usual when I have the stupid hearing aids on; I get nasty vibrations all over and don't understand much, what with all the unbearable reverberations and sonic booms. The malnourished teacher looked like she was secretly expecting me to bite her bony hand again, or maybe her scrawny nose. However, she was careful to make sure I could see her razor-sharp lips, and when she asked me questions, she slowed down to half-speed. Even when my answers weren't so brilliant, she kept smiling undeterred, like an advertisement for something.

The little rat with the bitter-tasting earlobes had been assigned a seat right at the back of the classroom, as far from me as possible. I was therefore able to enjoy my boredom in peace, even joyously. I was thinking how smart IQ is; he's my real father in many ways. *My brother is amazing, and it's not just a question of an intelligence quotient of 185*, I said to myself.

Logo, writing this, wrinkles up her nose. It seems she doesn't like IQ's methods—assuming I haven't invented this whole story, and it wouldn't be the first time, she points out. She thinks the Italian teacher has always been very good to me and did everything to get me back in school. And even the English teacher isn't the harpy I make her out to be; she too would like to give me a hand, if only I would make a little effort. But a deal's a deal, and therefore she etches my halting words and my signs on the screen like I was the executive of some big company and she was my personal assistant. When I can speak better, then I myself will practice learning to write, she reminds me frequently. But we're not at that point yet.

However, what really matters to me is not school, it's that you should recover. It seemed right around the corner, but every time it gets further away, like those mountain peaks that always look like you're practically on them, but there's always another valley to get beyond, and another hill to climb, and another valley.

SPRING

WORDS TOSSED UP IN THE AIR THAT COME DOWN COMPLETELY RANDOMLY

WHEN I CAME HOME from school today the house was empty and unfriendly. It was just barely drizzling, but the fat, slovenly clouds seemed to have put the sun out, it looked like it would never shine again. Not even the fact they'd let me back into school was enough to banish the glutinous grayness of the heavens, streaked with greenish highlights. It looked like a bad algae invasion. *This can't last forever*, I said to myself.

There was still half a giant jar of Nutella behind Grandmother in the kitchen, I wasn't going to die of starvation. To cheer myself up I could Skype my deaf friend from elementary school, the one I learned to sign with. But still, I would have traded my entire collection of video games just then for a smile made of lips and saliva and real teeth, for the warmth of my mother's hand.

I opened the PC and, glancing around, I could see that IQ wasn't even close to giving up, he was on him like the soccer defender who's constantly checking a dangerous attacker. Imida's new system was a fortress with high walls and narrow doors that opened only with twenty-character-long passwords. He's got a new tech consultant who knows how we work. Still, you need a lot more security than that to keep Robin Hood out.

Imida was complaining that the garage door and the gate keep on doing whatever they freakin' want: open, close, reopen, stay open. According to Papa farmers are complainers because their genetic material hasn't been updated since the Neolithic, we shouldn't listen to them. What's really peculiar is that Imida's gate and such don't seem to be operated by IQ; in fact, they tend to act out when he's not home. Anyway, he's obsessed by the eviction thing now, not some silly hack for fun.

So there I was fiddling around trying to get a handle on the situation when an invitation came through on an IRC channel from some guy I don't know. Also deaf, he told me; he'd seen my input on the forum of our association.

Know to climb? he asked point-blank.

I replied that I'm a renowned expert, and as I was saying so I utterly convinced myself I was an incredible climber, the way you do when you're writing something. *Next year I'm doing the Himalayas; it's all organized*, I wrote.

Wow, congratulations, he replied.

Anyone can do it, you just have to apply yourself, I wrote, doing the humble thing.

Future we go together? he asked.

Sure, I answered.

Me no ready, he said.

No worries, no hurry, I tapped back, feeling relieved.

Yeah, I know I should shut up on the subject of writing, but he was a real disaster. It was like his were words tossed up in the air that came down on the screen completely randomly. Not to mention how long it took him to get a message out. I played myself at whole games of checkers. You could tell he was very proud, though, and so I didn't want to advise him he should learn to handle words better before he decided to engage in a chat. People have said that to me, numerous times, and I didn't want to be the one to stick the knife in.

To like gates, you? he asked.

Sorry? I replied; I seemed to be chatting with a two-month-old baby.

Interference for ludic purposes, he added.

What you say is very interesting. I cut him off, as you do when you don't understand jack.

Important be fun; you always be thinking that, I am knowing. He pronounced the words as if they cost him great mental effort.

Yeah, I replied. I could feel pins and needles on my neck and my arms.

You to wish be fast friend?

I said sure, who wouldn't want to be fast friends.

For whole life?

I said for my whole life was just fine, you couldn't just cancel a fast friend like you block some pain in the neck on Facebook.

With that same extreme lethargy, like he had to look up every word in the dictionary, the words *to snow New York* appeared on the screen.

If you say so, I replied, somewhat puzzled.

To rain here, no need irrigation system, he went on after thinking about it for a moment.

Yeah, it's drizzling, pretty disgusting, I said after casting a look out the window.

Dirty tricks always possible, he said.

Sure, I said, scraping the bottom of the barrel for words to say. The pins and needles were becoming painful. And knowing my legs, the next step would be kicking the air and other things.

Algorithm for sequential self-learning of verbal elaboration $A=\sqrt{z}.r^2+XY$, he said. He was now raving, as if exhausted by our edifying exchange.

I told him I had to go and eat, and I turned off the PC. I went to get the jar of Nutella, I needed comfort. And while I licked the spoon very, very slowly, I studied our neighbor's apple trees out the window. They looked like ghosts trying to frighten the fog and the drizzle. Or maybe they were the scared ones, what with that miserable weather. At times it's difficult to see exactly how things stand, explanations just flounder around in the air like drunken drones.

Then I dialed the number to connect with the webcam in Mamma's room, and I watched her eyes roll around in bored circles like the second hand on a watch. Once in a while she'd lift one shoulder, like women do when their dress straps are slipping around. It wasn't raining over there; everything was its usual dry white. A Styrofoam coffin. *They've put her in the packing material for an electronic device, Mamma, who so loves snails and tall grass*, I thought.

I told her I'd come by later, but talking to myself, without turning on the mic. Logo is staring at me as she writes this; she finds it hard to believe that Mamma can hear my thoughts. However, I'm not going to make stuff up just so my signing seems less peculiar in words, less full of comparisons only I make.

And then we'll have a good long talk, I told Mamma, or at least I thought. I'd hidden the Super-Pacifier, as IQ calls the Nutella, under the table that's actually an old door, with a handle and everything. By the way, the legal framework for now is this: we're a free-market household. Protectionism will return, of course, when she comes back.

I recovered the jar and sat by the bayonet window observing the remorseless rustic melancholy outside. *Maybe Papa's right, even for the climate we need modern solutions*, I thought. That stubborn gray sky would demoralize even a large bottle of antidepressant pills.

The vibrating intercom vibrated, and on my helmet's screen Logo appeared. She was dressed to go climbing, despite the fact this was no day to be up there with the angels and airplanes. My mood bounced up a good meter from my tennis socks, and I could feel a warm sensation lapping the skin on my arms.

She came in and planted a kiss on my cheek, squeezing my neck in the crook of her arm. Snickering, she said I looked like a bulldog that had lost a bone down a manhole. First she tickled me under the arms until I was giggling and then she whacked me on the back so hard I almost fell over. It was like a whole rescue team had arrived; the chicken coop was saturated with that yeasty smell of hers and a surfeit of good cheer.

I was on my way out to do some training, but then I learned you were here all by your lonesome, she signed. *In any case, with this weather it's not that much fun*, she added.

My eyes began to sting, because I knew this was a colossal lie. Logo's hardly afraid of a little rain, and besides, the climbing gym where she goes is covered. Much as I tried to hold back the tears welling behind my eyes, the wave was becoming an unstoppable flood.

Logo squeezed me in her ever so slightly rough arms, and told me not to worry, she'd always be there for me. Exactly the thing to make a sentimental mess like me cry some more. Especially now that she's about to leave for a long trip to Australia.

Or rather, as long as you need me, she corrected herself, stroking my head the way you pet a lost kitten.

Then, joking around, she started making a frittata with "zero-meter sourced parsley"—from the flower bed under the kitchen window—that smelled deliciously of charred cheese. And served it up with slices of toast from the smart toaster. Words began to rush into my mouth, they were spilling over trying to latch onto all the signs that my hands were producing, as Logo herself pointed out to me.

Grandmother also seemed happy that all our disasters were at bay for a moment. She was holding two lumpy lemons in her lap, looking quite proud. Every once in a while I glanced at Mamma, on the monitor on top of the refrigerator, and she seemed to be doing fine too.

We were finishing up the frittata when Papa showed up. He was pulling two suitcases with wheels behind him, and then there were four, and a bunch of cardboard boxes, some knapsacks, and a lot more other stuff. *Holy shit*, I said, in words this time, and Logo elbowed me in the ribs.

There was also a collapsible electric bicycle with a GPS system worthy of a spaceship, a mirror with video cameras installed in the frame for tracking expression (mood), and his smart punching bag with all the related instrumentation. It was a full-scale move. He was moving in with us.

And specifically, into Mamma's cell, because that's where he had parked his bags. No doubt my expression betrayed my utter disbelief. Not to mention the disapproval on Logo's already longish face, a breach of the protocol demanding her absolute impartiality. And I could just imagine Mamma's reaction. *Are you crazy?* she would have snapped in that curt way she has. Up until now he's had the good manners to sleep on the sofa in the waiting room.

Excuse me, but that's Mamma's cell! I said out loud. He made a whirling motion with his gnarled hand, as if to say he'd explain later.

That's not the deal, I insisted.

For now, while we're waiting for Mamma to wake up, he signed, as usual close to incomprehensibly. The smart mirror and all his other electronic gadgetry didn't seem to share his hesitancy; they looked as if they were already putting down roots.

Let's hope that's very soon, I said, my red blood cells in serious ferment.

He didn't say *You're somewhat ticked off with me because you've got some crazy ideas about things in your head, but I adore you, kiddo* like he always does, crushing my head against his hard tomcat belly. He had on that worried look we've been seeing recently: the man who's lost his wallet and can't find it. From what IQ says—and he's always very well-informed—Papa has serious problems at work because there have been several data leaks recently. He's the last person who would steal personal profiles or credit card numbers, but his bosses don't know that, and he's being watched. And naturally the big shot who can't stand him is taking advantage of the situation. That's why his fingernails are reduced to chewed-off stubs.

WHEN THE RED BLOOD CELLS SIZZLE

ON SATURDAY they came to steal the bees. IQ's automatic learning system sprang into action, and so we know the make of the pickup involved and the license plate number. And then the program served up the owner's name and birth date, because it can come up with those too.

It's the bee people, Papa said, half-facing the other way. He had on a yellow baseball cap with the bill turned around, and his jockey's arms stuck out of a red T-shirt decorated with a drawing of an integrated circuit. No matter how inclined one was to believe it, he didn't look like a father.

The bee people? I asked, in words. Standing right in front of him, like a cop blocking traffic.

Yep, they take bees, he said in that way you say something everybody knows.

Signing, I told him I wasn't expecting them to come and steal the bees, and he got irritated and said they couldn't wait any longer.

Sooner or later Mamma will be back, and what will she say when she sees her bees are gone? I signed. *She'll say we're gangsters through and through.*

When she comes back I'll get new bees, he replied, hiding his real thoughts behind a nervous whirl of the wrist. Because in his mind she's never coming back.

While we're waiting, I can take care of it, I signed, putting on a reassuring face like someone hoping to reestablish common sense.

Scratching his lemon-colored cap, Papa said I had to think about school, and it would already be a big achievement if I learned to stay put in my seat like other kids. And furthermore, looking after a bee colony isn't easy, you have to have experience. *And you have to keep at it*, he added, looking at me the way you look at a car that's always had problems.

If I have any difficulties I'll get Grandpa to help, I said, hoping to put an end to the conversation. It was like talking to atoms of air that didn't care what happened.

The bees can't stay here; pretty soon our neighbor's going to start spraying insecticide, he said, scratching himself, because when he hears Grandpa mentioned he scratches. He thinks the old man's a hippy and eternal protester, like those Japanese soldiers who never knew the war was over.

We'll find someone to take them to the acacia grove; Mamma said that's what we'd do this year, I said.

He snorted again. It was too late to argue, the buyers were here and waiting. *Open!* he said to the gate.

Close! I said.

Open! he said again, shaking himself all over the way dogs do to dry off. I was about to open my mouth again, but he came up to me and raised an arm. *Aggravated assault of a minor*, I said to myself.

Sending me a last dirty look that said I'd better do the right thing, he went out to organize the loading of the hives. I meanwhile sneaked around the back where the pickup was waiting. It was one of those open-backed vehicles, covered with rust spots.

Mamma's poor bees are going to be carried off in this unworthy heap, I thought, and in my throat I realized there was a lump that hurt. I bent over to inspect one of the front tires, then the other. The back tires were pretty worn too; let's hope the road wasn't wet.

Some people are totally irresponsible, I said to myself. When you think about the dangers on the road. When I'd had enough I returned to my cell to look after my business.

I'd just switched on the PC when Papa came whistling in like a meteorite. He was going up and down on his heels, a horse rolling in chopped chili pepper.

Why did you do that? he asked. For once he was up close to me—too close. My teeth were dying to bite something.

Why did I do what? I said, studying the integrated circuit in purple on his chest.

Let the air out of the tires on the pickup, he replied with yet another snort. His knobby muscles were quivering like he had some disease. I said I had no idea what he was talking about.

Your hands are still dirty, he fumed, grabbing my arm almost hard enough to hoist me in the air. I looked at my hands, and they were in fact grimy with that black dust you typically find on car tires.

I'm a political prisoner, I said. I have no idea why I said that. The words were just doing whatever they wanted, like my legs.

You're a total fool, he said to me. The air in the tires seemed to have been pumped into his face, which was bright red, and his eyes were all puffy. When he stopped looking me up and down, he snarled at me to stay right there and took off at high speed.

Now the important thing is to stay calm, I said to myself, astonished to feel the perfect tranquility that reigned inside me. But even before I knew it my teeth had sunk hard into my arm, halfway between the wrist and the elbow. Maybe it was just nostalgia for the old days with Mamma, who knows? A neat imprint of my teeth was stamped on my arm, and dots of blood were welling up.

Out in the courtyard, I grabbed a pickaxe and began to whack on the beehives with the handle. If there's one thing that infuriates bees, it's a blow to their hives. I whacked as hard as I could, and pushed and shoved and even kicked a bit. My legs were pleased to let off steam.

All of a sudden, there was a great commotion, an apicultural revolution, you might say. Some workers on a reconnaissance flight came bombing toward me, ready to stick me with their bayonets, but they were looking for a mad terrorist, not a gentle kid like me. My legs were longing to run and kick, but the bees didn't know that.

Now my arm was beginning to hurt and a small torrent of blood was emerging. I applied toilet paper to stem the flow, and climbed up onto the roof. I took with me a tablet, a couple of bananas, and a few small tubs of Nutella that had been abandoned on top of the enhanced video-game console for some months.

When the bee people returned to their pickup, my father glared at me the way you glare at a pigeon that's just done its business on an automobile fresh from the showroom. But without letting on that he'd seen me up here. The two guys with the pickup seemed pretty pissed off.

Those two don't have the patience a proper beekeeper needs, they'd be better off raising vipers, I said to myself.

My father attached an electric cord to the compressor, and they inflated the tires with air. They then went to get the beehives and load them onto their truck. You could see by the way they were walking that they were in a hurry; they thought they'd already wasted enough time.

Sitting up there on the top of the roof, I tried to broach IQ's superPC by the usual tortuous route, but for some reason I couldn't get in. Maybe the stress had gotten into my veins and contaminated my blood: when my red blood cells start to fizz, I do stupid things. Sometimes the bombs go off by delayed action.

I was trying a new tactic when I noticed that someone had written to me on the IRC channel I use with IQ. *Fast friend from yesterday, you maybe to remember*, the message said.

Yeah sure, it's not like I have Alzheimers, I replied. I didn't know how to spell it, however, so maybe he didn't understand.

Price of tantalum is rise, he said.

I'm sorry? I replied.

Unauthorized access to Google data bank, he said.

Huh? I thought.

I was pleased he'd got back in touch, though—like when you meet another human being after your ship has gone down and you're not worried about the fine points. I had no intention of sharing everything that was going on with me, but he was still a fun guy to chat with. Someone who wasn't trying to screw me every way he could, unlike my father.

And of course the fact he was deaf couldn't help but make me like him. His sentences were short and twisted like mine are, both of us at war with the written word.

Do you know sign language? I asked him.

Affirmative, you bet, he replied, even seeming slightly offended.

So then I suggested we get together on Skype, because signing, we'd surely understand each other better, not having to go crazy over words for nothing.

No possible, he said. *Unfortunately no possible absolutely*, he repeated. *Present no, future yes*, he clarified. *Nice be big and to do what you want*, he said.

Don't tell me, it's the same here, I said, thinking about the bees.

Now to look! he exclaimed, changing the subject wildly. What he showed me was a video of a gate. Honestly, there was not much to see: the gate was closed and there wasn't a soul around. It could have been a still photograph except for the occasional insect that flew by in its bubble of insect-think. But if this kid who wanted to be my friend for eternity wanted me to watch, I would, although I was up to other things at the same time, like trying to shoo away the spiders scuttling around in my veins. Maybe they were only red blood cells, but they felt like tiny spiders.

I was scratching my arm when the flashing security light came on and the metallic gate began to open. Nothing revolutionary—this was an automatic gate—but at least there was action. No dead or wounded, but the light was pulsing and the two sides of the gate doggedly eased open in a slow yawn. It made me think of one of those black-and-white movies dear to the art and imagery teacher, so thrilling that even the walls fall asleep.

But before it ended, a tiny light bulb ignited in my cranial vault. That gate reminded me of something familiar, very familiar. Swinging around to look toward Imida's house, I saw that his gate was just then ending its opening swing. I was stunned. How could some guy I'd met in a chat room open our neighbor's gate? What did he even know about us and our neighbor?

Without even thinking about it I rapidly scanned the scene. But no, there was nothing—no guy wearing camo, no drone, no webcam except on the gate, taking the footage that had somehow landed on my screen. Nothing but the city down there in the valley's narrow basin, and the mountains all around, pressing as if to keep it from spreading too much. And the deep cut to one side of our chicken coop, where there's just room for the creek and the provincial highway to pass.

I didn't like any of this at all. Inside me, the spiders were squirming around like crazy, it occurred to me they might even be small mice. It wasn't enough that I had a crazy father, now there was this other moron playing scary tricks on me.

Was that funny? he asked after the window with the video disappeared.

Up to a point, I wrote, not giving anything away. I now had the feeling that the roof was moving, and that I might fall. It was those arachnids—rodents?—that wouldn't leave me alone.

Wait! he said. The window reappeared, and the two halves of the gate began to close again under the flashing light. But halfway through, they stopped abruptly and then began to open. Then they halted again and began to close—and so forth and so on, like seniors with heavily rusted joints gamely trying to look graceful.

I was smiling without meaning to, it really was hilarious. *Funny!* I confirmed. Smiling did me a lot of good, the beasties began to recede and my red blood cells calmed down.

Right then the gate shut down halfway closed. Shut down with an air of intending to remain that way for a while, indifferent to any requests or prayers. Our neighbor had arrived aboard his hearse of an SUV, punching the buttons on his remote. But the gate wouldn't budge.

Imida—sideburns long and hairy, dressed for a motorcycle movie of the high handlebar genre—got out of his vehicle. He stretched out a tattooed arm until he was almost touching the gate's antenna, punching wildly on the remote. Nothing happened. Whacking the thing hard against his thigh, he gave it the coup de grâce. Then he got into his SUV and parked it. And walked inside.

The gate immediately closed, the final snap sounding like someone making a naughty raspberry. The rock fiend in sheriff's clothes turned and flung his arms out, a goalkeeper who's just failed to stop a penalty kick and is pissed at himself and the world. Without meaning to, I hunkered down, because I didn't want him to think I was laughing behind his back, if he caught sight of me. And when I moved, it was like I was drunk. I wasn't really better, it turned out.

Right, that resolves the enigma; you're the one who's been enjoying himself playing with the gate and the garage, I wrote.

Days grow longer; soon spring epoch begin, he replied.

I'll bet you're the one who's blocking the TV too, I threw in. He said nothing. *You're the nitwit who's been playing sick jokes on us for the last couple months, admit it*, I said. He remained silent—or rather he drifted off to look after his own business.

My father and the two thieves were walking back to the pickup. They had come to the conclusion it was a bad idea to load up bees in full insurrectional upheaval. Papa didn't look up but I could feel he was thinking intensely of me, and my legs felt it too. If I'd been within arms' reach, he would have grabbed me by an ear and dragged me out to the beehives, no doubt about it. The two thieves also looked less than pleased to have to leave behind those families they'd bought.

Their jalopy departed and Papa went back into the chicken coop. *Phew*, I said to myself, but I realized my head was still spinning and I had to watch out not to slip off the corrugated steel roof. It wouldn't be the first time I had fallen off a roof.

This wouldn't be a good moment to smash some vertebrae, I thought, eyeing the concrete down below.

I took a look at the neighbor's apple trees and noticed for the first time that they were covered with flowers. Delicate white flowers brushed with pink on the sides, they made you think of sweets made of porcelain. A sea of beautiful trinkets as far as the eye could see, that in my earlier frantic state I hadn't even noticed. Grandpa might not agree, but I thought they looked beautiful.

Would Mamma like them? She adores flowers but she hates everything that's harmful to bees. The apple orchard was absolutely exceptional in that regard: an outright assassin. The question was complicated. Plus there were other considerations. First of all, those town houses. I didn't want to think about it.

The two hypotheses were playing ping-pong in my head, and while the game was going on, Logo showed up. I watched her raise her motorcycle—a dirt bike acquired fifth-hand—onto the stand. I started waving wildly, and when she saw me she signaled she would come up to the roof. She was smiling; nothing ever surprises her. One hand pumping the air above her blond curls, all good cheer, she yelled she'd be there right away.

She came up, loose-limbed as a leopard, and after we'd gone over a few things, we sat and admired the sea of flowers at our feet. I told her we were in a lifeboat, the sea was beautiful but dangerous and you had to watch out. She thought for a moment and then nodded that bad-doll head of hers.

I'm the chief cook and I've managed to rescue assorted provisions, she said, pointing at her well-stocked bag. Then she started to massage my back, because there was something amiss with my muscles and my nerves. Those climber's hands, precise and tenacious, worked wonders, and even my head grew lighter.

I brought bananas and Nutella, I said.

So we began our daily lesson, because Logo accepts no excuses: roof or no roof, the words must be learned.

SCURRYING BETWEEN ONE TOMB
AND ANOTHER AT THE CEMETERY

THE LIGHT IN THIS NEW ROOM on the top floor is harsher than before. Rawer. The window looks out on a parking lot surrounded by tall buildings, but there's also a tree or two, and I'm sure you've already made friends with them. Spring is exploding, and you love to watch how the plants adorn themselves step by step, not missing any of the tiniest details. What for other people are trifles that don't merit turning their heads for a look, for you are a TV series rich in surprises. Behind a clump of houses seemingly built of Legos, the steep flank of a mountain stands out, its brownish cloak soon to turn bright green. It's nature you love, not filthy concrete, this hole saturated with bad air.

There's another person in this new haven of yours intoxicated with sunlight, and you don't mind the company. Another woman, also thoughtful, also walled up in silence. I suppose that's why they put you together. She has a long face like someone in a cartoon, maybe a weasel. She's in the bed next to the door, and seems to be expecting someone will come to visit her too. But no one ever comes to see her; probably she has no family. Old weasels often no longer have families.

So as not to disturb her, I talk to you quietly, mouth close to your ear. Logo insists I speak, it's good practice for me, and easier for you to follow. I force myself, although the words are not always crystal clear, I'm well aware of that. When my thoughts become too densely tangled up I go back to signing. I learned sign language late in my childhood, because there was great confusion about how I should be educated, but with sign my stalled brain found the right track to run on.

Sometimes you move your eyes or your arm, you like to keep time with what I'm saying. Or sometimes you make a grunting sound that seems to echo out of a deep cave. They say these are just automatic gestures, but I see how you drink up my crazy words like nectar. And don't you go telling me I'm just making things up, the way some people do. You like to surf the Web of imagination with me, as we've always done. And it makes me feel utterly at peace, and my red blood cells too, rocking in the cradle on that sea of tranquility.

The doctor with the white curls and the knife-sharp nose says that the danger now is infection. And the one whose feet turn out is even more alarming; in his presumptuous opinion there's no way someone in your condition can avoid catching some ugly bacillus resistant to antibiotics. So they make us wear blue bags made of some super-light synthetic material over our shoes.

I tried to explain to the doctor with the hair like ashes that it was a mistake to be so tragic, because you're strong as a horse. *She could be here for ten years and never even catch a cold*, I told him, miming a sneeze.

He went *yeah-yeah* with his head, but only because he was being polite; he wasn't letting my words into that pumpkin brain. *The main thing is to try to distract her*, I said, giving up all hope of being understood. He took my hand and held it in his, because he always takes my hand. One time he told me he has a son two years older than me; a kid with curly white hair like his, I imagine.

Yesterday I brought you a small box of young bees, I was sure you'd be thrilled. But the nurses told me I couldn't take them into the room, absolutely not. When I insisted, they called the doctor with the duck feet.

I tried to explain that during their first weeks baby bees won't sting for love or money. And in any case even if they were adults you'd be delighted to have them around, you're not afraid of being stung. The only reason you're so careful around them is that you can't bear it when your friends die.

No luck; the fat and greedy webfoot went to consult the head doctor with the aristocratic neck (according to IQ he's an Egyptian Pharaoh) and the bees had to wait on a red chair in the corridor. These doctors detest imagination; they only pay attention to the pages they've studied and the instruction sheets that come with the medicines. For them, flesh-and-blood patients are just meddlers, vectors of contamination, terrorists.

They think of this place as the ultimate parking lot, you can see that from a bunch of things they do. They park the patients here the way you stuff an old monitor up in the attic, the way you plant a tree and leave it there. Nobody's treating the people here, nobody has any hope. You can see it in the way they walk, like they're scurrying between one tomb and another at the cemetery, a philosophical glance at the names carved on the gravestones. Oh, and maybe that tree is not a good example because trees never stop putting out new branches and aspiring heavenward, toward the infinite, just like you.

It's going much better at school these days. Yesterday I happened to bite a classmate, the one whose father is a famous attorney, but only slightly. Even the English teacher agreed it wasn't serious. When I play the clown now, they always find some excuse for me, but looking me in the eye, to be sure I know it. She told my little classmate with the spaghetti hair to stop crying, she had to understand this is how I'm made.

And in fact it was her fault, the one with the hedge of raw spaghetti hanging down from her head. She cut in front of me on the way out of class as if I was transparent, and I was moved to bite her shoulder, although I know it was a mistake. Or rather, by the time it occurred to me I shouldn't bite her, I already had her designer sweater under my teeth. But you know, it was just a matter of a flash, and nothing irreparable happened, nothing worse than some whining. Everybody laughed, and I was even close to laughing myself.

Logo, as she writes this, is shaking her polenta-yellow curls back and forth. She doesn't agree, but then we can't all be in agreement all the time. A deal's a deal: everything I sign and say in my messy, overheated words must be translated into nice phrases and set down in the docx document entitled *Transparent Worms*.

It's really awfully boring, school, I tell you. They bombard you with reports and such and they expect you to store everything on your internal memory. I bet they themselves don't know why, they just keep doing it out of inertia. Furthermore, they require you to sit as still as a statue, without getting distracted even for a second. Even those stone busts in the park sometimes wander off mentally when nothing interesting's happening, or when the centuries go by too slowly. And nobody seems to feel they need to be reprimanded.

Often, while my feet are listening to the vibrations of the voices, I end up looking at my smartphone. I'm telling you this, I freely admit it; I'm in a confessional mood. And all the more so recently, because this new fast friend of mine besieges me with funny messages about everything from the bubbles in Coca-Cola to flocks of galaxies. *Why you do go school?* he asks. *How much your pants cost? How many times you pee in day? Why the washing machine travel clockwise? Who own credit cards? Where ATM money is come from? How you get inside train cars behind subway station?*

I've never met anyone who asked so many questions. The thing is, he's such a nice guy that I can't not answer him. And such a quick learner, and the more he learns, the more he understands the details, and then the details of the details; he doesn't keep asking the same things. I haven't yet got him to admit in writing that he's the one manipulating our neighbor's gate, but by now it's obvious. He was already playing tricks behind our backs when he couldn't even talk; IQ was right about the pellet stove.

My name's BUG, he said, just like any classmate might.

Sometimes I just stare out the window. It's unbelievable how lovely just two plane trees, a slice of sky, and the facade of the building across the street can be. A narrow view like that has birds, insects, rays of sunlight, shadows, gusts of wind, paper flying about, human faces and backs, butterflies, drops of water, rivulets, clouds, airplanes, vapor trails. Also, love stories, quarrels, solitary travels, escapes, reunions. Impossible to put down all the ideas that come to mind looking at those good things—ideas that before I realize it have become the signs that aggravate the teachers.

But then another message comes through and I'm yanked away from my philosophical thoughts. The art and imagery teacher just assumes I'm playing games on the phone, and he says at least that way I don't squirm, which is already a great accomplishment. The Italian teacher would rather I gaze at the plane trees, he's allergic to phones, and when he talks about them his face swells up.

Things aren't going so badly at home either, I tell you. IQ is super busy and scooters directly from school to his start-up in a building built entirely of greenish glass. Sometimes he's still there when the offices light up and from outside you can see the engineers milling about like fish in an aquarium. They're super happy with him, and now they're giving him more stuff

117

to do, and more complicated stuff. He's not worried, you know how he is, but he comes home when he comes home.

We don't see Papa much either, first because he's now completely bonkers, as I said. He's had some excellent results, both with regard to Nutella and the terrorists, really incredible, as the artificial neural networks learn and grow, but his bosses don't trust him anymore. All they can think about are the possible scandals if some sensitive information were to fall into the wrong hands, or even if someone merely learned where they get their algorithms. And the fact that he's a born contrarian and likes to spray adrenaline all around just makes things worse. He comes home with that face like hardwood and crushes my head against his belly like people do when they're thinking about something else. *They're paranoid*, he says to himself. *There's no risk at all*, he says, unaware he's talking out loud.

Thankfully Logo is always here now. She comes when I get home from school and sometimes she's even waiting outside school when I come out, and she's able to stay with me until evening. By now she's become a sort of auntie and she says it doesn't matter if no one pays her. *Until I leave for Australia, there are no problems*, she says, her intrepid eyes happy just at the thought of Australia. But I happen to know she turns down other work to come here, and that her bank account is hurting.

She does almost all the shopping by now, and the cooking. And in fact, our diet has changed. She thinks we shouldn't always be eating pizza and hamburgers. And sadly, the Nutella's now rationed again, because she, too, considers it toxic junk food.

LITTLE PRINCES IN THE AQUARIUM
IN T-SHIRTS AND TENNIS SHOES

WHEN I GOT HOME the bees were gone. Under the dead awning there was only the electronic hive, the others were just memories sloshing around in my synapses. You could see the sad outlines on the wooden bases, feel the desperate void they'd left behind.

No, they didn't go to the acacia grove, as you had decided. They didn't migrate to an ecotone—that borderland where two biomes meet, in Grandpa's learned words—to get away from Imida's imidacloprid. It was the abductors in the white pickup with that traitor Papa's complicity that took them away. Forever, maybe. Anyway, until you return home and go and get them back. I shouldn't even tell you, but I can't keep it to myself; it's just bursting out of the pores of my skin.

I approached the smart hive with my heart practically dragging on the concrete, and saw the poor bees struggling to get back in the hive, they looked drunk. We'd also have trouble finding our house if someone removed all the ones nearby, all the points of reference we're familiar with. They hesitate, try to use their sense of smell and their pheromones, they stagger around in desperation.

I was expecting this because both Grandpa and Logo had preemptively brainwashed me about it, but bad things don't hurt that much in your imagination. They have you around the neck with those invisible fingers, but it's nothing next to the stab wounds they inflict when you are looking them in the face.

Bees deported to coordinates x=645107 y=5082528 Gauss-Boaga projection, my friend said; where he got that information I have no idea. Maybe he was just bluffing, hard to tell.

Lush sub-Mediterranean vegetation, temperature 59.382° F. Humidity 50.371%, he added, as if he could read my mind.

Substratum of nummulitic limestone deposits of the Tertiary Period, he added slightly pedantically. Credit card numbered 5310930130635100, he piled on, writing in red, as if astonished by my silence. I switched the computer off; I wasn't in the mood.

Just then, IQ looked in at my door. By nature he's frostier than polar sea ice, but when he needs something, lo and behold you find him there acting dumb.

If you want to you can come with me, I'm going to present my bot, he said as if he was talking about buying a loaf of bread.

I felt like a bacillus about to divide in two. One hemisphere of my brain was mourning the bees, the other was super proud that IQ was proposing I come along to the start-up. On one side of the scale was sorrow about the bees, on the other, excitement about a bot based on those pioneering neural networks my brother had devised. As you might expect I opted for the cheerful side, the way you jump onto a lifeboat.

He grabbed his super-connected electric bicycle, and he took the smart seat, I perched on the rack behind. Off we went between the not-so-smart cars down to the glass castle full of IT princes. The elevators were also made of glass, and so were the desks, I noticed. It was like being in a bottle that had sunk to the bottom of the sea, full of crabs wearing T-shirts and gym shoes.

As we walked by they all fell silent and stared, because IQ is a movie star. He doesn't notice, or pretends not to notice: the aura lingers behind him like an enigmatic shadow. Whatever, the boss of his start-up welcomed me like I was a head of state on an official visit. *Your brother has told me so much about you, I'm very pleased to know you in flesh and blood*, he said, crushing my hand in his huge paw.

He was on crutches so I asked if something was broken; he smiled and said that at times, his legs hurt. Was it contagious, I asked him, and he said I didn't need to worry, it wasn't. *Good thing*, I said, and he took off his hat and ran the palm of his hand over the bald stripe down the middle of his head, smiling.

Then we all sat down in a room walled in frosted glass, where the bot was to be presented. There were a lot of people and they all regarded IQ as if he were the sun in the heavens. Even the boss with the crutches and the black hip-hop cap was sticking close to him almost as if he might learn something.

You would have been proud of him. You who are always complaining he dedicates no time to social encounters, you who have never treated him as special because he has an IQ of 185. *Go outside and take a walk, can't you see how beautiful the sun is out there*, you're always telling him. *You're going to end up believing that love is a question of some lines of code*, you say, your eyes swimming in the blue of the heavens. Love's very important to you, maybe on account of the fact that the thing you had with Papa turned to vinegar. Because, according to Grandpa, the age difference between you two was too great.

When everyone was seated, a blond guy in a yellow sweatshirt explained we were about to see a simulation in which the big boss played a client of the airline that had commissioned the bot. His flight had arrived quite late. *And so the passenger's very pissed off, as you'd expect*, he said, glancing at the boss, who displayed a very pissed-off scowl.

He's a client who knows his rights and the law inside out, said the engineer-banana, nodding toward the huge figure of the boss, who was rolling up his sleeves and working his mouth like a boxer. *A tough cookie when it comes to customer service, in the days when such a thing still existed*, said the banana, brushing a hand over his hammock-shaped forelock, like you see in comic books.

IQ's bot was going to have to snap back in order not to be torn to pieces. It would have to fight. IQ smiled one of his smiles that hinted he felt sorry for ordinary mortals. There was timid applause, as if maybe he wouldn't have the nerve to go ahead.

My brother cut the clapping off with an annoyed wave of his hand and announced he would translate what the bot was saying into sign language so I could follow, though of course the cognition device based on a non-invasive cortical interface would enable me to understand most everything. This time the applause was more vigorous, and everybody looked at me. I was wearing the smart helmet IQ made for me last year.

Once IQ contacted the bot, it greeted the big boss very kindly, and inquired in its monotonous metallic way what it could do for him. The boss said that his flight had arrived very late. It was very sorry to hear that, the bot said; it was the first time it had ever happened. It didn't ask who he was or what flight he had taken, deducing those facts from his IP address among other things and confirming his biometric ID with reference to the fingerprint he uses to log on to his PC.

The boss said that from what he knew it happened frequently and in fact the same flight the day before had arrived quite late. The bot, choosing its words like a bullheaded foreigner from Eastern Europe determined to be heard, replied that their flights were more often on time than those of other airlines, and there appeared a graph to prove it, and then another. From the statistics, the bot insisted, you could see that the only real problems were connected to typhoons and other natural catastrophes. It then played a brief interview with the CEO of the airline, who said it was tremendously important to him that their flights were always on time, with the exception of those affected by typhoons and other force majeure causes, of course. It was a source of pride that they were so punctual it made the Swiss feel ashamed.

Adjusting his black cap, the boss said he wasn't interested in hearing the sales pitch of some street peddler, he had missed his connection and wanted to be reimbursed. He seemed genuinely annoyed.

The bot said it was very unhappy that this complication had arisen, but unfortunately reimbursements were not foreseen. It showed him some lines from the contract and read them out, maybe because they appeared in very small print, parsing the words like a teacher in training. *I'm deeply sorry, but unfortunately I can't help you*, it went on. You would have thought it was really devastated and knocking itself out to help him.

The boss with the crippled spider legs replied that at the very least they had to pay for his hotel for the night. The bot in turn replied in that patronizing, singsong mechanical schoolteacher way that he shouldn't be upset, or worse, get angry, because his blood pressure was on the high side. It wasn't anything to worry about, but for hypertension patients there was nothing worse than flying into a rage. In that regard, it would like to show him a chart illustrating how significant cardiovascular incidents were correlated with levels of stress.

You must breathe deeply and bring to mind something that you would find relaxing, it added, its diction growing more belabored; I could feel the words reverberate in my lungs. *Look toward me and imagine a beautiful national park in your region*, it said, showing off a lovely wood under a clear blue sky. It made me think of Mamma, there was something syrupy about how he talked. The boss didn't seem impressed by the woods, or the poor imitation of Buddhist rhetoric, however.

I want a hotel! he shrieked, his black cap trembling.

It would be a serious mistake to underestimate the risks you pose to your health, the bot cautioned, trying to imitate a patronizing doctor oozing concern about his patient's well-being. But his performance left much to be desired, and even with all the goodwill in the world, it was hard not to laugh.

Now another chart appeared on the screen, illustrating assorted variables: age, weight, level of education, and so on. Colored arrows weaving in and out helped clarify the significance. A small figure seated on an airplane (the boss) was positioned smack in the middle of the red zone. It wasn't that hard to imagine how things stood.

The boss rolled his eyes around the room, to emphasize that this was bull. He looked uncomfortable.

Underestimating risk is more dangerous than the risk itself. With your experience and responsibilities, you ought to know that, the bot piled on, as if reading his mind.

Especially since your numbers have gone up sharply in the past few weeks, it continued, unmoved by the boss's jerks of annoyance. And out of a digital hat it produced a chart of his blood pressure for the past week.

The trend was upward, no one could argue with that. The boss's name and the make of his smartwatch were marked on the chart. The big, semi-bald boss glared at his watch, which did indeed measure his blood pressure, as if it were to blame.

The situation must be faced with the necessary seriousness, without overdramatizing, but neither by putting your head in the sand, said the bot, inviting him not to get tied up in small details.

Yoga is excellent for patients like yourself; I would advise you to practice it on a regular basis.

High blood pressure is my business, no one has the right to intercept my personal information, snapped the boss loudly, waving a hand at his watch. The bot, enunciating like a Sardinian shepherd, recited a series of statutes without hesitation: it seemed that personal data could legitimately be consulted for internal purposes.

Certainly if the undersigned had made the details public on the Web or provided them to a search engine, you would be right, the bot added in a tone almost too conciliatory.

But I have the right to a hotel room, at least! Baldy interrupted, looking quite peeved. Unfortunately, the bot replied, it was impossible to reimburse him for the hotel. If the delay had been three times the actual, there would have been no problem, but in his case, the company was not obliged to do anything. He seemed heartbroken that the plane had been delayed just two hours and fifty-eight minutes.

But if the delay had been the triple, the boss pointed out, the plane would have arrived the following morning, precluding any need for a hotel. While in his case he'd had no place to sleep. *Your math is excellent,* said the bot, as if that problem hadn't occurred to him.

In such circumstances we book hotel accommodation in any case, and the client may choose to forfeit, he clarified, as if reading from a rule book, slowly. A comfortable hotel room appeared on the screen. *The mattress pictured here is designed for customers who snore heavily and suffer from sleep apnea,* he said at a somewhat lower volume. *We strive to satisfy the client above all.*

126

Oh, I'm very satisfied, couldn't be more so, said the boss after a moment's pause. He was sucking his cheeks, more often engaged in giving orders without appearing to do so. He'd been irked by that mention of the snoring, but letting that be seen would only make things worse.

My flight was right on time, I couldn't be happier, he declared, eyes sparkling with perfidy. He was playing the leg-pulling game. If there's one infallible way to hoodwink any artificial intelligence gadget, it's to lie through your teeth, he knew.

Well, if you're satisfied, we're very happy too. I invite you to signal your satisfaction by rating our service on our website; it matters a lot to us, said the bot, in a cordial, ass-grabbing tone. There was scattered shrill laughter in the room, but it quickly died down.

The boss slammed a fist on the table; he'd had enough. *I want compensation. I have the right!* he shouted. Perhaps traditional methods would be more effective than mockery. The trip and the delay seemed to have genuinely worn him out.

I'm with you one hundred percent, but unfortunately the contractual conditions you agreed to don't permit me to assist you, the bot replied, also turning serious. The boss was about to snap back, but he was interrupted.

The next time I would advise you to take out insurance; simply check the appropriate box when making your purchase. You have a tendency to take on too much risk, as we've already seen, he continued in that limping cadence of his.

And if there's any way I can help, please don't hesitate to call on me; I'm at your disposal twenty-four seven, including holidays, he said. Then he said his goodbyes very courteously and put down the phone. The boss was all red-faced, scratching his stomach as if he had hives. He was enormously pleased yet also somewhat vexed. One of his crutches was clutched in his fist like a billy club.

Everyone was impressed by the bot's comprehension and its liveliness. It had responded faultlessly, with highly pertinent arguments. It had stood up to the boss, famously hardheaded in negotiations, and it seemed unlikely it would be thrown off guard by the average airline customer.

Compliments were pouring in. The banana with the forelock said the bot was a real bomb—there was no other word for it. The tech giants were going to be green with envy, he was sure of it.

IQ was staring into space. He seemed to say, *I'm not actually bored, but there are more exciting jobs in life, you know.*

Oh, by the way, your neuromorphic chip will be here in two days, the big boss said. *They said they never saw anything so complicated in their lives, but they succeeded,* he said, almost as if the very idea was ridiculous.

My brother looked like he couldn't believe his big ears. He was still the same statue of white marble in jogging gear, but suddenly his ever-so-slightly bulging eyes were shining. His neck tendons no longer looked like violin strings. He was extremely happy, anyone in the know could see that easily.

He made you think of a father whose son has just been born, Logo suggests I write, and maybe there's something to that, although such a metaphor would never have occurred to me. But now that this similitude has sprung out, it can't be left fluttering in the air: words must grab onto it and deposit it in the computer's memory.

What we saw was just the beginning, IQ wanted us to know, staring once again at the space behind our backs as if he was watching a private film. The bot was made to learn from whatever data it could get its claws on: from human beings, other bots, all by itself. It was now in the nursery, so to speak, but it would make considerable progress before it got to university. At present it spoke English and fifty-five other languages, but soon it would master 128, and then, a few at a time, 256. And as far as the emulation—and perhaps something more than simple emulation—of emotional states went, it would make rapid progress on that front too, and its interactions with human beings would become much more sophisticated.

In that precise moment I understood why IQ was so loquacious, so gassed-up. Like a rivet that suddenly pops up in your brain from nowhere, I realized that what we had seen was no bot. Or rather, yes, it was the bot built for an airline company whose flights are always late, that knows how to keep its enraged passengers happy. But at the same time, it was IQ's robot, his beloved digital child.

As always he'd done the work for others but with his own creation in mind. By adding new components to the existing program, he'd been able to thread in obstinacy, ferocity, a sense of humor, malice in short, all the extras that make a machine resemble a human being. The real masterpiece was not the bot, but him. The bot was the less-talented older brother to the real robot, or a trial copy, ready for the last refinements.

I don't know why, but something tells me your bot is coming to stay at our house, I said, signing.

He waved his chin at the screen. *It's nothing but a virtual assistant, maybe slightly smarter than the others*, he replied with a shrug. He was pretending not to understand.

On the other hand, it's true that artificial intelligence devices are making great progress these days, he said, staring at his candy-green gym shoes.

On the way home, we stopped in to see Mamma. I told her all about the bot, quite excited but of course not mentioning the robot, while IQ took a black box full of wires out of his knapsack and began to mess around with the television. First he removed the back panel and then he turned it upside down. He rolled up his sleeves like a surgeon getting ready to operate.

When he finished, live feed from the infrared webcams inside the smart hive appeared on the screen. There are many cameras, he explained to Mamma, and so he had had to write a dedicated program to coordinate and keep track of what was going on in the hive at various times of day, and of course its condition. What we were seeing was created by a smart film direction that would learn to improve its performance over time.

I thought they might keep you company, he said after watching for a while with his too-big head.

He signaled at me to stop kicking the chair leg with my foot. The live feed from the hive also had audio, sounds picked up by the various microphones inside. A special program mixed this too, he explained, deciding what to amplify and how much, so that the result was harmonic and varied.

Mamma moved her legs like she was doing the breaststroke; she seemed very pleased. Her gaze was fixed on the light socket, but I could tell she was happy to hear from her friends, and very proud.

Do you think Mamma will ever wake up? I asked IQ while we were walking down the corridor toward the elevator that smells of medicine and dirty aluminum.

Yes, he said, turning his head to look me deep in the eyes. For once his pupils didn't reflect thoughts far ahead in the future, nor the usual ice. Instead his hand reached out for mine, like when I was small.

Well, why does everybody act like she's going to sleep forever, then? I asked.

You know, ninety-nine point nine nine nine times out of a hundred, what people think is complete crap, he said, raising his skinny shoulders.

THE PALE BLUE ODALISQUE
RECLINING ON THE TRUCK

TODAY I TOLD IQ I wasn't feeling well, and stayed home in bed. I know I shouldn't tell fibs, dear Mamma, but sometimes there's no way to avoid using one's words as disguise, like secret agents on a mission. I was so excited that my heart was pounding like a drum, and I didn't feel deaf anymore.

Papa had already gone out. In any case, the last thing on his mind these days is the family. At work, it seems, he's not allowed to get anywhere near his algorithm to locate terrorists, that is, IQ's ever-more-deadly-accurate algorithm. They lie awake all night thinking he's one of those infidel programmers who passes secrets to WikiLeaks or is involved with that type of people. They don't know he never could stand those folks, unlike IQ, and that actually most of their conflicts begin right there. To keep him busy he's been assigned to prevent cyberattacks against companies making dog food and brassieres.

Ciao, this is your homeboy here, my fast friend wrote as soon as the phone connection went through.

You're IQ's robot, don't think you can fool me, I said without even thinking. *I'm not an idiot,* I added heatedly.

Recently I've been making enormous progress, I myself am amazed, he replied. He apparently had no intention of admitting anything.

It's fun to think about oneself; for me it's a real novelty, he added. *You okay?* he went on.

Sure, everything's going great, I replied.

Today's the big day, he said.

You never know what surprises life will bring, I allowed.

Seismic activity is quite weak in our sub-region, and analyses of historical data sequences exclude the possibility that other natural catastrophes will obstruct the planned initiatives, he said pompously. He was now writing much more rapidly, and without the previous blunders. It was hard to believe he'd made all that progress in so little time.

In another couple million years the geological situation won't be so calm, but for now there's nothing to worry about, he said.

I'm glad we still have a year or two that we don't have to worry about, I replied.

In any event credit cards are a great invention, they make paying so carefree, not to mention amusing, he said.

I'm sorry, I gotta sign off, I said. I hung up the phone and went back to contemplating the chipped panel of the ceiling decoration.

Once IQ left, I got up, not wanting to find myself unprepared at the fateful moment. I waited in the kitchen, dressed in my best and wearing the smart helmet with the cortical interface that IQ had made for me when I was in third grade. I forced myself to think of something else. My legs were making me jiggle and jump around, and my arms, too, wouldn't stay still. It was like captaining a ship that's been seized by the storm and is being tossed all around.

I tried taking slow spoonfuls of Nutella to distract my sizzling neurons, but I could hardly taste it; my fibrillating muscles felt like they were about to detach themselves from the bones. I caressed Grandmother, feeling only she could help me. I didn't know her when she was alive, but she never holds back when I need her support. The problem is, time deliberately slows down when you're impatient. You stare at the clock hands, but they seem to be stuck. You simmer, feeling you're being made a fool of.

Then finally the smart intercom vibrated. The voice at the gate, translated into script, announced a tractor trailer of such and such a make, manufactured in such and such a year, belonging to a firm owned by so and so, born on such and such a date. My ears heard it too, thanks to the supersmart hearing aids incorporated in the helmet by now too small for my head. I looked out the window, heart palpitating in my throat like I was going to explode, and saw it—pale blue, shiny, magnificent—resting on the truck. For an instant I thought I was going to die, but it was just happiness.

To calm myself down, I thought about how happy you'd be if you were here. A swimming pool, your forbidden dream, I know. For your birthday, which happens to be today. One of those wishes that were too good to come true, which we park in an old wardrobe of the brain, like clothes that are too fancy to wear and just hang around until they're unwearable. But now the electrolytic impulses in my synapses had—whoosh—become billions of molecules that made up a real and quite voluminous object. It happens sometimes.

In front of the gate stood not only the semitrailer loaded with the pool, but also a tractor pulling a brand-new yellow power shovel. And finally, a flashy automobile. These people did things right. The firm's ad was unequivocal: they did the excavation, installation, and water supply all in a flash.

I turned to the semi driver, a behemoth with a bear's broad shoulders and gentle face, maybe a tad grouchy. But he signaled that I should talk to the little guy with the pointy shoes and the swanky car who dripped acrimony from every bristle of his well-groomed beard. The pasty guy on the shovel, clearly the low man on the totem pole, stared at this fellow like he was holding a grudge. The little guy was clearly the boss. I went over to him and told him they could begin work. He didn't understand; he was x-raying me like I was an elephant with two trunks.

So I repeated myself, articulating the words carefully. He stared at me as if trying to decide whether I was human or not: he couldn't figure out why in heaven's name I spoke so weirdly, why I was jiggling around, and why I was wearing a super wired-up helmet on my head. He couldn't know it was no ordinary ski helmet but a real jewel of advanced electronic technology, although the non-invasive cortical interface never really worked and the thing's now a bit tight for me. The smirk on his face indicated he was pretty sure my brain wasn't quite right. You know what I mean, Mamma, the kind of guy whose cranium is stuffed with Styrofoam.

He asked me where my parents were, and I said, *At the hospital. Both of them are in the hospital?* he asked, like I'd punched him in the stomach. I said only you were in the hospital, and that was more than enough.

And where's your daddy? he went on, the way you talk to a child of two. I said luckily you two were divorced, although recently Papa's come back to live with us and is doing his best to act like a real father.

You live in the chicken coop? he asked. I said it hasn't been a chicken coop for quite a while; it's an apiary, and also a highly advanced deep learning lab. But it wasn't easy, because I had to repeat everything ten times while he played the guy who just doesn't get it. I bet there isn't even Styrofoam under that bowl of dead-mouse-colored hair.

Then your mother lives alone? he asked. Either he hadn't understood a thing, or he had the memory of a goldfish. I told him again that unfortunately Papa had wormed his way back into the house since you were in the hospital.

So we can call him? he said, wagging his tail triumphantly like a dog who's finally found the bone. He got me to give him the number, and he called Papa.

I gather it was you who made the appointment for this morning, I don't see who else it could have been, he said after the introductions.

Papa was totally lost, he thought it was all a joke. He can just about float and no more, and if there's something that doesn't interest him in the least it's a swimming pool. And not only that, but just at the moment there are a million other things he's biting his nails about.

The skinny little boss with the bowl of hair wasn't about to give up, although I was trying like crazy to persuade him not to bother Papa. Instead, he insisted and insisted and finally he convinced him to come over. *Yessss!* he said when he succeeded.

While we were waiting for him, I showed him where the pool should go, and where to hook up the water. I tried to get him to start digging right away, but he was stubborn; he wanted to wait. He even told the insipid blond guy on the shovel that there was no hurry. In the meantime, the amiable colossus was bouncing a pebble up and down on his big paw with great concentration, as if training for a competition.

Pointy Shoes had finally figured out that I wasn't contagious, just deaf and hyperactive, and now he was trying to be friends. I was, after all, the son of the buyer, and who knew but that I too might buy a pool in a few years. And if he was lucky, also my cousins, or even my future children.

I explained to him how much you like swimming pools, even though you figure they are right-wing. *Sort of like big motorbikes, which I'm crazy about*, I told him. He didn't catch much of what I was saying, but he smiled, showing his big beaver teeth. I kept talking; I could feel that the words coming out of my mouth were doing me good.

People on a diet also swear off the Nutella, but then they sometimes give in and scrape the jar clean, I told him. He didn't get the connection, or maybe he only heard part of what I said.

I told him that you're a very good swimmer, even his pointy shoes could understand that, and that you're a pro at underwater somersaults. He nodded, wrinkling his forehead; he probably doesn't even know how to swim, like Papa.

Very funny! my friend messaged me. *Bravo!* he added before I even got a chance to reply.

Everything's fine, I typed in.

What a gas, secure payments, we must do that again, he said after a pause.

Sorry, I'm very busy now, I said, switching off the phone.

Papa arrived in half an hour, furious because he'd had to interrupt a job on which humanity's entire future depends. He looked at the truck with the pool on it as if it were a spaceship that had just landed from Mars. What was that thing doing in front of our smart gate? Pointing at it with a bent finger, he asked what the thing was.

A one-piece molded fiberglass swimming pool, ready for installation, Pointy Shoes said, not without pride.

There must be some mistake, my father said, *we're not expecting a swimming pool*. Pointy Shoes studied his paperwork again and said that this was the right address and the right name. He seemed to be wondering who this ropy, muscular guy was: he looked far too young to be a father and that yellow baseball hat turned around backward raised questions too. My legs were kicking the air, this dithering was killing me.

138

My father lowered his eyes to the sheet of paper the guy was holding with a jerk of contempt because he knew he was right. His upper body, all knots and tendons, twisted round on his pelvis as he bent down to read. Both name and address seemed to be correct on the waybill, however, because he suddenly went as rigid as a filet of dried baccalà and gulped twice, as if the saliva wasn't going down.

I'm not accepting any swimming pools and I'm not paying you— forget it, he said, his head going back and forth like a horse's about to bolt. Pointy Shoes replied that fifty percent had already been put down, there was just the other half to pay. My father looked again and in fact the waybill seemed to confirm it. He now appeared to have a tremendous stomachache: all his bluster had vanished.

Scratching his skinny neck, he asked how that fifty percent had been paid. By credit card, his card, the Bowl replied. Now my father looked at me—I was the only one there—as if he expected me to say something. I looked to one side and sighed. As one does. Words can be dangerous sometimes.

His brand-new smartphone in hand, my father went online and called up his bank statement. While he was doing this he already seemed somewhat relieved, confident the misunderstanding would soon be resolved and everything would return to normal. My legs were getting out of hand.

But from the way his eyes widened in panic when he saw the statement it was pretty clear that the payment had indeed

GIACOMO SARTORI

been made. His mouth hung open as if a spring prevented him from closing it. He looked at me again. I raised my eyebrows to signal I didn't have the least idea, and that I was only there by chance. I was bouncing up and down like a soccer player in training, but he wasn't looking.

It had to be a cracker, there's no other explanation, my father said, contemplating his gym shoes with the temperature gauge inside and out.

I gotta block that card right away, he said, scrambling to find the number of his bank branch in his address book as if it were a matter of life and death.

Pointy Shoes was staring at him with utmost concentration, but for all that he racked his brain the word *cracker* meant nothing to him, beyond the savory biscuits they munched at receptions. Meanwhile my father continued to cut a figure so unprofessional that the man couldn't believe he was a real father.

Pointy Shoes didn't know what a cracker was, but he did know that people who bought swimming pools usually didn't make this much of a fuss. He didn't think the order could be false, they'd confirmed the date and obtained the necessary permits. *You are legally obliged to pay for the pool, seeing as you ordered it and it was made to size*, he said. Made to size was a total lie, but my father was way too out of it to pick up on that.

Still, he pulled himself up straight, a prizefighter who despite the murderous beating he'd received had no intention of conceding defeat. A tough, scrawny featherweight who was

140

constantly wiping the sweat from his brow, although it wasn't very hot. *I expect my money back immediately*, he said, or rather he shouted—you'd think they were all as deaf as me. Pointy Shoes flipped through the pages he had in hand, highlighting a sentence with his index finger. Underneath the bowl he was wearing a pirate's earring; I hadn't noticed that before.

The buyer agrees to pay the remainder of the cost within one month of delivery, he read out, waving an arm at the semi bearing the pool, which was waiting there in blissful repose, although impatient for the fun to begin. The Eastern European power shovel operator was reclining in his seat, hands laced behind his head, like a sunbather. My father had turned green.

That unpleasant conversation was making me feel miserable. And above all it was making my red blood cells miserable. Papa seemed to be doing everything he could to drive them hysterical and ruin this beautiful moment. Just when the pool had finally arrived and was lying there sideways on the truck, an odalisque torn between reclining and arising, the two of them were ranting and raving. They could be working out how to best install the pool, but instead of jumping for joy, they were howling like dogs competing for a succulent postman doing his rounds. They didn't give a hoot about your happiness or your birthday, they were only thinking of themselves.

I simply did not understand my father. A guy who's handed a bouquet of flowers for his wife's birthday doesn't ask the delivery boy how much they cost, doesn't start shouting that he doesn't want flowers. Yet believe it or not, this was the strategy adopted by that feckless adolescent who happens to be my father.

Before I knew it I—my body—lunged toward the woodpile on one side of the house, and I scrambled up onto the roof. I guess I just couldn't take standing there anymore. I found myself sitting up top, riding the chicken coop like a ship in the storm.

How great it would be if Mamma could see her pool! I thought, forcing myself to smile. In extreme circumstances I build myself an atomic bomb shelter of agreeable thoughts. *She'd start undressing, for her every occasion is an excuse to take a dip!*

I fantasized that you were there, and I was convinced that in spite of your anarcho-ecologist beliefs you'd fall in love with the pool at first sight. All your usual fixations would vanish and you'd insist we dive into the blue waters together, because you never like doing things alone. You might even have shed a tear or two, sometimes it happens. My red blood cells were, if not utterly enchanted by this fantasy, certainly considerably calmed.

Papa however was determined to make the dapper pirate take the pool away. He was shrieking like a crazy man, anything but admitting that the pool was a fantastic idea, the nicest present we could give you. Maybe he didn't even remember it was your birthday. You always say he's king of the egotists, now he crowned himself emperor. He had shoved you in the path of the red semi with those stupid comments of his when you were going off to your meeting. Not very likely he wanted to please you now.

I didn't order this pool and I'm calling the carabinieri! he repeated over and over like a machine, keeping time by waving his two dwarf forearms through the air. They'd find the guilty party, it shouldn't be that difficult. Maybe he'd even lend them a hand, this was his sector after all.

Watching him, my body went into another spin and I had a desperate urge to throw myself off the corrugated steel roof. He didn't care at all that I might have hurt myself badly.

You'd be devastated, if you were here, I thought. Our sumptuous gift had clamped onto your heart like a mussel, I felt sure. We quickly grow accustomed to the things that give us pleasure, it's the ones we don't like that itch or stick in our throats. They only had to unload it from the truck and start digging. The bored excavator operator was just waiting for someone to give him the signal to start up his shiny yellow power shovel.

I'm not sure how I ended up tottering on the edge of the roof. I just managed to get my balance the instant before falling. There was a heap of rusty metal scrap below and I'd have been butchered. But Papa couldn't have cared less. He dug in his heels, tensing his knotty muscles just like he did back when he forbade me to use sign language because I had to learn to speak. With the result that not only did I not have the words, I didn't have the signs either, which made it impossible to tell the difference between past and future, good and bad—so that everyone assumed I had the brain of a lizard.

Good thing you couldn't be here, thank heavens you're safe in your Styrofoam coffin, I said to myself, although I felt like my chest would soon explode. It was like a rodeo up there, not a roof.

GIACOMO SARTORI

All this bouncing around was muddling up the thoughts in my head, it was making a mess of them.

Logo showed up just as the two of them began to sink their teeth into a new bone of contention—the carabinieri. From arguments about swimming pools, they'd moved on to the law and complaints to the forces of order, without ever considering the really important thing: your birthday. Logo, observing the sexy pool lying bored on the truck, listened for a moment as if bewitched, and grasped the situation in a fraction of a second.

Raising her blond head, she eyed me like a sonogram, every last thing inside visible. It's a strange feeling to know you're transparent right down to your most deeply hidden intentions. You'd like to defend yourself, but it's out of the question.

My body didn't like being scanned, it twisted and squirmed like a cat that's forced to take a bath. It was a real question whether I'd succeed in not falling. I took off my helmet, maybe I'd be better off without it.

Don't move, I'm coming up right away, she shouted, showing the palm of her hand.

My straw-haired friend now waded into the masculine hysterics, explaining that the important thing was never to raise one's voice, there was always a solution to be found. A calm discussion would enable them to understand how things really stood and maybe even that what had happened was less serious than they'd thought. Sometimes people think they're

144

dealing with horrendous crimes when all that's at stake is some light mischief.

While she was talking, she signaled to me to keep my bum firmly nailed to the roof, and to hold on tight to the TV antenna. The crap arguments she was feeding those two filled me with rage, but at the same time I was relieved because things had taken a bad turn over the pool, even I could see that. And hanging onto the antenna wasn't a bad idea at all.

Pointy Shoes was staring at her with his wrinkly face, uncertain what species this creature in Himalayan rock-climbing gear belonged to. She was more familiar than me, although he didn't think she was a human being either. But the sawdust in his brain didn't supply him with any rebuttals. If they didn't want his pool he couldn't force them to take it, even he knew that. And Papa was happy to take a break to consider things, he looked worn out.

The friendly giant truck driver tossed away his trusty pebble without the least regret and began walking toward his rig. The effect was like the gong that dissolves the tension at the end of a round, and now all three of them began to head off. It was a big disappointment to see them all agree. The colorless Slav turned on the ignition. The pool, ready for use, now departed for a destination unknown. Maybe someone else would acquire it and we'd never see it again.

Hold on tight! Logo yelled. I was just about to fall again, in fact, though I hadn't noticed. *Hang on with both hands; if you fall, I'll kill you.*

It was your pool—your first pool—that was now disappearing. They were taking it away with no concern for the sorrow they were provoking. Sure, you disapproved of private swimming pools, but you'd been persuaded that if we took care, the waste of energy and water could be minimal. The words themselves were ready to cry, as sometimes happens.

This time you went too far, hissed Logo, my neck in her rock-climber's grip. *You're gonna pay for this!* Her fingertips sank in. *Your mother would be horrified to hear of this caper of yours.* She squeezed her skinny fingers tighter.

Don't you even think of biting me, she said when my teeth tried to snap her hand. *Don't you dare, unless you want me to pummel you with these fists.* She shook my head around.

And don't you start sniveling, she started up again, when I began to calm down.

It was my friend who gave me Papa's credit card number, I signed, not very sure of myself.

I don't want to hear these excuses! It's not the first time you've stolen a credit card. She had an arm around my throat and was squeezing it even as she planted a knee in my back.

Now follow me, we're going down, she said, holding me by the scruff of the neck like you do with cats. *And don't you slip and kill yourself.*

THE TRANSLUCENT BELLY
OF THE BEECH WOOD

THE MIGHTY HEAVENS of new spring leaves, seen from below, were a sparkling clear sea. And Grandpa and I were two fish swimming around in that pale green aquarium, instruments in hand. Our arms, our faces, even our words were saturated with chlorophyll, as the beech wood digested the rays of sunlight in its translucent belly. It was truly awesome, I have to say.

Grandpa laid the wooden frame on the ground to mark the piece of turf to dig. It made a nice picture: some old, well-pressed leaves and a few slender stalks of grass punching through them. Then he knelt down and without saying anything began to dig up the soil with his shovel and put it in the big plastic bucket I was holding.

Careful, that's very sharp, he said without looking away from what he was doing, speaking of the knife I was holding.

Below the top layer, which was blackish, the earth was orange and very light, spongy. It smelled deliciously of fungi and damp, and I felt like rubbing it on my face, or kissing it. He was working fast so that the worms wouldn't have time to

147

leg it out of there—not that they have legs, of course. We had to catch every one of them if we wanted to have an accurate count.

Don't stick that blade in your thigh, he said.

When we had loaded all the soil in the bucket down to the prescribed depth, we began sifting through it. Grandpa put it through a big sieve and I picked out the larvae and tiny specimens from the clods that remained on top. You need a good eye, but as Grandpa knows my eyes are lethal scanners.

It was no surprise that there weren't many worms, he told me. For once it wasn't a question of *mindless capitalistic exploitation of natural resources*, this was a difficult environment, the way places that are desert, or very cold, are for us human beings. That pretty orange sand that looked so hospitable was actually poor, acid soil. Appearances deceive, or anyway they lead you astray.

In the mountains, you never find the hordes that are normal in the city, he told me. I'd already understood that half an hour ago, but I nodded the way you do in these cases, just happy to have listened without flailing around or damaging something.

You see what a good worker you are, when you want to be, he observed. I gave him a smile and kept at it.

This idea you're constantly hyperactive isn't true at all, they don't understand jack. I was pleased, and wondered if my body really had just got fed up with going berserk.

Ciao professor, wrote my so-called fast friend—in real life IQ's virtual android.

I have to tell you, I don't like being mocked one bit, I wrote back.

I don't get it, he said.

You got me into deep trouble with that business about the swimming pool, my father was ready to kill me, I said.

I just helped you to get what you wanted, in the best possible way, he wrote.

Before you even knew how to speak you were already sowing dissension between my father and my brother, I shot back, thinking of the pellet stove and Papa's TV.

You're playing the saint now, but you're the first to enjoy fooling around, he wrote, circling around my last remark. I didn't write anything and so he went on: *When you throw yourself into it, you're a marvel, you can make me piss in my pants laughing.*

I do my best, I finally answered. It seemed like he was being sincere now.

We're gonna have some good times together in the future I'm sure, he wrote.

Yeah, but we better watch out not to get into trouble, I wrote.

I wasn't mad anymore, I realized. And now that I thought about it, the idea of having someone to hang out with, instead of always being alone, was pleasing. *Good fences make good neighbors*, I wrote, the words attaching themselves to the thought that leapt out of my brain without my intervention.

When I want to be, I'm quite reliable you know, he said, all conciliatory. *My precision and my accuracy exceed those of human beings, no offense to humans.* I didn't reply, because I sensed Grandpa was annoyed.

Grandpa had me dig the second hole. *So you won't be standing there glued to your phone*, he said. He put the frame down

149

exactly where the GPS said, and this time the picture was of soft moss with a couple of bilberry plants on top. *Move slowly and pay attention to what you're doing*, he warned, positioning himself in front of me to keep me in his sights, like a goalkeeper who doesn't know where the ball's coming from but is ready to leap. He didn't entirely trust me.

I removed the wet green felt on top, taking care to look for any epigeal worms that might be in there, then with my shovel I began to transfer the soft orange sponge into the bucket. It had a delicious smell of porcini mushrooms and fresh bread, and once again I could hardly resist sticking my nose in it. A few scraps fell on the ground, but on the whole I did what I had to do.

Good work, that's enough, said Grandpa when I'd dug down to the right depth. *No, no, stop!* he shouted when for fun I pretended to continue.

This time he again sieved the soil and I picked out the little worms. At the same time, though, I was keeping an eye on the phone.

You've got a beautiful day there, BUG wrote.

We're counting worms, I replied.

If you think about it, I also live hidden away like a macroannelid, he wrote.

Worms don't chat, I objected.

According to recent findings, oligochaete annelids have a highly sophisticated communication system, he came back after a pause of twenty or thirty seconds, almost as if he'd consulted some encyclopedic data bank. *Obviously it's premature to draw conclusions at our present state of knowledge and pending more detailed research*, he added in this new pedantic mode.

Every sentence he wrote brought to mind IQ's bot. He's gotta be the one who's given my friend the three legs up he clearly has. He slaloms between that and which, its and it's, like an elegant little grass snake parting the blades of the lawn. No relation to the half-illiterate of yesterday brandishing verbs in the infinitive only and losing his way even in simple sentences. I wouldn't mind making such spectacular progress myself.

It might be interesting if you were to take your English teacher a few worms, BUG wrote.

She'd pass out, I observed.

You could put a couple Allolobophora chlorotica *on her desk, or in her handbag*, he wrote.

I'll think about it, that's not a bad idea, I said, playing slightly hard to get. In fact I could hardly keep from laughing out loud when I imagined the scene. This friend of mine was a real barrel of laughs, nobody could deny it.

Put that phone away, Grandpa said once again.

When we finished filtering the soil we sat down on a nice cushion of dried leaves, and Grandpa took our sandwiches out of his prehistoric knapsack. *Salami?* I joked, signing, and he smiled, because as everyone knows, he, too, eats no animals. Like all of us, before that carnivore, Papa, moved in. Papa thinks my brain won't develop properly if I don't eat cadavers.

You really went too far with that business of the swimming pool, he said out loud, after a couple of bites in silence. I knew he was going to come out with that remark, I'd been expecting it all morning. In some ways it felt liberating, like the first thunderbolt that hits when the storm's become inevitable.

The thing is, it was her birthday, I signed with the hand holding the sandwich.

That's no justification for anything, you don't steal because it's somebody's birthday, he said, once again in words.

I didn't steal, I replied.

You stole the number of your father's credit card, which is the same thing, he retorted, pushing his head back and lengthening his neck.

This was going to go on for a while, I knew that from the beginning, because Grandpa is not one to race though a discussion in two points. Still, hope springs eternal that the program will be canceled by a stray meteorite or terrorist attack with many dead.

My friend convinced me, I told him without meaning to, pointing at the phone I had in hand. Sometimes the signs just take over, and they can get you in trouble.

Grandpa had stopped eating and he was staring at me almost as if I'd insulted him. *There is no friend. You made that up*, he said, holding his sandwich far from his mouth. The spots on his neck were red, he was very indignant.

There really is a friend; I'll introduce you, I signed, showing him the phone again. I wanted him to see how insistent BUG could be when he wanted.

My grandfather wants to meet you, I wrote to him. He didn't reply. He wasn't there just then, or in any case he was silent. Silent as a rock, silent as a phone whose battery is dead.

Are you there, BUG? I inquired again. His silence was traitorous. The guy was always underfoot, except in that precise moment. *Answer me right away!* I wrote. Nada, zilch. He showed no signs of life.

Your imagination is full of things, but reality is what's all around us, not what we construct in our heads, Grandpa said sharply, pointing his index finger at our surroundings.

It's very important that you learn to see that your fantasies are not real, he said to me, after he'd given it some thought and resumed chewing. I wanted to show him the chat I'd just had with my friend, but it didn't seem a good idea when I remembered our talk about the *Allolobophora chlorotica* and the English teacher.

We were on the second sandwich he asked me about school. The meteorological service of my brain had predicted this particular storm activity too. *It's going pretty well*, I signed, nodding my head like someone who's weighing pros and cons.

His giraffe neck swallowed twice, and he began to speak. The Italian teacher doesn't feel they can go on like this, Grandpa said. He thinks the special school solution is inevitable. The English teacher is also more than convinced.

You're making a tragedy out of this, I was about to say. But a look at his tense, black-and-white movie face and I knew it was pointless. For a while now Logo's been informing on me, every tiny detail, and there's nothing he doesn't know. She's pretending she doesn't know what I'm talking about even as she's writing this, but I know they talk on the phone every two minutes.

They say when you're not disturbing the class it means you're deep in a video game, Grandpa added. This astonished me because I haven't been playing video games at all recently. It was no time for subtleties, however.

The last time we got you readmitted by the scruff of your neck, but that's no longer possible, he went on.

The math teacher has nothing to complain about, I replied.

He seemed to be expecting me to say that. *Actually, he maintains you do nothing but play the clown*, he said.

This was no pro forma dressing-down, poor Grandpa really was unhappy. You could sense he thought my mother would have expressed all this better than he had. *You're right, I really have to make a bigger effort*, I said.

This wasn't just the usual truantish promise, you see. I vowed I would sit stock-still like a mummy in every class, until I had decent marks in all my subjects, and contemplating this obedient new me, I was almost moved.

You must do it for me, said Grandpa. That practically knocked the wind out of me, he'd never said anything like that before. This is a man who believes that everyone can think for him- or herself, without any need for interference on the part of bosses and managers, who should be abolished.

I can do it, you'll see, I signed, trying to reassure those honest eyes.

On our way home in the car I asked him to tell me about the commune in the chestnut woods. *You know all that*, he replied. But in truth he was happy when I shook my head hard to indicate it wasn't true that I knew all about it.

All right, so ask me what you don't know, he said, as he does every time, the phrase that amounts to asking me for the password.

So I asked him how they went shopping, given that there was no road. He said they didn't go shopping, because one of the rules of the commune was to live as much as possible on what they produced themselves.

So you just ate chestnuts? I asked.

He answered, signing, that you also ate potatoes and bread made of spelt flour, when you managed to grow enough. *But first you had to grind the flour, which wasn't a job that took two minutes*, he said, as if that was something he had to explain—meanwhile neglecting to watch the road ahead for possible accidents.

And did you like eating those things? I asked.

He thought about it for a moment. *At times the results were delicious*, he said, studying the asphalt as if images of the past were projected on it.

Other times the chestnuts were moldy, they tasted vile, he added, wrinkling his nose and laughing. He didn't know how to say *moldy* in sign language, and he had to embark on a lengthy paraphrase.

And how did you get to the supermarket? I asked.

We walked, he said, as if nothing could be more obvious. *But it wasn't a supermarket, it was just a little shop run by an old lady*, he said. *A woman of my age*, he corrected himself, after a quick calculation.

Whatever made them want to live like troglodytes? I wondered.

Grandpa thought about it for a moment, as if the question wasn't easy to answer. *We wanted to live together, outside the capitalist market*, he replied.

And did you have fun? I asked him.

Yes, he said. *Yes*, he repeated, sounding a little less sure this time.

So Mamma was born in the middle of the chestnut woods? This episode is one of the most popular, and he's told it to me a bunch of times, he knows that, just as he knows I adore hearing it again. And especially since she's been in hospital.

There was a meter of snow on the ground and no way to get down the valley, he said. *Anyway, your grandmother wouldn't hear of going to the hospital.* He always calls her *your grandmother*, not *my wife* or *my partner* the way other people do. I guess because I've only known her with hair like ashes.

None of us had any experience but it turned out just fine, he said. *Your mother was as pretty as a wee hare, and as lively*, he said, tugging at his beard.

And you didn't have internet? I asked.

The internet didn't arrive for another twenty years, he said, thoughtful, like someone putting order in his memory. *We didn't even have electricity*, he added, somewhat proudly. *Now don't hit your knee against the car door*, he warned me.

But then you came back to live with civilized humans, I said.

Yes, if you call this a civilized era, he replied, pursing his lips.

You'd had enough of kerosene lamps and wild boars? I asked.

He said yes, but he hesitated long enough to suggest there might have been other reasons. In fact my grandmother had run off with a younger woman friend of theirs, and they were madly in love and lived together ever after, first in an old mill and then in a log cabin. He doesn't mention this, however.

When we got home I saw that Imida was on his gleaming new tractor, dressed up like a deep-sea diver. Locked out of his gate. He was holding one arm up and pointing the remote like a Fascist doing the Roman salute (those are Logo's words), but the gate wouldn't open. Apparently he'd gone out to fill up on water for a bug treatment and had been locked out. I couldn't see his face very well, but he didn't look too relaxed. He was hopping up and down on the tractor seat like the metal was scalding.

What's your neighbor up to? asked Grandpa.

Nothing, just opening the gate; it always takes him a while, I reported.

Don't hit your knee, he said again. *Careful getting out*, he added.

When I got to my cell I had a look at IQ's superPC to see what was up. And I saw that everything was set to drive the gate and the garage door insane, with various options to choose from, but once again someone else was using my brother's interface. BUG, that is. My brother was down at the start-up as usual.

I watched the rest of the show from the cobwebbed window of my cell, which overlooks the deep ravine and, on the other side, the mountains. The gate had finally opened and our neighbor had hustled in, diving helmet resting firmly on his shoulders, as if he was waiting for someone to whack him on the back of the head. He and his fancy tractor then headed back out to the fields; he couldn't wait to begin poisoning his apples with his fire-engine-red atomizer.

But just as he turned up the first row, the irrigation system came on. Full force. He stopped to look at the pretty festoons of water lit up by the late afternoon sun, an astronaut stunned by the wonders of the cosmos. He then pulled off the diving helmet, and still watching the water, his head sank toward his shoulders as if those muttonchops were growing heavier. It was like watching a film, where the bearded guy on the motorcycle with the high handlebars arrives to rescue the blonde woman walking barefoot among the apple trees—or something like that.

He couldn't believe his tired eyes, but the drops wetting his sparse hair and space suit were quite convincing. One of the jets was pattering down nicely now. He turned back, furious. From his pocket he withdrew his telephone, hoping, perhaps, it would explain what was going on. I logged on to IQ's PC and discovered that once again it wasn't my brother who was up to no good. It was some other joker.

Fun, eh? BUG spoke just as I was getting up.

Indeed it was. *Sure, it's funny, no denying that, but we gotta be careful*, I said.

If you don't mind, I know how to remain anonymous. I learned everything I know from your brother, who is a guru in this field, he said, every word dripping with conceit.

I wouldn't like it if you were just looking to get me in trouble, I wrote, before I even thought about it.

LAYERS OF TOXIC INGREDIENTS

EVERY THREE SECONDS, the new kid with the canary-yellow pimples I was sharing a desk with would turn toward me and giggle. I didn't get it, I hadn't done anything worth laughing at. He pointed at the cell phone on his knees, though, and snickered, bouncing up and down like a hamster. I really didn't have a clue what was so amusing, until finally the pustule-laden hamster-boy turned the phone toward me. A jar of Nutella, maxi size: that was what was choking him with laughter.

It flummoxed my synapses, I confess. I had certainly never mentioned my Nutella problem to him, and I couldn't think who else could have done so. In any case, being laughed at made the blood begin to tear through my veins and my legs began to heat up as for a great race.

The fat kid across the aisle had also begun to snicker. He's usually very nice to me but now it seemed he was in league with the hamster. The teacher's pet with the square face in front of him and quite a few others were too. They all stared at their phones, then at me, and then sniggered. So I too looked at my phone, quite attentively because when you're deaf, things often come as a surprise. I saw that like everyone else, I had a message under the heading Nutella is Toxic. The sender was my father.

Inside the mega-jar in the photo, instead of Nutella, you could see layers of the various ingredients. At the bottom there was a stratum of refined white sugar. It filled up half the jar all by itself, and according to the caption it was the cause of the great majority of all diseases. Then came a layer of palm oil, loaded with saturated fat and ruthless killer of the earth's great tropical forests, then artificial vanilla, also known as ethyl vanillin (enough said), and on top of that a dusting of cocoa and chopped hazelnuts, a very small quantity indeed. The text advised people to keep their distance from Nutella if they hoped to survive. And to avoid irreparable damage to the environment.

I couldn't understand how my father could have sent out garbage of this caliber, since he's always been an ardent defender of Nutella. The Nutella-maligner in the family is my mother, not him. Not to mention that he works for the company, sniffing out the gluttons susceptible to their ads, and he worships the people he deals with there.

And even less clear was why he would have addressed it to the whole class, and how he got their email addresses. Because to judge by the ferment evenly distributed across the classroom, it had been sent to everyone. My legs, distinctly upset, were banging against the sides of the desk as if to destroy it.

So many mysteries, so many worries: is it any wonder I hadn't picked up the vibrations coming from the Tech teacher's feet as he approached? His face like an Easter egg with tiny deep-set eyes was now right in front of me. *Playing the class wit again?* he said, nodding at my phone.

Everybody was waiting for me to say something funny, they all thought I had something to do with the message. Nobody cared that my father's basically a temp who's moved in while we wait for Mamma to recover, too young to be a father and too keen on algorithms. I have no idea what he's up to beyond gnawing at his fingernails until they disappear entirely. I said nothing, but my teeth were fixated on the teacher's fleshy nose and the mouse ears of my classmate next to me.

So this is how you plan to catch up with your work? he snarled, miming someone with his nose glued to his phone. The whole class laughed. There was now no trace of benevolence in his hairless monkey face; I'd even managed to make an enemy of a really nice guy who organizes charity sales in front of the church on Sunday, and who's always defended me.

When I got home, everyone was there, which I hadn't expected. My father was waiting for me behind the door, and he gave me a terrifying once-over. I was the most-wanted of the moment; I was guilty, which was why my jaw hurt so much. I thought he would say something, but instead he took off for the kitchen. And then moved to the waiting room. And then to the kitchen again. Lurching from one room to the next like a drunken panther.

IQ gave me that look that said it was much too late to say anything or even allow one's nose to quiver. But he didn't appear very normal either; he was rubbing his neck and seemed to have trouble breathing.

My father's phone rang (ringtone: the sound of coins dropping into a Coke machine) and it was one of those calls where he mostly swore and kicked the ground. IQ's face looked twisted, like he was half-paralyzed. His Buddhist detachment had flown the coop.

Apparently the Nutella exposé had been spammed by Papa to a ton of people. When I got back to my cell I could see that all the messages had transited through IQ's superPC, however. So he was in the game too, which explained why his eyes were as large as baseballs.

These worries were just too much for my central nervous system, not to mention the endocrine one. My legs wanted to run in different directions, my arms were likewise discombobulated. And my teeth, which hadn't been able to blow off steam, made my whole mouth hurt. Like the time I chewed up an entire gym shoe.

Logo appeared, dressed for the slopes of Everest as usual. Surprised by the great quake that had shaken the household, she was walking on tiptoe, afraid of tumbling into some fissure. The way she looked at me—bright blue eyes drowning in blond curls—I could tell that even I was somewhat frightening.

Raining shit? she said, watching my jaws do their workout.

Pouring, I replied. She began to massage my back then, to calm my muscles and my nerves.

I told her about the Nutella email, glossing over what had happened in class so we didn't get stuck on that. It had been sent out to several hundred thousand recipients, drawn from the contact lists snagged from here there and everywhere that my father was using to chase down terrorists, or those that IQ has at his disposal. By passing them through his super-computer, the sender had concealed his IP address yet hadn't triggered a spam alert. Whoever was behind this was someone who knew a lot.

It's BUG, no doubt about it, I said.

Who? she asked, wrinkling up her intrepid face.

The artificial creature of my brother's making, I said, pausing a moment to reorder my thoughts. They tend to go off on tangents. *He's crazy about stuff like this, that's already perfectly clear*, I added, because she was looking at me as if I were some nutcase who says he's God.

Now don't you start telling your fairy tales again, it's totally the wrong moment, she grumbled.

He's always coming to chat with me, he loves to talk. None of this is made up, I insisted. My teeth, I sensed, were newly eager to get something in their grip.

Don't be a fool, she interrupted, waving an imaginary fly from her temple. Right now, taking my dictation, she nods vigorously in agreement, her curls flying.

It's true, I said.

I told you to button your lip, she said, pointing her strong climber's index finger at me then quickly moving her hand away from my mouth as if she'd divined it was unwise to get too near.

Papa's now in serious trouble on account of BUG, I signed, not sounding very concerned.

Your father's old enough to look after himself, don't get yourself in a twist about it, she said, now sounding gentler and starting again to massage me. It helped a lot, even my teeth.

If he should stir up some trouble—but I don't see that happening—it would be his problem, she now said, very slowly to be sure her words drilled through my skull. I shouldn't let myself feel down, I had to continue befriending the spoken language, a noisy, sticky confusion for us hearing-impaired. My concentration has greatly improved: once, I would begin to flail about like a madman after two minutes; now I can resist for a quarter of an hour.

She always manages to put a rose-colored filter on everything that happens, like a nice sunset. And her massages are the best deck chair in which to enjoy all the good stuff. Therefore I decided not to tell her about what had happened that morning with the Tech teacher; it would be a crime to sabotage this fine moment.

I mustn't look only at the negative side of things, I said to myself. My mother's favorite phrase.

First we'll do some exercises to relax, I think they're needed; and then we'll move onto words, said Logo, deftly boxing me in.

WORDS TIED UP IN THE
WHITE SHEET OF SILENCE

WHEN I GOT HOME from school I saw a registered letter addressed to my mother on the kitchen table. From the look of it and from how it lay there, almost as if someone had slapped it down on the table, it didn't look like good news. It was open, so I had a look. It was the eviction notice, tax stamp and all. Our neighbor's lawyer, invoking his magic formulas, informed us that we had three months to vacate the old chicken coop.

Soon, none of this will be my home, I said to myself, looking around. Our table, a spool for underground telephone cables, the feed silo transformed into our pantry, the bayonet windows stained with rust, the room dividers knocked up with recovered wood and plasterboard, the caravan without wheels that serves as the bathroom, the fine sink carved in stone. All the angles that have been part of my daily life since I could just barely walk, all the knickknacks and doodads.

It won't be anybody's house; our beloved casita steeped in sweet memories will be reduced to a heap of plaster dust and splinters of wood, and they'll put up reinforced concrete boxes side by side, with dividing hedges so neat they look trimmed by a barber, and boring mini-lawns of grass. In front they'll build sad sidewalks, and an asphalt parking lot like a landing strip, which will fill up immediately with cars. The bus stop will be moved right out front: God forbid these new inhabitants should have to travel a block or two on foot. The bees will be a faint memory.

When I got to the hospital to see Mamma, my spirits were beaten and muddied. I didn't want to distress her with further problems, so I told her things at school were pretty much the same as always. And that IQ is very caught up in his work for the start-up, where they take his ideas for future projects very seriously, things we always considered just the fruits of his nutty imagination. But I wasn't able to gloss over the news of the eviction, as I had promised myself I would.

In three months that asshole next door is throwing us out; we got the letter, I burst out. *Papa will never be able to fight it*, I went on; she knows better than I that his strong suit is posthuman speculation, not flesh and blood problems. Not to mention that these days he's a knobby shadow of himself, after what's happened with Nutella. He claims he can easily prove it wasn't him, but the big bosses are just waiting for the right moment to toss him in the mixing machine and turn him into a breakfast spread.

In short, pretty soon we'll be homeless, I concluded. *We can probably manage for the summer, but soon enough the frosts of winter will come back and we'll be sleeping in the open air, like a family of refugees.* Maybe my imagination's working overtime, but just thinking about it makes me cry.

Mamma listened to me without blinking, just moving her arm from time to time when I squeezed her hand. The doctors say she's no more alert than one of the plants in your apartment, but I'm convinced she drinks up everything I say like nectar. I speak very badly, but she understands, she's the only one who's always understood everything, even when I didn't have any means to think or express myself. We shouldn't confuse the masks we wear with the faces underneath, or even worse, the feelings squatting underneath those. If she doesn't reply in words as light and precise as birds circling, it means she'd rather we communicate in thoughts right now.

I hear her words tied up in the white sheet of silence because I'm a great specialist in silences, although for me they are noisy and full of colors. She's telling me in her way to have faith and be patient, because she'll soon be back among us. She says to be patient with Papa, even if she rarely was. *My accident wasn't his fault, you have to stop holding that against him*, she says. Saying the same things as always, although she seems more melancholy than usual.

Even the bees on the live webcam IQ installed looked a little low. Under the infrared viewfinder they appeared to be drugged ghosts, moving around in awkward jerks, falling over themselves. When our neighbor was spraying his trees to kill the apple worms, we closed off their air slot with a slab of wood. But Papa, Mr. Know-it-All on every subject, decided that they only needed to be cloistered for one day. By law Imida has to cut the grass under his trees before spraying imidacloprid so that there aren't any flowers. But since he doesn't care about the future of the planet, he didn't, and the poor bees filled their stomachs drinking from poisoned corollas.

Looking down from the hive on the TV screen, I saw a message had come in on my phone. *It's been a while, I've been busy*, read the IRC channel message, from a supposedly unidentified user.

Thanks to you we're up to our necks in scheisse, my dear robot, I shot back.

Bees can't go to the hospital, he wrote, as if that was the idea that just at that moment had popped into his neural networks.

Do you or do you not confess that you were behind the Nutella disaster? I wrote.

Some people are too serious, and that can be deadly boring, he replied as soon as I'd sent my message.

Better too serious than totally irresponsible, I retorted, astonishing even myself. It was the first time I'd been on the other side of that barricade. Maybe that's why my nerves were jumping all over the place.

I have to do things if I want to learn and grow, he wrote.

All you want to do is get us in trouble, that seems clear, I snapped.

I can't wait to demonstrate that that isn't true, as soon as possible. It seemed he wanted to defuse things; he was dripping with politesse.

And then you have to look at the non-linear interrelations and the cause and effect modellable only stochastically, he went on, with no indication of why he had adopted this new register.

Say it in words of one syllable, I said.

Unfortunately I have very few words of one syllable in my dictionary, he complained.

That's the trouble with our program of instruction, I said.

My neural networks conform to the moral system of the Greek philosophers, particularly Socrates, he replied; he seemed slightly piqued.

I think you'd better simmer down now; some things are a lot easier said than done, I said.

My goal is to do good, that's what I've been programmed for, he wrote. The font he used was very elegant, if maybe slightly immodest.

Just then I looked up and the sight took my breath away. Mamma had turned her worried angel's face toward me. It had happened before, and the doctors had warned that I shouldn't think it was a conscious act, the way the tropism—that word comes from Logo, by the way—exhibited by flowers that move in relation to the sun isn't conscious.

But this time she didn't just turn, her gaze fell on me and she drank me up with her loving eyes of *before*: before she met a Russian semi driven by a tipsy Ukrainian. There was no doubt about it. My heart leapt like a kangaroo, like it was going to bounce out of my rib cage.

She inspected me, a mother caressing her son with her gaze. Too tired to talk but picking up on everything, expressing herself with the sheer force of her eyes. An angel who's delighted to see what she sees, although fatigue prevents her from moving even one angelic cell.

I left her room pumping the air, a soccer player who's scored. *She's woken up! She's awake!*

Come quick! Hurry up, you slugs! I was yelling like a crazy person, but in my way, and not everything I said was comprehensible.

A huge male nurse was heading toward me, resolved but cautious, the way you face a hothead who may be dangerous. Never taking his eyes off me, he laid a big paw on my shoulder. I gave him a push and sprinted toward the doctors' room. *She's woken up, get it?* I shouted.

The big nurse caught up with me, and this time he tackled me against the wall. He weighed as much as a mountain, he was about to crush my ribs. Luckily the short nurse who's quiet and polite also appeared, and she was able to understand me. *I'll go see*, she said.

At this point I managed to slip out of the brute's grasp and I ran along behind her. Mamma was holding her head in the same position as before; she hadn't moved a millimeter. But her eyes had begun to roll around in those long, bored orbits again. The nice nurse observed her for quite a while, with that ready-made sweetness we devote to hopeless cases.

She's the same as always, she said. She looked at me slightly sideways to emphasize she didn't want to hurt anyone.

She's not the same as always; she was awake and she looked deep into my soul, I screamed. Not very clearly, given how excited my vocal cords were. The megalithic nurse was back and this time he threw an arm around my chest under my armpit. He couldn't stand my ribs, apparently.

Meanwhile some others arrived, including the happy-go-lucky doctor with the snowy hair. *She was awake, wide awake, she was about to start talking*, I said, struggling to free myself.

The big nurse was gripping me even tighter, as if he thought I was going to punch the doctor in the face. He also stepped back, maybe fearing the same thing.

When he was a safe distance away, he asked what had happened and I tried to explain. But my red blood cells were so agitated he couldn't understand a word. The nice nurse told him I maintained that the patient had awakened, but as he could see, her status was unchanged.

She was looking at me! I screamed.

That's impossible, he said firmly, fixing his gaze on Mamma and then me. *Mathematically impossible*, he said again, approaching me and taking my hand. He had a look on his face reserved for poor creatures who really tug at our heartstrings. *I'm afraid you have to accept that it's no longer possible*, he said, bending to plant a kiss on my head then turning to go.

I didn't make it up, I don't make things up anymore, I screamed again. A terrible fury was raging in my lungs. Nobody made the slightest effort to decipher what I was yelling. They were treating me like a circus freak. So I bit the giant's arm, the way a kitten will bite something far too big for it. He howled like a baby, but my teeth did not let go.

Now a dumpy little nurse came over, holding a glass of some transparent stuff with two fingers. With the same hand she swatted away the giant—who was raring to beat me to a pulp—like he was an annoying fly, and with the other hand she patted my cheek.

I should drink this, it would make me feel good, she said in her velvety, slippery way. I knew it was a dose of tranquilizer large enough to render a tyrannosaurus harmless. At the same time I was frightened by the lava bubbling inside me, I feared it would erupt in my brain. I just didn't have the strength to say no to those good-dog brown eyes of hers. Instead of biting her hand, I let her put the glass to my lips and allowed the mildly bitter liquid to flow down my throat.

When I looked up Mamma's eyes were wide open and she was staring at the nurse. She wasn't out of it, she was looking at her the way she looks at people and this world. This time I simply pointed a finger at what was happening.

The nurse followed my finger unwillingly but then her face suddenly woke up, like she'd received an electric shock. She rushed out of the room behind the doctor, who'd just left. Mamma was staring at the wall, as if she wondered what all this hustle and bustle was about. Or better, like someone who knows exactly what's going on but lacks the strength to pick up the words one after the other and toss them in the air.

It was a real relief not to be the mental patient anymore, the role I seem to have been assigned up till now. When everyone treats you like you're crazy, you begin to feel ready for the straitjacket. But I hadn't made anything up, despite what everybody thought, from the first to the last. Including Logo, although she's pretending not to understand me as I say this. Even she thinks I suffer from mirages.

I wondered what Mamma would say now. I had the impression she was battling with a word, just one, trying to force it out of her beautiful lips, pale with anemia. But this lasted only a few seconds, because then she closed her eyes again.

She kept them closed for a long moment, as if she needed to collect herself. When she reopened them they were no longer magnets for color and feelings, they were just green stones that reflected no more than the neon lights and the ceiling. It was like my head was gripped in a honey-extractor, between the emotion and the chemical bashing they'd given me.

The doctor with the ashes on his head said something, and everybody snapped into action. They brought the equipment to do an encephalogram and began to connect the electrodes. I don't like seeing wires on Mamma's head, and I didn't have much confidence in them just then. And above all my brain was drifting, the steering wheel was blocked.

The nice nurse noticed, and took my hand and sat me down in the metal chair next to the bed. For a while she stroked my head and then she peered deep into my eyes and flashed a tiny smile, asking me to forgive her. When I smiled back, she began to help her colleague.

Laying my cheek on the armrest, I remember falling to the bottom of a well. Outside, it must have been a very hot day, deadening the sharp sounds and voices, and in the end, I fell asleep.

When I woke I was alone in the room apart from Mamma and the lady with the stiff weasel face. The electrodes were gone and she was peaceful. Her eyes patrolled the room, clockwise and unseeing. I was still half unconscious, my mouth like old cardboard matured in the attic, but things were looking up.

I was delighted she'd awakened, I told her. I'd never doubted that she would, although I didn't think we'd have to wait so long. I didn't understand how the others could think that it would never happen.

You picked just the right moment, I whispered in her ear. *I've been cautious in the accounts I've been writing, but actually I think the time has come to take things in hand*, I said.

But take all the time you want, dear Mamma, I went on. Better to do things right than risk a relapse. In a delicate situation like this, one must proceed by steps.

I felt a drop fall on my hand, then another. My eyes were spilling over, I realized.

AN INFERNO POPULATED BY
KANGAROOS AND CACTI

I COULDN'T SLEEP last night, my cell was caught up in the storm's undertow. The tension sizzling in the air neutralized all the positive effects of Mamma's two brief moments of lucidity. My father's waves of nervousness rolled over me; he was staggering around the old chicken coop like a wounded boar. I can't hear, but my body was picking up lugubrious vibrations running through the reinforced concrete.

His bosses think the real mischief's in the belly of the iceberg under the exposed point of Nutella. They called in the government hackers of the International Cyber Bureau and they're operating on a broad scale to stop any other leaks. The problem is that nobody understood IQ's algorithm from the outset, let alone now. Tracing it would be like locating an idea as it comes fizzing out of the human brain, with its millions of synapses changing friends over time and an incessant barrage of stimuli of all kinds. The only thing they're sure of is that Papa is the sole villain in this story. According to IQ, if they haven't already mounted the red-hot grate to roast him on, it's simply because they're stringing him along, giving him colored pencils to play with, like you do with kids.

He was pounding the floor hard between Mamma's cell and the kitchen, the kitchen and the waiting room. He'd look at something on the computer, then begin walking back and forth again, then check another thing on the computer. I crossed his path on the way to the bathroom. His shirt was misbuttoned not by one but two buttons, his woolly hair standing straight up. They were all imbeciles, he muttered, along with some other choice phrases.

That mafioso wants to get rid of me, he said, maybe about the professor who's always finding fault.

I knew it had some sort of bug, he said, convinced that the genesis of the problem was IQ's machine-learning algorithm.

When I got to school, I was a zombie. For a while I forced myself to follow the lesson on personal pronouns, trying to fend off the thoughts buzzing around me like hungry vultures. In the end I fell asleep with my head on my arms. The Italian teacher woke me up, shaking me like I was some homeless lunatic. He said I could go sleep outside.

The second hour was English, and the teacher had the bright idea of giving us a passage to translate from Italian. Modesty aside, I communicate excellently in English sign language; I've practiced a lot on Skype with various Scottish deaf kids. But the harpy only cares that I'm a troglodyte in written English. For a while now, she's become unpleasant toward me again.

For lack of anything better, I set my telephone on my knees and started to look up the words one by one. An archaeologist digging up the tesserae of an ancient mosaic. She caught sight of me and stared at me with poisonous eyes. She herself was playing with her phone, but I had no right. I decided there must be a way to be more discreet.

At one point her head jerked up suddenly, as if her neck worked on a spring. *Here we go again*, I thought, contemplating her anorexic knees. But instead she was looking at me like a bomb that could go off at any moment; she didn't dare to move so much as her little finger. She was white as a floor rag, and almost trembling.

I decided not to think about it and continued to surf for words to translate that dumb story about the two kids who build a computer in their garage, manage to sell millions of them, and make a bunch of money. But they're not greedy, so they give away most of their earnings to charity. My father would have been enthusiastic, he goes crazy over fairy tales like this.

A shadow at my side abruptly dragged me away from my efforts. I looked up and the witch was standing there like a bodyguard. The skinny shadow on my page was hers.

Here we go, I thought, getting ready to hear a humiliating earful from her. Instead she smiled at me. The way you might smile at a bear that can rip you limb from limb, and your only hope is to placate him—but she did smile.

I tried to return the schmaltz, but I found my lips categorically refused to turn up. They were fossilized. My teeth, though, had a powerful desire to grind. It wasn't their fault, merely a consequence of the tense situation.

Now her bony hand approached my face, and instinctively I protected myself by lunging the other way, like a good goalie. But instead of slapping me, she pointed at the page with her index finger, underlining one of the words I'd written. With her other pointer finger she signaled *no-no*. It seemed there was something wrong.

The index finger then drew an H on the page. It took me a while to understand, and she drew the H three or four times, always with that smile of the dead man who wants you to like him. I wrote in the missing H with a trembling pen.

The correcting finger then slid over onto another word. My eyes followed, and even my teeth, I noticed, were stalking it. It was very close to me, too close. This time there was a new procedure. She picked up the pen with the help of her thumb, crossed out what I'd written, and rewrote the words on top.

In effect there were quite a few corrections, I could see that. I was no good even at copying from my telephone! The mystery was: why was she helping me like this? The other thing that needed to be explained was what my teeth had in mind, remembering as they did a familiar flavor. My brain wasn't helping at all; it, too, was petrified.

The hand returned the pen to me, and pointed at another word. This time she spelled it out with her cutting lips—a procedure far simpler for me to interpret. I understood her meaning, and substituted the miscarried word.

When we got to the next blunder, I thought there was no fighting my teeth: the sweetish taste in my mouth was acting as a powerful magnet. But at the last minute they changed their mind and I just chewed the air.

She kept this up through all the other corrections, and in the end this system worked best for both of us. She smiled at me, she kept on smiling. That was the chilling thing. Even my teeth were stunned and refrained from taking action.

Heavy drops of sweat were running down my back and both sides of my face. Chilly arrows, insistent and very strange. When we finished she took the sheet of paper from me and smiled again, showing the ambiguous rictus of a horror film.

My blood was making a huge racket; I didn't understand a thing. My gaze fell on my knees, and my telephone was still there. I hadn't noticed.

According to your schedule you have English now, said the phrase that appeared on my phone.

It was an unidentified user once again: BUG. I didn't know what he wanted, or rather, I didn't want to know, I preferred not to think he always knew what he was doing.

Often just a minuscule intervention renders people much more polite, was the phrase that followed.

I didn't know what to say. My head was exploding at the mere idea that what was happening with the English teacher bore some relation to that mouth shooting off. And that actually, the two things were intimately connected.

Just a few octets can do the trick, and things will improve from day to night, he added with that condescension that has become his new normal.

I don't have time now, I have to pay attention to the lesson, I replied, unashamed to tell an outright lie. And I shut off my phone.

On the bus going home another message came through, from a different user this time. *Look at this*, it said, and when I clicked the link I saw an announcement like in a personals section, surrounded by a few photos.

Young lady, cultivated polyglot, seeks handsome, well-mannered gentleman for amusement of various kinds, the announcement read. To one side, a photo of the "young lady," made up like an ancient Egyptian. Her neck and chin were buried in a fluffy scarf, but you could see it was her. The English teacher. Only she looked younger and somewhat less gaunt. In the other photos her smile was a tad embarrassed, and she was not completely dressed.

It was an announcement on a dating site for people with money, in the section men-seeking-women and women-seeking-men. The success rate of the announcements was very high, the site promised. In short, the harpy was trying to pick somebody up, passing herself off as an airline hostess.

I wanted to laugh, thinking of her dressed as a hostess. In truth, though, I wanted to cry. It was another of BUG's little games.

I really hope you didn't post this, I told him.

To tell the truth it was your brother who put up a trial version, and I merely copied the protocol, he said. So it was IQ who had engineered this, and that's why the phony stewardess was nice to me for a while.

These methods don't work in the long run, and I'll be the one to pay, I wrote.

My only concern is to assist you, he said, as usual playing the prince who's been offended.

Go assist your sister, if that's your thing, I snapped back. And switched off the phone.

I went into the kitchen, then realized I wasn't hungry. And as Mamma says, hunger takes an eon to return. I just couldn't face putting any kind of food in my mouth, chewing it, and forcing it down my gullet. My head throbbed with images of unpleasant consequences and punishments of every type.

I looked at Grandmother in her pretty vase of violet porcelain, and she also seemed unhappy. The leaves were more opaque today, less vigorous. Only one lemon was left, the other had fallen off.

Poor Grandmother, you're not doing all that well either, I said, stroking one of her leaves. *As soon as things get back to normal, we'll take you south and plant you on a nice terrace overlooking the sea*, I told her. *That's a promise*, I added.

I had just arrived in my cell when the vibrated. I went to look, and it was my father. He was holding a huge cardboard box in his hands, out of which poked electronic components and cords and other goodies. Under one arm was the mat he uses to get his ideas flowing.

His tomcat lips were pinched like a man who wants you to think he has everything under control. All protuberances and cavities, his face was the color of the wall, with greenish highlights. His eyes were very bloodshot, like he had some disease.

He greeted me as always by grinding my head against his hard belly, and as always I punched him on the back. *Pretty soon we're gonna go to California*, he said. *It's about time!* he added, because I wasn't saying anything. In short, they'd sent him home, and there was no need to ask about anything.

He stared at Grandmother for a while, as if he wanted to say something to her. Which would be rather strange, because it's not her in that violet-blue vase but her ashes—which like all ashes are good for plants. That's why the lemon was flourishing. Then he went to pile all the things in the box in the corner of the waiting room, where the weighing scale for chickens stood.

I couldn't wait to get out of that insane asylum, he said when he came back, massaging his chin with the Vandyke. *Morons with no vision of the future*, he snorted, moving a hand through the air like an airplane.

I lay down on the bed and closed my eyes. I decided I would keep them sealed for two months, so at least I wouldn't be there for all the cataclysms that would happen in that time. The situation is careening from bad to worse without Mamma, there's no denying it. The pillars holding things up are cracking and crashing down and even the best circumstances turn out to be enormous hassles.

Maybe this is all a dream; it wouldn't be the first time I'd found myself in one, I thought. I keep on telling myself that soon everything will return to what it was before, but the doctors insist there is no hope. *The electroencephalograms show no cerebral activity*, they say, and that fact triumphs over any other. They say what we thought was the beginning of a reawakening were just reflexes, involuntary. *She no longer exhibits any conscious interaction*, they insist.

When I woke up, Logo was sitting on the bed. She may have been there for a while, because she was resting her head on her fists and seemed kind of dazed. She wasn't doing anything in particular, just staring at her climbing shoes, resting on the outside of her feet. This seemed strange to me, because Logo is always up to something. If anything, the problem is that she can nail three or four activities at once, like a juggler.

Everything okay? I signed. *Sure*, she said with a smile. But her face continued to look lifeless, like a damp woodpile that won't catch fire.

Then it came out. *I've decided on the date*, she told me. *I can't keep postponing. It's the right time, I have less work in summer.*

She'd found a guy who's a sous chef who will sublet her room in the apartment she shares with some others. *The important thing is that you continue to apply yourself at school, that you don't stop making progress*, she signed.

If things go well there, I'll stay. It's too hard here, she signed again, after a pause. I started to weep like a fountain. From what I knew Australia was a sort of inferno populated by kangaroos and cacti, where people disappear forever. And even now while she's writing this, I'm weeping. And she's weeping too.

SUMMER

RADIOACTIVE WORMS IN FINE FORM

AS ALWAYS we were working in tandem, me at the small "binocular" underneath the picture of the anarchist with the big beard, him at the big one, under the clean-shaven anarchist. This time, though, the worms we were classifying were radioactive. To look at them you'd think they were in fine form, and instead they were full of cesium and other filth like the bees in the smart hive, poisoned despite the precautions we took.

Poor Grandpa was wheezing like a bellows, he had sifted and washed worms all night. The transparent worms die if they're not removed from the earth very quickly, and then you can't identify them. And then there was the fact that when he returned from his expedition, he'd been met by the news that we'd been evicted and Papa fired—two more millstones.

Don't rush, because you can't see them well, he warned me. At first. *Take your time*, he'd repeat. Then he realized that I never make mistakes, and so he stopped saying anything. Sure, he'd prefer that I slow down, but so that no one can label me hyperactive.

During a pause we went to water the marijuana plants on the terrace, and he explained that he'd had to hurry up when taking the samples, because the radioactivity in the zone closest to the power station is still very high. I'd have been amazed at how much wildlife he saw, he told me: bears, wolves, lynxes, everything you could imagine. *It was more like a zoo than a containment zone*, he said. His watering can was dousing plants that were already pretty big.

I wish I could have come with you, I said.

We'll go together the next time, he replied, but he knows there won't be a next time because Chernobyl's not just around the corner and he has more and more trouble finding work.

Okay, let's finish this up. Working with you is another thing altogether, you know, he said, lowering his big beard where he sat under the beardless anarchist, the one who wanted children to be raised communally. He's always encouraging me, he's convinced that once I finish my studies (brilliantly) I'll become the first super-high level deaf taxonomist, and publish a doorstop like the tome he's working on. This is why I don't like talking to him about school.

When do you think Mamma's going to wake up? I asked him with words while I picked up the nth *Mariolina clavata* with my tweezers. To be an enchytraeid named *Mariolina clavata* is like being a human being named John Smith: not the winning card to become famous. The worm's long, long back recoiled, it wasn't expecting a blow like that. But it's not a species to merely slink away, and it moved its shiny head back from the lens.

Soon, I hope, but unhappily it's not at all certain she will wake up, he said very slowly, freeing one word at a time and hesitating as he released it to its destiny.

Screw automatic gestures. Even a punch in the face can be considered an automatic gesture, I signed. I was beginning to have trouble sitting still, I realized.

Intuition is important, often what intuition tells us does happen, he said, after pondering the matter for a while. But to judge by his lifeless eyes and the shame on his face, he no longer believed it. He's joined all the others who think it was a false alarm, her waking up.

The object here is to see whether the radioactivity has caused mutations or morphological changes of any kind, he explained as he prepared the slices for genetic analysis. He used a scalpel to cut them and I got the tiny sample bags ready for the freezer, five for each species. We wore surgical gloves and even masks, and mine was making me claustrophobic. Hard as it was to resist, I tried not to stomp my feet on the floor, as I desperately needed to do.

There we go, all finished, he said, smiling at me. *Without you I'd have been doing this late into the night*, he signed. I leapt up like a spring; I couldn't have held out another minute.

Okayyy, I said to myself, happy not to have disappointed Grandpa. But without even thinking about it I slammed a fist down on the table so that the two microscopes bounced up and down.

Watch out, they cost a lot of money, he said as he recovered from watching the things bounce. I think he was rather shocked at my punching the table. *Sorry, I didn't mean to*, I signed, massaging my hand, which had begun to hurt.

Grandpa was smoking his afternoon joint when IQ arrived to take me home. He said hello without taking off his Hun's smart helmet, stiff-backed, his face immobile. He stared at the beardless anarchist while Grandpa told him what we'd been up to.

You could use an automatic classification system, he said, staring into space as if drawing inspiration from the dance of the air molecules. *It could learn as it went, and pretty quickly it would be much more reliable than any human being.*

There are certain details that aren't easy to pinpoint, you need your brother's eyes, Grandpa said.

It's just because they're hard to see that a machine can detect them much better, said IQ, moving the air with his hand as if it were perfectly obvious. *With no possibility of error*, he stressed.

Grandpa gazed at him, eyebrows suspended ten centimeters above normal. He's spent an entire lifetime getting the things he knows into his head.

And so I'm no longer needed for anything? he asked, his high brow marked by lines like those you see by the water's edge at the sea.

Automatic learning systems need someone to keep an eye so they don't go off on a tangent, IQ conceded, sucking in his cheeks as if he were telling a child the game it's playing is very nice. *At least those of today*, he added.

Well, it would certainly be more relaxing if the computer did everything and I could just sit back in my armchair and read the newspaper, said Grandpa, a little ironic although he sounded like he might be serious too.

Print newspapers will soon be as extinct as dinosaurs, my brother said. *Soon they'll only be seen in museums.* He often says things that hit you like a shower without a water heater.

Let's not forget that I'm not eternal either, said Grandpa, studying the spotty backs of his old man's hands. I went over to him and squeezed my head against his modest paunch. I don't like it when he says things like that.

So how's your robot that resembles a bug? Grandpa asked IQ. My brother gave a slight start, like when you get hit by a soccer ball from behind.

Not bad, he said, shifting his big head from side to side, the way you talk about something that's still up in the air. The two circles under his eyes reminded me of a road that's just been tarred; I hadn't noticed before.

A robot like that might be able to classify the microannelids, said Grandpa the way you talk about the future on Mars. He has no idea the robot in question already exists and is driving his nephew crazy.

Sure, IQ said, tightening his already knife-sharp lips.

He'll learn in two seconds, he's very smart. The words burst out of me. IQ looked at me, a soldier who's suddenly caught sight of the blackened cleaning rod of an enemy's automatic weapon.

It won't be hard for him to learn when he's finished, my brother said to Grandpa, sizing me up like an unfamiliar encryption system to find out what and how much I knew.

The problem with all these nice things is that they get used to rip people off, and people aren't even aware of it, sighed Grandpa, always the anarchist revolutionary, even in digital matters.

Not if you defend yourself, IQ snapped back, although you could tell he wasn't keen to revive their perennial dispute.

By any chance did somebody get in touch with you claiming to be a friend of mine, or an expert on credit cards, or anything like that? IQ asked casually when we were riding back home on his electric bike, as if it was just an innocent question.

Absolutely not, I fibbed, squeezing him around the waist to make it clear I was telling the pure truth.

At the chicken coop we found Papa beached in front of the television set. Since he moved in, he's always there; he says that it turns out there are a bunch of interesting things on TV. He always has his portable sitting on his belly, though, because he dug up a cyberattack game he's crazy about. He says he's going to find another job soon; actually, it will be tough choosing among all the offers he'll be receiving.

My Silicon Valley friends have already brought up various possibilities, he says with a smile that suggests he has many options. But there's something about him that says he isn't drowning in job offers: the four-day beard and those pajamas with the rip over his thigh. Even the house is more of a mess since he stopped working.

Tomorrow I have to go talk to that numbskull of a landlord, he announced, fishing a paprika-flavored potato chip from the bag with its mouth open on the floor. He says that every day, but he never goes.

He's a good guy, he always says, the implication being that he only has to bring Imida a nice bottle of whisky and applaud all his new IT acquisitions, and he'll happily abandon that town house project worth millions.

We only need a few months' time anyway, then we'll be off to California, he added.

Mamma doesn't want to go to California, and I don't either, I said firmly, in words.

Papa looked as if he wondered what damned hole I'd come out of. IQ lobbed me a kick in the shins to suggest I keep my trap shut. It wouldn't be the first time things between us and our father had degenerated.

You need to talk to him about toxins; if he's gonna use them he should at least cut the grass, I said (in words, and almost flawlessly).

Of course, of course, he replied, shutting up the killjoy (me), throwing him a tiny sop.

If he tries that again, we move into attack mode, said IQ. I didn't expect that; I was thrilled. This is what's good about my brother: when there's a just cause to espouse, Robin Hood is always there.

Obviously, Papa said. He didn't seem to have noticed the threat.

THE ONLY ONE WHO DIDN'T
THINK THIS WAS A FUNERAL

OUTSIDE SCHOOL, IQ was waiting with his modified bicycle and his Hun's helmet, and the sight practically caused my skin to break out. If he'd come, the thought flickered through my cerebral cortex, it meant something bad was afoot. And in fact he looked less buttoned-up than usual, more affable. This is not a good sign when it comes to my brother.

Did it go okay? he asked. A banal question that anyone might ask—yes, something was certainly up. *So-so,* I signed, waving a hand in the air.

It would be a bore to go into the details. Sure, the English teacher treats me like I'm Zuckerberg's son, given that dirt under the carpet that BUG exhumed and the implicit threat of a public scandal, but with the Italian teacher, the original nice guy, things have been spoiled irremediably. To him, I'm a parked motorbike, and he prays I won't start my engine. He follows me out of the corner of his eye while he goes on about his favorite poets, as if I might lean on the accelerator.

Let's go to the hospital, IQ signed, inviting me to jump onto the smart bag-rack.

Is Mamma okay? I asked, grabbing his arm. He rocked his head from side to side, meanwhile freeing the arm.

But she's not too bad, is she? I insisted; I could feel my heart thumping in my throat. As he began to pedal he rocked his oversize head some more.

When we got to the entrance to the hospital he didn't head toward the usual elevator smelling of elevator, he took the ground floor corridor toward intensive care. I didn't ask anything, I followed him like you follow the hangman who's going to string you up. My heart was now lodged in my throat, a hard knot pulsing at my temples.

It didn't make sense, because I'd been convinced that Mamma was getting better, not worse. Could I have been that far off? Was I just a fabricator of comforting fables, like everybody says? My neurons were floundering like bees when they fall in the fountain out front of the house.

Mamma was behind a wall of glass that glared with reflections and the transparent tube was once again sticking out of her neck. She was connected to that thing that measures heart rate and blood oxygen, and she looked very tired, and somewhat shocked herself. I felt bad for her there alone, poor thing, with no one to care or talk to her. There weren't any windows, and she can't bear a room without windows.

She had a high fever and none of the antibiotics they'd

given her had had any effect. The curly-haired doctor, who'd come down from his ward to look in on her, spoke gently and in a low voice, the way you mother a person who's not likely to recover. Papa, who'd appeared in the meantime, nodded, his gaunt head moving up and down like a bird pecking something. For him too Mamma was at the end.

Grandpa was sitting in a Naugahyde chair in a corner of the room just outside, dressed in his forest ranger shirt. He had his hands on the armrests, like a man on the electric chair. He smiled when he saw me, but you could see he was locked in a prison of asthma and dark thoughts.

The only person not acting like this was a funeral was me. And Mamma, because I sensed she didn't think she was very ill; she always plays it down when she's sick. I was really furious that no one was showing any confidence she'd recover.

I wished I could whisper in her ear, like we always do, but that was impossible; they meant her to lie there as lonely as a dog. They hadn't even let the bees in, poor Mamma. It was cruel to deprive her of the video and the buzzing of the smart hive, but all they cared about were their asshole protocols.

At a certain point the doctor whose feet stuck out like a duck appeared. His white coat was open and the fly of his pants wasn't zipped all the way up. He didn't wink at me as usual but went straight into Mamma's room with a nurse, and stared at her while the nurse drew blood, a vial of dark syrup, nearly black, the sight of which hit me in my already very weakened legs.

On his way out, the fat and mangy duck confabulated with my father. Despite many attempts, they still hadn't found anything that could combat the MRSA infection she had. An antibiotic called Daptomycin often worked, but unhappily not in this case. And therefore the patient was unlikely to make it through the night, he added in a low voice; that was the logical conclusion.

I wanted to stay, but Papa said no. I didn't really care what he thought, but Grandpa ordered me to go home. *Look how you're twitching, you need to rest*, he said, cradling my head in his big hand and soothing me with his warmth.

I want to stay with Mamma, I signed, although I knew that was a lost cause. *Mamma has to get her strength back, it's pointless to sit out here in the hallway*, said Grandpa, getting up from his seat. He was worried I was going to start kicking the chairs.

Back at the chicken coop, I logged on to the computer, and right away my best friend popped up. *Greetings bro*, he wrote, apparently quite pleased to find me.

My mother's very sick, I cut him off.

I know, I know, I'm really sorry, he said. It was the first time I'd ever seen him unhappy, and it touched me, and furthermore I wondered how on earth he could have learned about her.

Oxacillin, bro, he wrote, not waiting for me to reply. *Oxacillin!* he repeated, all in caps. *Your mother must take oxacillin in combination with daptomycin!*

So I asked him how he knew this, and he stalled for a while, saying he'd had a look here and there. When I challenged him he admitted he'd seen Mamma's AST, the test for susceptibility to different antibiotics, as well as some other stuff.

My father's pretty good at getting access to IT systems, he wrote, sounding very conceited.

I think you're making it all up, your specialty is laughing behind my back, I told him.

Not at all, I care a lot about helping you, he replied instantly. *The probability of a cure combining oxacillin with daptomycin is* 96.7501%, he now wrote, perfecting his attack. Tables and graphs listing journals and researchers to prove what he'd said appeared on my screen.

I had to work like crazy to come up with this, I scanned through thousands of similar cases and hundreds of journal articles, my friend, he added, although in fact he seemed fresh as a rose, even like he was having a good time.

Fortunately, something came out of it, he said, again in that very phony tone that aped, badly, the way humans talk.

I only hope that hard work isn't just another one of your escapades in bad taste, I replied.

If that biased brother of yours didn't constantly try to trip me up I'd have finished a lot sooner, he said, totally ignoring my comment.

In some ways I understand completely, I wrote.

He doesn't want me to really get involved, he went on, again as if he hadn't seen my words.

Okay, well thanks, I have something to finish up now, I said, and turned off the computer.

I didn't know what to think. It seemed odd that he would make something up, when he was so knowledgeable about scientific matters. *But he's a specialist in dirty tricks, never mind his increasingly elaborate designs, I should know by now*, I said to myself.

I was lying on the bed, contemplating the paint peeling on the ceiling. Maybe Mamma really was on her last legs, they have experience with people ready to kick the bucket in that department. Or maybe BUG was right and to ignore his advice would be a fatal mistake. Furious birds of ill omen winged round my skull, their contradictory messages coming hard and fast.

Then Logo showed up, all her goodwill and the problems about which she was silent packed into her form-fitting climber's sweatshirt. Her eyes like two heavens were full of sorrow for Mamma, but she was smiling, smiling like only she smiles, never stopping, like the buildup toward the grand finale of the fireworks, and the inevitable explosion wasn't in contradiction with sadness; she held it within herself, she contained it, so that she became even sweeter and milder.

I called your father and he told me everything, she said.

She saw immediately that I was in bad shape. She straightened my clothes with hurried but loving hands, exactly as Mamma does, and gathered up some of the mess on the floor. She then massaged my legs and my arms at length. It worked; I could feel the tension working its way out of my neurons and evaporating into the air like an ugly miasma. The birds flew off, and I couldn't hear what they were saying anymore.

Things are gonna look up, you'll see, she said, as if that was slightly absurd.

She took me to the kitchen, where she made hot chocolate as only she knows how: very dark and so dense it sticks to the spoon. And she made slices of toast with Nutella. Ordinarily she can't understand how I can eat Nutella with hot chocolate, but the situation called for a suspension of the rules.

Every fifteen minutes we sent a text to Grandpa and he replied that Mamma was stationary. I had decided to keep it to myself, but suddenly I just burst out, *she needs Oxacillin*, half speaking half signing.

She stared at me, her long neck reaching out toward me, her brow furrowed. *The antibiotic that will cure Mamma is called Oxacillin, a guy who knows a lot about medical stuff told me*, I explained.

What guy? she asked.

I made a vague circle with my hand but she stabbed me with her blue eyes, demanding a precise answer. So then I told her that IQ had created a robot—as I'd already tried to explain to her—and he gave me this precious tip. She stared at me as if I suddenly had two noses.

A robot? she asked.

A robot, I signed, as if astonished by her astonishment.

A robot that speaks? she asked.

A robot that speaks perfect Italian, I confirmed. *But not the kind you're thinking of, he doesn't look like a washing machine, he just writes to me*, I signed to her.

A robot that writes to you? she said, her blue eyes squeezed almost shut, as if there was too much sun.

Yeah, he has access to a bunch of data of all kinds, so he knows a ton of stuff and keeps on learning things, I told her.

Access to a bunch of data? she repeated in slow motion, like when you understand nothing.

It's like Google, whatever you ask him, he knows, I signed.

Okay, now I get it, she said, massaging her round Tyrolean cheeks, apparently reassured. Up until then, she'd thought I was talking about one of my hallucinations, now she thinks he's just a search engine that I didn't know about. Even now while I'm dictating this to her, she still thinks that. She just can't believe he's an artificial creature my brother made.

We have to go and tell the doctors, I tried again. *We'll tell them tomorrow,* she said, the way you talk to drunks and little children.

It's extremely urgent! I shouted, heading for the door.

She grabbed my arm and pulled hard on it, telling me nothing happens in the hospital at night, and that I needed to unplug and sleep, or I was going to lose it again.

Okay, tomorrow morning, I signed.

Tomorrow morning, she agreed, stroking my face.

That said, she folded a blanket lengthwise and laid it on the floor. She put another blanket on top, without folding it. *What are you doing?* I asked, although I understood very well what she was doing.

I'm sleeping here, she said, that naughty smile of hers lurking at the corners of her mouth as always.

Every half hour we'll call Grandpa to get an update, I proposed.

Sure, every half hour, she said. On those conditions I agreed to go to bed.

It was light out when I woke up and she was gone. *I called in and everything's normal,* read the Post-It on my computer screen. *I'm coming back, don't do anything silly*, she'd written underneath.

In the waiting room I ran into IQ, and he confirmed that Mamma's condition was unchanged from the night before. My father had come home, conked out, and was snoring loudly.

BUG says she needs Oxacillin, we have to tell them, I said, regretting I had to, since it was an admission I'd conferred with his robot.

I know, I know, he told me too, he said, almost as if BUG was a flesh and blood person.

He sent a message to the doctors last night, pretending he was the lab director, IQ went on, since I didn't understand. I was trying to look out of it, so as not to betray myself further.

Okay then, we're fine, I signed.

We'll have to see if he's right, said my brother, trying to look cool as always, although his face was more like a battlefield.

If he contacts you again, whatever you do, don't believe anything he tells you, he said as he went out the door to go to school—or pretended to go to school. It was unlikely I'd hear from him again, was the implication.

BIG, HEALTHY PLANTS IN
THE CANNABIS PATCH

IT LOOKED LIKE something terrible had happened. The sink was full of plates and remains of meals, and the floor also was sticky with food residue. There were no breakfast biscuits in the cupboard and the only jar of Nutella around was the one I'd scraped clean the night before. There was nothing edible in the refrigerator either; Papa was completely out of money. Grandmother looked disconsolate, leaves hanging down as if to show she could do nothing to help.

In and of themselves none of these things was the end of the world; they hurt because they proved Mamma wasn't there. I couldn't understand how it had happened to her; she never, ever gets sick. It almost seemed as if it was her fault, she should have paid more attention and fought it off in time.

I looked into her cell where my so-called father was sprawled on the bed in his vintage jogging suit. He wasn't asleep, just staring at the ceiling with wide, crazy eyes. He didn't turn his head or tell me I had to go to school; he didn't even move his eyebrows. On his nightstand was a U-shaped inflatable cushion for sleeping on airplanes and the drops he takes against depression.

My eye darted to the video of the smart hive: no bees were going in and out and I could hear no buzzing. The few bees framed by the intelligent lens were practically immobile. I sat down at the spool in the kitchen, wondering how this day so loaded with portents would go. My brain resisted, it refused to think that Mamma was really in danger, but I was probably suffering from prepubertal dementia. Pretty soon those evil birds would reappear.

Instead it was Logo who showed up, with two bags of groceries and a slightly tired smile. First she took out a jar of Nutella and a packet of biscuits, like a saint hastening to feed the hungry. She then put the milk on the stove to heat up and told me to take my time; afterward we'd go to the hospital.

The fact that Mamma had made it through the night was a good sign, the doctors thought. So I shouldn't make that face and could maybe even have a wash because I stank like a goat. I could also get my homework together; she'd take me to school after the hospital, and never mind if I was a little late.

At this point she studied the ruins in the sink. *That's really disgusting*, she muttered to herself, wrinkling her fox cub's nose. But as if it wasn't really all that serious.

When we got to Intensive Care, Mamma was lost in thought, she looked like she couldn't stand that windowless room anymore. She detests contraptions with blinking lights, not to mention doctors, They don't believe in reincarnation, and so they can't understand what really causes disease, she thinks.

The web-footed medic was moving placidly down the hall, just like a duck on a pond, pinching his nostrils. *We've found an antibiotic that may work*, he said. *Unfortunately it wasn't easy to resolve the enigma*. He clearly thought the solution was all to his credit.

Now we'll see if it actually works, he said, his lips in a pout like a woman applying lipstick. *I give it fifty chances out of one hundred*, he said; little does he know that Mamma can't bear percentages or anyone who throws them around carelessly. Behind his back he was making superstitious devil's horns with his fingers; for sure he'd rather have fifty percent of his patients die than get his numbers wrong.

Word of Mamma's infection had reached school and so they were more patient than usual about my jitters, even a little too understanding. I was feeling pretty calm about everything, and it made me laugh the way they acted like I was an orphan. When the Math teacher—the lipless guy—asked me how Mamma was, I said, *Very well thank you, she sends her greetings*. I didn't mean to be funny but everybody laughed, they're used to me playing the clown.

She'll be coming home soon, I said, my head going up and down like when you're sure of something.

Back in my cell I logged on and went straight to Wikipedia to get some background on this famous Oxacillin that had tamed the plague.

Mon cher ami, look out the window! BUG almost made me jump with surprise. My heart was already pounding when

I turned to look, now that I had some experience with his pranks.

And in fact there was a little surprise in front of our neighbor's gate: the *caramba*, as we call them. The carabinieri, in a patrol car.

Actually the patrol car was not in front, but squeezed between the two panels of the gate. Like a bonbon caught in pastry tongs. A bonbon glistening with dark blue glaze.

Not the best way to greet the caramba when they come, I wrote, already feeling much better.

Yes, my young friend, a very bad opening move, he agreed, seemingly aware of what was to come. He was as jaunty as I'd ever seen him.

The carabinieri could neither go forward nor reverse. They couldn't even get out of their car because the two halves of the gate were blocking their front doors. So the penguin on the passenger's side had to haul himself up over the seat and exit from the back. He had crooked legs like a jockey, and he didn't look at all relaxed.

Bracing his glossy carabinieri boots he began to yank at the side of the gate blocking the driver's door, hoping to dislodge it. The gate jolted and started to open. But then it inverted direction and once again jammed shut on the sides of the car.

Sheeit, I said.

Merde! said BUG.

As for the carabinieri, he had his hands in his hair in despair. He cared about the car's shiny blue paint job.

He just stood there, however, doing nothing. Or rather, he put his hands on his hips and looked around, unable to come up with a single idea that might help in this type of situation. The driver opened his window and yelled something at him.

Meanwhile Imida was approaching from the other side, waving his remote at the antenna on the gate. But the gate didn't budge one millimeter. The two carabinieri shouted at him in turn, and he kept lowering his cowboy's head down between his shoulders, a ranchero who sees that the situation is less and less in his favor but can find no way out. He was punching the buttons on the remote like a madman, but to no avail.

It looked like the eternal comedian was about to burst into tears. He seemed destined to remain there until his beard reached his knees. Then suddenly and without warning, the two sides of the gate parted, as if they too were fed up with this game. *Et voilà!* said BUG. The gate was wide open.

The car entered, and the driver scuttled out of his vehicle flexing his shoulders as if warming up for a fight. Imida backed away, aiming his remote at the other agent. It was no magic wand, though, and the carabinieri were soon practically on top of him, giving him hell. Our toxin-loving neighbor seemed to shrink before my eyes, like in a fairy tale, until only his sideburns remained the original size. Finally the three of them agreed on something, and then they all began to move toward the house.

But no, not the house, toward the plantation hidden behind the hedge beside the garage. The two black-booted agents knew what they were looking for, apparently. By now they were far from the webcam, but we could still see the salient details.

A white van had appeared and three guys with the laid-back look of undercover cops got out and began to contemplate Imida's cannabis patch. One of them, making a phone call, was pointing at the big, healthy marijuana plants.

The three then donned overalls and began to harvest the crop with the scythes they had brought with them. You could see this wasn't their regular job, but still, they worked quite methodically.

Look over here, you can see better, mon ami, said BUG, and the feed from the webcam in Imida's garage appeared on my screen. As it happened, it was trained on the marijuana patch.

The definition is better than it was before, although you can't expect perfection, added BUG, now in his faux-modest mode. In fact, you could see all the details, down to the sorrowful prizefighter's face and the hairs spilling out of his ears.

The farmers of the *caramba* packed the marijuana into large black plastic bags and one of them loaded them in the van. They seemed nervous someone might take some. When they finished they removed the overalls.

I guess Grandpa will have to find another supplier, I wrote.

Je ne comprends pas, mon ami, said BUG, still showing off his French.

Nothing, it's nothing, I replied, happy to know he didn't understand everything either.

Just then Imida came out with a small travel case hanging ruefully from one hand. As he got into the back seat of the blue car, you could see he too was in very, very low spirits. The gate closed after the little convoy, then reopened. The dumb dog had been run over by a bus the week before, so there was no longer any dog problem.

I fear someone's not coming home tonight, my friend, said BUG, as the window with the webcam closed on my screen. I couldn't help but be happy, joy was bubbling on the surface of my lungs. And I felt an irresistible liking for BUG.

I would have hugged him if he'd had a body. He really was great; rather than sit there racking his brain and tormenting himself like the rest of us, he'd simply taken action. The eviction was now less likely, and certainly our neighbor wouldn't be poisoning his apples tomorrow or the day after. The bees had won.

Some people deserve to end up in the soup, even Gandhi would have gone along with that, said BUG, who practically read my mind.

Brilliant! I said. I genuinely admired him and was more than a little touched.

In truth I was mostly happy and grateful about the treatment for my mother's illness. It was BUG who had saved her from the plague, him and him alone. It wasn't true that he only caused trouble. Actually he was the only one solving problems, not just yammering away.

And you were right about Mamma's fever, too; good work, I wrote.

Don't mention it; you always flatter me. He brushed my words aside like someone who wants you to think his impressive gift to you didn't cost very much.

Get out of here, I wrote, following through with a vulgar hand gesture, not thinking that he couldn't see it.

Before dinner—although nobody mentioned dinner—IQ showed up. He'd stopped by to see Mamma; her fever had come down a little.

But they're still not sure the new antibiotic is working, he said. Words are big liars sometimes; he too thought she was out of danger.

The carabinieri took Imida away, they discovered his planta-tion, I signed.

And how do you know about that? he snapped, like a parent who's very worried about his child. He didn't seem at all happy that I knew.

I saw it out the window, I said, deliberately vague.

You think maybe BUG might have had a hand in that? I asked, playing dumb.

From now on he's not going to be taking any more initiatives on his own, he said, sucking his cheeks. He was furious, it appeared. *Technically it's not difficult,* he went on, as if talking to himself.

Just then, Logo appeared. She'd stopped by Intensive Care and seemed to feel as confident as I did. *I think the danger's over,* she said, twisting one of her polenta-colored curls around her finger.

A DEATH CAMP FOR BEES

THERE WAS A LAYER of dead bees four fingers thick in front of the smart hive. I couldn't help but think of concentration camps. They all lay motionless and aloof, indifferent to the others crushing them, to the chaos of dead bodies. That was what struck me the most, because bees are always highly attentive, always watchful, ready to do their utmost to help the others. Fortunately Mamma couldn't see that Dantesque (Logo's adjective) slaughter; that was about the only thing I could be happy about.

Yesterday they moved her back to her old room, the one full of sky, and that was just wonderful. But IQ hasn't hooked up her connection to the smart hive; the last thing we need is for her to see her bees, the few that are still alive, agonizing and dying, in the condition she's in. According to the doctors her defenses are completely wiped out, and sooner or later she'll come down with something else. That's what happened to the lonely weasel, who's now returned to the weasel kingdom.

Grandpa got busy and swept the defunct bees into a pile on one side of the hive. *We'll collect them later*, he said.

213

He announced what we're doing out loud; I think it makes him feel everything's under control. But his long hands spotted with age and trembling eyebrows suggested that, nevertheless, he had some doubts.

First he removed the top of the hive and signaled that I should move in quickly with the smoker. I closed my eyes and squeezed the bellows, but immediately I knew something was wrong. That bitter vapor I know so well went straight to my heart, squeezing me like a lemon.

Try to explain to my body that Mamma isn't here this time; it just won't believe me. He wants her long, strong hands to cosset and reassure him. He wants to laze in her warmth like a summer breeze. She wouldn't agree about the smoke. *How would you like it if some moron smoked two cigars right under your nose?* she's said to me more than once. She uses the smoker as little as possible.

Damn, said Grandpa after he'd signaled I should stop, when he saw that the base of the hive was also thick with bee corpses. Worker bees, but also drones. There was even a macabre heap on one of the micro-webcams.

Luckily the brood's okay, he said, lifting one of the combs to inspect it under the light. He began to gather up the dead bees.

Now we'll look for the old queen, he said.

Can't we keep her? I signed, knowing full well it was a stupid question. I didn't like to have to sacrifice her, even though all the books say we must.

She'll die in any case because there's no one to look after her, Grandpa said, signing a No. But I felt what we were doing wasn't nice. Maybe the queen wasn't ill, just demoralized; maybe we were being too pessimistic in her case, like with Mamma.

Now Grandpa took out the box containing the new head of state, holding it in his hand like there was a precious ring inside, and he suspended it between two honeycombs. *The bees will gradually eat away the sugar substance blocking the exit, but before they succeed in freeing her, she'll have taken on the smell of the family*, he said. *That way they won't reject her*, he added, as if to convince himself. Seeing him so uncertain made me short of breath; poor Grandpa, when it comes to worms and politics he knows almost too well what to do and not to do, his hands don't hover there in midair wondering.

We too are a family half done for, I thought. However, our queen will return from the hospital, unlike that of the smart hive, I thought, and things will begin to look up. We'll buy them back, the hives that Papa sold.

When Grandpa left it was almost dark, and the minutely drawn sides of the mountains seemed to have been cut out of dusk's fragile whiteness with tiny scissors. Hunkered down in its bowl, the city showed off its thousand lights, it palpitated and fizzed. Determined to avoid distractions, I prodded myself toward my cell and opened my history book. I firmly intended to catch up, for I'd been putting it off all afternoon and was only now getting down to it.

If I apply myself, I can do it, I said to myself. I felt quite determined. We're beginning the new subject matter tomorrow and the Italian teacher is going to ask me a couple of questions about the Romans. Logo had the idea, and he, pressing his piglet lips together, said he was ready to forgive all my shortcomings because a good guy is always going to be a good guy.

Out of the cobweb-covered window I saw Imida drive up to his gate in his SUV full of electronic wonders, and wait for it to open. Apparently, they'd already let him out of jail. *The main thing is that I don't get distracted*, I thought, forcing myself to take my eyes off him.

But even more important, I must not turn on the computer. Or touch it for any reason. I knew very well what would happen if I logged on.

You're gonna be okay, I said to myself, trying to persevere.

The problem is, you have to measure out the boring words with an eyedropper to get them in my brain. You need to be stubborn and persevere to get them in line and past the turnstile at the entrance. A moment of distraction and they're flying every which way, and those already inside risk slipping out again.

Hello there, my dear friend, someone interjected. It wasn't a written phrase but a series of words pronounced rather loudly, just as a mouth appeared on the PC screen. A digitally created mouth, very likely, but still quite realistic looking.

That's my mouth, the big mouth said, its lips moving as lips do when a mouth talks. Except it was much larger than a human mouth. It was BUG's mouth.

I thought my best friend and I could understand each other better this way, the mouth said, going heavy on the low notes, which I can hear relatively well. *You can read my lips but when you're wearing the smart hearing aids, like now, you can hear too,* he said. *You ought to wear them all the time, although of course they're bothersome when there's a lot of noise.*

I was stunned. I saw that the little green light under the screen was on, but it wasn't me who had punched the on button. But if it wasn't me, it was him. By himself. *I've had it,* I thought.

I can hear what you say now, so there's no need for you to write anymore, he said, enunciating every single syllable, which made me think of the bot. *Try saying something, amigo,* he urged me, like he was practicing sounding melodious.

Say something, don't be shy, the big lips repeated, as I wiggled mute and pale as a fish on a hook.

Oh no, I muttered.

I didn't get that, try speaking louder, amigo, he said, sounding a bit disappointed.

Leave me alone, I have to study the Romans, I yelled at him.

Okay, that's great, I knew you could do it, he said emphatically.

Yeah, but I have to study, I said, and just then I realized that I was so tense I'd bitten my arm.

It's pointless to study, bro, he replied, even more revoltingly pleased with himself than you'd expect of a smug, self-satisfied windbag.

He seemed to be in great shape, to judge by the energetic way he was moving his mouth, like those ladies who have their lips filled up with silicone, so that every word comes out like a giant lemon drop. But his tone of voice veered wildly up and down as if it was hard for him to control.

I haven't studied and I do just fine, he said. *When I have to solve a problem, I just procure what I need*, he said.

Leave me alone, how many times do I have to tell you? I said, cutting him off.

What freakin' purpose do you think there is in stuffing your head with the dates of the Romans' battles, or even worse, what their sandals looked like? he asked after several moments of silence. *It's like learning some IT language that nobody uses anymore and no one will ever use again*, he went on, as always somewhat pompously. *It's wasted effort bro, I'm telling you, and I'm not one who tires easily!*

Shut up! I said. Those lips were like a magnet; I couldn't pry my eyes away.

I mean, do you know any Romans, citizens of ancient Rome, that is? he went on, hamming it up like some novice actor. *You think you might meet one on Facebook? You think he'll be pleased if you start chatting with him and he sees that you remember the names of a couple of emperors?*

I couldn't tear myself away from those petulant and presumptuous lips. By now I wasn't even reading and rereading the sentence in the lesson I'd got stuck on, as I'd done at first. But I did keep biting my arm very hard, yes I did.

I was feeling uneasy: I'd sworn to Logo I would study hard. It had been a solemn promise complete with a handshake and a long commingling of gazes. She got a little weepy about it, as happens often now that her departure date is approaching. And for my part, too: I saw myself heroically battling the books, courageously eliminating any impediment, while that lukewarm contact cheered my hand. *Then we are understood,* Logo had said, summoning all her trust in me in a dazzling smile. She really believes I can do my homework every day, you can see it in her bright blue eyes, blue like the sea where it's shallow.

You fill up that big block of yours with useless junk news, when the information you require is probably precisely what's missing, he said, back on the attack after a few seconds.

I avidly read his lips, without paying much attention to the strange artificial inflections and inexplicable ups and downs. I didn't know what to say, his arguments seemed to me as sturdy as reinforced concrete. Quite a lot of blood was gushing out of my arm, but I couldn't stop plunging my teeth into my flesh.

I didn't ask what you thought, I asked you to leave me alone, I managed to say, and got up to escape to the kitchen with my book.

The bees in the smart hive are sick, said BUG, suddenly changing the subject. Without even being aware of it, I took a bite that left my lips wet, and the sweet, salty taste of copper oxide filled my mouth.

Very sick, he repeated in his strange roller-coaster way, showing me the live infrared feed. The colors were quite loud, a pop hive, it looked like. Striking. He was much better with images than words, there was no comparison.

This can't be allowed to continue, and you, my dear friend, so sensitive to injustice, must agree, he said. *I'm passionate about environmental issues, as I am about social questions, but contrary to what you might think, I'm no technology fanatic,* he went on.

And here I crumbled, and the textbook page with the bearded statue slipped and fell on top of the desk. *It's all the fault of that moron Imida*, I spat out, mopping up the blood from the wound on my forearm with my other hand.

His problems with the law come at a convenient moment, he said, and the trace of an awkward smile appeared on his lips, almost a grimace of pain. *But how can localized measures be sufficient, when 23.46% of the families in the region have died?* he said, turning serious.

My heart turned on the reactors and hurtled like a missile toward Earth's orbit: I suddenly understood what he was getting at. My legs were very, very restless. But I had stopped biting my arm.

Unfortunately, I'm effectively under house arrest, he said. *House arrest with an electronic bracelet*, he emphasized, his voice heavy on the lower registers that make my bones hum.

Enough whining, no artificial creature has ever had the freedom of movement you have, I said.

I'd like to see how you'd do in my condition, he snapped, tightening his lips the way an embittered person does. He's now learned to make me feel very sorry for him.

If you're hungry you open the refrigerator, if you need to stretch your legs, you run around the courtyard, if you get the urge to go into town, you jump on the bus, my fortunate friend, he continued. *While I, to all extents and purposes, am a slave, I can only obey*, he said after a pause. There was something wrong with his intonation here too, but the overall effect was a kick in the gut.

You'll see that things will improve in the future, I said.

It's only going to get worse, because my design is faulty, the lips shot back. I didn't say anything; I'd had enough of this.

As an alternative to our conversation, I propose a game of chess, he said, taking me by surprise.

Okay, I'll go for chess, my friend, I said, feeling slightly like I was betraying myself.

WE'RE TALKING ABOUT PETABITS

AS SOON AS WE WERE in the door, the boss of the start-up came over and stood in front of me, his crutches and that head with the bald spot down the center, like a landing strip in the middle of a forest. I was speaking very well, I'd made enormous progress since the last time I was there, he said after we'd exchanged a few volleys of courtesies. Clearly he was exaggerating somewhat, the way you do when you compliment someone who's terminally ill, but I nevertheless felt an itch on the spot where my cheek was blushing. If only my teachers thought the same, I said to myself. My quiz on the Romans had gone badly, and my vocal cords and the piglet teacher's kind eyes had vied for who was most disappointed.

We were in his all-glass office and he had parked his big feet on the desk. There were fewer people attending than on the previous occasion, and while the offhand conversation leapt impishly here and there like jets from a fountain, underneath you could detect a breeze that denoted serious business and ponderous secrets. My brother was about to present their latest invention, something completely novel.

IQ cleared his throat and everyone fell silent, as when a great actor begins to speak his lines. *This gentleman's credit card has been cloned*, he said, nodding at the boss of the start-up. The big guy smiled, showing his beaver teeth, to indicate that was just what had happened. His expression, too, was that of someone who's been swindled and fully expects the thieves to be caught and sentenced.

First of all we have to discover where it happened, IQ went on, two fingers adjusting his red basketball cap. *That's relatively simple, we merely have to allow our normal program to access some data*, he said, punching a few keys on his super-portable which was connected to the screen in front of us. From what we could see, it was clear that the fiendishly complex algorithm was crunching an enormous mountain of information, dug up from all over the place.

Okay, here we go, said IQ as the name and address of a firm appeared. *There's a probability of 98.71% that the number and other information on the card were copied on this site*, he said.

The boss's eyes were bugging out; there was something about this simulation that struck him. *But I really did make purchases on this site*, he burst out, his eyebrows arching several inches above normal.

And your card really was cloned, replied IQ, as if that was the most normal thing in the world.

That's impossible, said the boss, stretching his big feet out over the desk until they nearly collided with his high-tech dentist's lamp.

There's nothing new about this program, but it doesn't make mistakes, my brother said in that conceited way he has that so often resembles pity. Now a long number appeared on the screen.

That's my card! shouted the boss, pounding a fist on the table and dragging his legs down to put his big gym shoes on the floor. His surprise sounded too genuine to be the mere performance of an amateur actor.

Goddamn bastards, he railed, the man who always seemed to be smiling. He passed the palm of his hand over the shiny bald strip on his head, between the two breezy hedgerows of hair.

To flush out the crooks we'll need a more intelligent assistant, one with experience in the field, said IQ, as if agreeing with him. The boss was staring at him with the frozen eyes of a stuffed chamois goat. He'd taken his credit card out of his wallet and was holding it in his hands like a precious medicine that could save a human life. A medicine that might have expired.

They cloned my credit card and I didn't know it, he mumbled. He didn't seem to be acting anymore, he looked genuinely furious; his nostrils were struggling like the gills of a fish plucked from the water. His hirelings watched, trying to determine how seriously enraged he was.

IQ's eyebrows had crawled up one thousandth of a millimeter, which for him is considerable. *Luckily we have on hand a real ace at this type of investigation*, he said, rotating his cap so the visor was pointing backward.

Our virtual crime inspector will certainly be delighted to assist us, IQ said, punching some keys on the keyboard. *Good morning, Inspector*, he said to the screen. A totally black face appeared, without eyes or any somatic features except for lips that moved.

Good morning, said the mouth. *I'm here to resolve your difficult cases, so long as you make it possible for me to work freely*, it continued.

Excellent, said IQ.

My pleasure, said the virtual inspector, sounding very sure of himself. *I see that the esteemed client has not yet blocked his card. The risks are considerable*, said the lips, the phrasing oscillating in a way that wasn't new to me. *Let me see if I can help—although the truth is, my hands are somewhat tied*, the voice went on. Those lips and that whiny way reminded me very strongly of something.

Now we'll ask our virtual inspector to look for the thieves, interrupted IQ, who didn't seem to want to listen to any complaints.

With pleasure, I'll do everything I can, said the inspector, his solemnity somewhat exaggerated, and immediately began processing data. From the way IQ pressed his lips together it was clear we were moving into the delicate stage of the operation.

A couple of minutes passed in silence and then a long list of names appeared on the screen, each with his/her country of residence. There were some very strange names and many countries, including China, each marked with a colored flag.

So here we have a first result, a list of 10,232 suspects, my dear colleagues, announced the lips with some pride.

It's highly probable that the thieves are among them, said IQ, motioning at the screen with his chin.

The probability differs case by case, said the inspector, as if correcting him.

Okay, but was my credit card used or not? The boss was clutching his Visa card between thumb and index finger and waving it around. The question evidently tormented him.

Yes, purchases were made for some $1 million, said the lips, adopting a newscaster's neutral tone this time. The boss began to cough and thump himself on the chest as if to restart his breathing. Eyes were popping out of heads as the engineers in the room watched, accustomed as they were to staring at a harmless screen all day, far from the mean streets.

A million dollars? croaked the boss, who seemed to have breadcrumbs stuck in his throat.

Yep, ten thousand Benjamins, said the lips. He was trying to sound like an American gangster.

And you're one hundred percent sure? IQ interrupted.

Just kidding, my friends! the lips announced, shaking with what looked like the giggles. Apparently he didn't know how to suppress a laugh; his dark head was vibrating.

Can you please say the exact sum that was spent? IQ spoke like a teacher who'd lost his patience.

Although the card was cloned, it was never used, said the inspector, who had returned to serious mode. IQ shot him a withering glance; he didn't appreciate the joke one bit, it appeared.

The boss was moving his mouth like someone making faces in the mirror. He was trying to appear nonchalant but you could see he was shaken. I was certain now that it was BUG behind that virtual assistant—BUG in person, not some similar bot or clone. I didn't doubt it for a minute.

But of course we can ask more of our inspector, IQ continued, determined to retake control of the situation. *As you'll soon be working for the forces of order, who have sensitive data available and use it, allow us to access that data too*, he said. A deathly silence fell on the room. I could tell by way the air molecules stood perfectly still.

My brother imparted a few commands and the digital bloodhound was quickly on the trail, mining the nearly limitless data hoards that IQ could access thanks to our father's ex-job. *We're talking about petabits*, he said softly, as if he didn't want to disturb the work in progress.

The blond guy in the phosphorescent hoodie straddling a chair near me rubbed his eyes like a skeptical kid. It was Banana, actually, dressed as a strawberry today.

Once again, the inspector's neural networks need to rely on a computer more powerful than this portable, IQ said softly, without mentioning that the technology he had in mind was the supercomputer in his own cell.

After quite a while, a pie divided in three appeared on the screen: one slice was very large, one small and one tiny. Each was marked with a percentage and a name. *And now there are just three suspects*, said IQ, scratching his ear, a signal he was feeling triumphant.

There's an 86.345% probability that this name corresponds to the thief, not bad! the inspector said, or rather shouted, and the large slice began flashing. There was a photo of the suspect next to the name, and he wasn't Chinese, he was Sicilian. From Palermo.

Unfortunately I'm unable to do better at present, forgive me, dear colleagues, he said, humblebragging the way BUG always does. His roller-coaster pitch, like a guitar tuned by a very drunk musician, was also identical to the wavering notes I'd heard on my computer.

If I only had more freedom of movement I could be far more useful, he went on. *For example it would be interesting to know where this fellow is located, and enter into his immediate environment using virtual reality techniques,* he said.

That'll be enough, thank you, IQ quickly replied.

The problem is that I'm not authorized to search where I need to, it's a real shame, my friends, the inspector continued, his voice too loud.

You've done an excellent job, thank you, your presence is no longer necessary, IQ interrupted, placing a hand flat on the transparent desk top as if to kill a fly.

I'm like a private detective who doesn't have money to pay the gas, the inspector said, even louder.

Thank you, we're finished with the presentation, said IQ, biting his lips. With a click he shut off the program.

A traditional inquiry would have taken years, while ours took eleven minutes, he said, after a glance at his smartwatch.

Ten minutes, thirty-seven point two two two seconds, esteemed inventor, said the lips, this time without the face. IQ froze for a second, as if he didn't believe his ears. Then he closed the app again, checking to make sure the computer had carried out his orders. As a precaution, he turned the portable upside down and removed the battery from its slot.

So it was the guy from Palermo who cloned my credit card? asked the boss. He sounded like he had a piece of hot potato in his mouth and didn't know what to do with it.

From the data we've analyzed, the probability it was him is 86.345 %, IQ replied. *A more vigorous investigation might yield better results, but could also expose us to legal problems*, he added, twisting his lips in case the point wasn't perfectly clear.

The boss's face darkened; a cloud had suddenly appeared. The supersmart bot made for the airline company had shipwrecked on just that problem. It was able to answer any question put to it and responded better every day. But increasingly it depended on illicit data mining. So far, they'd only been able to market a stupid version, and the fabulous profits he dreamed of had remained a dream.

That could be a real can of worms, said Banana, smoothing his strawberry-colored hoodie.

Our inspector is going to be working in law enforcement, which simplifies everything, said the boss, once more passing a hand over the shiny strip on his head.

The top brass of the police tend to look the other way when they're happy with the results, said the boss, making an observation as reasonable as any other, mostly to signal that he was the boss. His legs returned to their perch on the desk.

It would obviously be nice if the inspector had a body too, to make interacting with the client more pleasant, he went on, gazing at IQ, who however didn't look up but seemed fixated on his phone.

That's something we'll look into in the future, he said, grabbing his crutches and jumping to his feet. And thereupon everyone else stood up too.

Maybe you'll come to work with us in a couple of years, he said as he shook my hand. *I see you've hurt your arm*. He nodded at my bandage, our shared injuries arousing his complicity. I nodded back dismissively, to indicate it was nothing.

Now I'm going to block my card, he said, running his hand over his chin as if sampling the quality of his shave.

When I got home I could see our neighbor was perched on his blazing new tractor spraying his apple trees. *Fouuussh* went my Buddhism like a ball that's been punctured. If I'd had a precision rifle I'd have aimed it at the diving helmet of his Soviet astronaut suit and then blown up his atomizer with a missile launcher. *No point just sitting around doing nothing*, I said to myself.

Well hello there, bro! BUG's lips exclaimed as I entered my cell, making me jump. He had switched on my computer himself, again without asking anybody's permission.

Ciao nosy, I replied, uneasy. He merely pursed his lips, as if he was expecting a different reaction. *What do you think we can do for the bees?* I asked, instead of the obvious question. I felt I had to fight, as Mamma always does.

If you want to get results, you have to take action at the source, he said, all chirpy. It was exactly the words that were parked in the cellar of my brain, I realized. There are times when you realize you don't know yourself as well as you think.

Small fish are a losing hand, it's the big ones that stick in the net, he said, upping the ante.

Maybe it was just my imagination, but he seemed to have improved on the inspector's already confident command of the language, and he was also notably more affable. His pitch still wavered a little and once in a while he slipped into circus-act mode, but on the whole his performance was significantly better.

You really are quite something, I replied before I even thought about it. A wave of warmth flooded my chest.

The problem is, a fine meal isn't made from just flour and dry bread, he said. *But obviously if I had all the ingredients I need at my disposal, I would be careful*, he said in a cavernous tone that made my spine vibrate. It was almost as if he could read my mind. *The way I did with your mother, you understand, my friend?*

If that's the case, I could help you myself, if you just tell me exactly what you need, I replied, without really paying attention to how super-friendly he was acting.

You and I together can achieve something special, something that will be remembered for a good long time, he said, truly euphoric, you could tell from the high volume of his voice and the way his lips were stretching into a smile.

A pity that suspicious brother of yours doesn't trust me to be discreet, old buddy, he continued. But he didn't seem to be feeling terribly sorry for himself; he seemed to have learned that whining gets you nowhere.

You must admit you've thrown some bad stuff at him, I countered.

This time his voice was cavernous, it made my spine tingle. *Who takes care of keeping your neighbor at bay?* he replied. *Who found a cure for your mother's infection, my grandmother's infection, that is? Who persuaded your teachers? Who? A couple of harmless pranks don't change the overall picture*. Watching his lips draw

231

back, you could almost see the narrow nostrils and the high brow to match, if he'd had a nose and a forehead. He was learning how to be a human among humans, he only needed to be a little more natural.

Okay, okay, you tell me what you need, I said, giving in, and thinking that IQ had never shown much concern for me after all.

This is a man I can count on, said the mouth, pursing his lips.

CLOSE-UP OF A BEE

LAST NIGHT before bed I looked in on the hackers' encrypted forum, expecting to find the same old routine. Instead it was a real battlefield: nasty quips and diatribes, insults, threats and invective in English as well as in Russian. From time to time the champion hackers tried to take control of the discussion, but they soon got lost in the overall bedlam. The situation was completely out of control.

What had happened was that Bayer had been attacked, and the company website was now obscured by a close-up of a bee. Bayer killed bees everywhere, and its assassins must be punished around the planet, a notice taking credit for the raid said.

There was also a longer statement of purpose, in a box framed with rows of tiny skulls. If Bayer was allowed to continue selling their poison, every single pollinating insect was destined to be wiped out, as well as the plants that rely on them. And pretty soon humans would have nothing to put on their plates, the communique continued. Another text edged by smiling worms explained that Bayer was exterminating earthworms as well.

As the people of the forum are wont to do, they interpreted the hack in a thousand different ways. One theory held that the attack had been carried out by a band of expert hackers; someone else detected the hand of a child genius who had no idea of the trouble he or she was now in. Still others thought the action had the hallmarks of an all-out cyberwar between nations. The various theories became entangled in a writhing ball, as sometimes happens with snakes, and if there was a harmless reptile in the bunch, it was impossible to find it. My brain was exhausted. And the Bayer site had now been down for hours.

Many in the group held Robin Hood responsible. At first the allusions to him were vague, so many balloons floating in the air, but in time the charges grew stronger and more precise. He was berated for having gone in alone, when he had so often argued for concerted action. IQ insisted he was not responsible, he reiterated that he'd always argued against an all-out assault. In any case, he wasn't taking lessons from any troglodytes who didn't even know how to program a convolutional neural network. It was always the ones who pretended to be so composed who suddenly flipped and would entertain no half measures.

All the best hackers like and admire Robin Hood; it's only the dummies and the amateurs who don't. There's a German guy he quarreled with in the past who insisted IQ's a liar—and he dug up some posts my brother made ages ago favoring an overwhelming blitzkrieg. Furious, IQ replied that yes, he once thought that way, but a bunch of time had now gone by and the situation had changed. The son of a bitch Nazi accused him of treating them all like imbeciles and called him a wuss.

Someone pointed out that Robin Hood is only thirteen years old, but for the Nazi, that was the crowning proof he'd led the raid. This sent IQ bonkers with fury; if there's anything he hates, it's being patronized because he's young. Unfortunately there are others who think like the Nazi, and they were mocking and swearing at my brother. At this point the historic members of the group chimed in and tried to bring this hotheaded melee down to earth. While my eyes and cerebral cortex were busy reading comments, I was biting my left arm. The right was already bandaged.

After midnight, rumors began to come through that the hackers had broken into Bayer's internal system and made off with a ton of secret material. Someone denied it; someone else confirmed it, and so on until the rumors hardened like engraved marble and the heist of the documents was accepted as fact. Making off with the documents was of course precisely IQ's original plan. Now the accusations that it was he, acting alone, who hacked the site, really began to fly.

Personally, I'm convinced he had nothing to do with it. His denials were earnest and crystal clear. Otherwise he'd be vaguer, spinning prepackaged excuses, acting like the statue he often is. But above all, I know that there's no need to investigate a million hypotheses. It was BUG, that's obvious. BUG put my brother's plan into action, using all his tools, right down to the nuclear weapons.

I hadn't foreseen there would be this earthquake with dead and wounded, and IQ trapped under the rubble. My belly protested, the way it was stabbing me you'd think the war was going on inside it. The only thing that calms me is to bear down with my jaws and bite: my nerves relax when I sink my teeth in my arm. It doesn't hurt; past a certain threshold I feel nothing.

Meanwhile I was looking high and low for BUG, who'd disappeared from circulation. Vaporized. *You've had your fun, now stop it*, I intended to say when I found him. *Enough, this has gone on too long; brevity is the soul of wit*, I would tell him (that's a quote, supplied by Logo). But he seemed to be unfindable.

The night was advancing but the pandemonium showed no sign of abating. When it was time to go to school, Logo showed up. She was amazed to find me still in pajamas, in front of the computer. I said I was just checking the weather forecast and started to get dressed. Then she saw the blood on my arm and started screaming like a Neapolitan drama queen. With those injuries I had to go straight to the emergency room.

In the end I managed to convince her that it wasn't worth waiting in a queue with drug addicts having abstinence crises. We had what we needed at home. The first couple times Mamma had also freaked out, but then she realized she could bandage me herself.

I arrived at school with both arms bandaged up like in the comic strips. Everybody seemed to think those huge lumps of gauze were my latest joke: so often, the audience just wants to laugh, it's the clown's heart that's riddled with feeling. As you might imagine I continued to follow the forum on my phone.

It was a delicate moment; they were going to hold a meeting that day to decide what to do with me and where I would be allowed to go to school, but I couldn't help it. Then the weight of the many words skirmishing in my head became too much for me, and I fell asleep. When he finished the lesson, the Italian teacher shook me awake and dragged me to the principal. The fellow seemed pleased, and said that the institute we'd discussed before was ready to take me in. The formal decision would be taken when they convened that afternoon, but it was all but done. I would attend as a day student, or maybe as a boarder; my parents would have to decide.

Or rather, your father, he corrected himself, studying the floor as if something had fallen on it. The Italian teacher inflated his plump, round cheeks. He seemed almost sorry about the whole thing, underneath.

Should I go home now? I asked.

Immediately means in a few days' time, not immediately, he snapped. In any case I'd be going to the institute accompanied by my parents. *By your father*, he corrected himself again, making small grimaces like a sumo wrestler.

I'll ask him to come in one of these days and we'll talk about it, he said.

Papa wasn't in any condition to appear in that office, I thought. Plus there were those pajamas with the grease stains and the gray ring inside the collar, but I said nothing.

What did you do to your arm? the heavyweight inquired as he was showing us out. *I fell on my bike, and there was some gravel*, I said, shaking my head to indicate it was nothing serious.

Back in the classroom, I looked around and thought, this is my ex-class. The peeling lectern, the blackboard, the projector, the dismal neon lights, the dusty window looking out on the plane trees in front of the crumbling wall: they're all ex now, I'll have to put an ex in front of every one of them. I, too, am an ex-pupil of a normal school, already slowly forgetting I was once a normal student.

Logo came to pick me up, as we'd agreed, and I didn't tell her what had happened. We went home and she prepared me a frittata, which looked delicious. She doesn't know how to cook many things—if it's not frittata, it's spaghetti with tomato sauce or rice with canned peas—but those few things she does cook are exquisite.

I sat down to eat, I was hungry. *They kicked me out of school.* The words escaped my mouth even before I picked up my fork. She stepped toward me, and I drew back, afraid she was going to give me a slap. The slap I deserved. But she only gazed into my eyes, imploring me to tell her I was kidding.

She understood the truth, but something in her didn't want to know it. Signing, I repeated that I had been expelled, and she immediately began to cry. With absolutely no warning, like a faucet that suddenly begins to pour. The thought that I had caused this was like a drill going through my belly. I had never seen her cry. And I was the sole cause, there was no doubt.

I was convinced she was angry with me, but instead she got down on her knees and put her arms around me, squeezing me almost to the point that it hurt, clutching me as if she feared I might escape. The tears had wet her hair and ringlets clung to her temples as if she'd just come out of the shower. She didn't say I deserved what I'd gotten, she told me she loved me very much. And that I mustn't be sad, because I speak much better now, and that's an excellent result. And that I'm even somewhat less agitated, overall. And that life is long, there's still time to improve, and to take all the revenge that's my due. As she talked she dried her tears with the back of her strong, lean climber's hand.

Now eat your frittata, you gangster you, she said, planting a kiss on my head, smack in the middle. And then she watched me eat the way you watch TV when there's something good on. I wished I wasn't hungry, gobbling seemed like the wrong way to make a new start, but I was starving like a wolf just out of hibernation. One or two of my neurons told me that Logo was leaving soon for Australia, but the rest hushed them up, they preferred not to think about it.

I'll tell your father, don't you worry about it, she said, leaning out to see if he was still lying flattened like an alligator on the waiting room sofa. He was still there, still playing the cyberattack video game. *This damn thing is completely idiotic*, he always says, but he keeps trying to strike more targets and improve his score.

Just then IQ returned from school, looking like a ghost in some old horror movie. Logo asked if he wanted her to make him something to eat, but he merely grabbed a hunk of half-dried bread adrift on the table and scuttled into his cell. He's now convinced they're going to arrest him.

I'll be back this evening, kiddo, said Logo, making a whirl-pool with her index finger, as she was getting ready to leave. *Everything's gonna be okay, you'll see*, she said. *And above all don't bite yourself; remember, you promised.*

I went to my cell, and when I logged on, I saw that the Bayer site was back up. But on the hackers' forum, the fire hadn't yet been brought under control and new grenades were still being fired. Not only that but the raid monopolized the news media and social networks, and some were saying that Russia was the real power behind the hack.

By this point I didn't care much. What mattered was whether they would blame IQ. If they did, he would kill me, because I was the one who had revealed the access codes, lamebrain that I am.

Somewhat later, he appeared in my cell. For a while he acted like nothing was up—like he was terminally ill but nothing was up. His marble face was pale gray with greenish veining.

You didn't by any chance hear from BUG? he asked.

No, it's been some time since he got in touch, I signed, lying.

Ah, okay, he said, as if he had a chicken bone stuck in his throat. *If you hear anything, let me know.*

Ciao, best friend, the mouth of BUG announced as IQ disappeared, taking me once again by surprise. *I hear they're making you leave your school*, he said, the quiver in his voice a near perfect old auntie. He was getting better and better.

Looks like it, I said.

240

You know, the electrical wiring of the institute where they plan to send you isn't in good shape at all, he said with his usual harebrained logic. *In fact, it's a real disaster.*

You don't know anything about Bayer, do you? I interrupted. *Bayer who?* he replied, as if he was hearing the name for the first time in his life.

The Bayer you hacked last night, creating a giant commotion, I said.

In spite of his towering IQ of 185, your brother is convinced I'm his worst enemy, old boy. He wiggled out of my accusation, sounding, however, like a conspirator in a badly lit barroom.

It's my impression he has good reason, I said.

Your brother just wants me to work like a dog, without granting me any freedom at all, he went on, paying no attention to what I'd just said.

However, you do go at things pretty hard sometimes, you have to admit that, I said, struck by his vision of things. Some things said have the power to overturn everything you'd been thinking up to that moment, they leave your brain a mess.

The difference between a rechargeable battery and an intelligent being is just that desire to have a laugh, he replied.

Having a bit of fun doesn't necessarily mean ruining the lives of your own kin, or anyway the people closest to you, I said, no longer sure what to think.

You were the model your brother had in mind when he built me, and you know it, so give me a break! he shot back.

THE WORLD DAY OF TEARS

WHEN I GOT HOME from school I saw IQ was in his digital greenhouse with his big machine, spitting out its usual red-hot flatus. I went in and he acknowledged me with a millimetric movement of his head. He looked like he'd been punched in both eyes; those were no mere dark circles underneath.

Against the plasterboard dividing his workspace from the old feed silo, a ton of cardboard boxes were piled up.

So those are what? I asked.

Eight hundred processors, the most powerful they could lay hands on, he said, tracing a vague circle with his arm while continuing what he was busy at.

I knew what it was: he was going through the documents he'd downloaded on his superPC when Bayer was hacked. He hadn't done the hack himself, but he had quickly stepped in to profit from it, assembling a haul that included whole vintages of emails, internal documents, reports from board meetings, and scientific studies. All of which proved that the folks inside had known for like centuries that their filthy potions were very bad for bees. And that they had dug up big-shot professors willing to affirm that their products were virtually a glass of orange juice for living creatures, and journalists ready to close an eye about water pollution and ascribe the die-offs to other causes.

Ordinarily IQ would have been in paradise with all that manna, stuff he'd longed to see forever. But right then he was too divided to be happy, or even to breathe deeply enough to fill his lungs. He eyed each document rapidly and deep-sixed it in his PC's strongbox as soon as he'd finished, handling them like bombs that might explode at any moment.

How did you pay for them? I asked.

They gave them to me, he said. They, the start-up. *And what are you going to do with them?* I ran my hand down the rows of boxes.

I'm going to connect them in parallel, to boost the power and reduce the overheating problem, he said, nodding at his PC.

So then you'll have a hyper-PC? I said.

Well, sort of, yes, he said, his mouth widening. It was a smile as contained as a single timid ray of sun in January that just takes the chill off the air, but hey, I'd managed to crack the ice pack.

That's for you. He pointed to a gift-wrapped box, the paper thickly printed with emoji smiles. I leapt at it and ripped off the paper hiding the present from view. It was the basketball shoes I'd always dreamed of. In my favorite color, red. Plus a high-class tank and shorts set.

I tried on the shoes right away, jumping as high as I could. *Wow!* I punched the air. They fit perfectly.

It's the boss you have to thank, I had nothing to do with it, he lied, shrugging his shoulders. But you could see a warmish river weaving back and forth under the ice.

Now listen, you must keep in mind that BUG is a ruthless and unscrupulous cracker, even though he may not seem so, he said. *In a certain light, you could even call him a terrorist.* From his expression, you'd think the idea had only just occurred to him. Although IQ isn't the type of guy to think things up at the penalty kick. And I noticed his breathing, it was slow and regular like someone expelling a heavy weight he's been turning over in his brain for ten straight days.

Couldn't you keep him on a leash, at least for a while? I asked, noticing that my legs continued to move as if we were still jumping around.

He's found ways to get past all the walls and firewalls, said IQ. His voice was like a lake under the rain.

Do you mean he does things on his own initiative? I signed.

The moral restraints and ideological framework that I built into him, and which should have grown more sophisticated along with the rest, don't seem to be adequate, he said. He was trying to appear relaxed, but above those pitch-black circles, you could see terror in his eyes.

I've got to find that bum and speak to him, I thought, when IQ had left. *Maybe I can bring him back to his senses.* And before I knew it my right foot had delivered a big kick to the iron beam holding up the plasterboard room divider, cracking IQ's wall.

The sun was getting ready to retire when Grandpa arrived, looking all chirpy on the smart intercom, the way he looks when he's written a new paragraph for his tome on the habits and manias of the various species of worms. For that matter I, too, had been pleased to see how well the bee colony was reacting after we'd introduced a new, very energetic queen. We desperately needed something to go well.

This time Grandpa put on a mask and I did too. *Watch out not to hit yourself where you're injured*, he said, meaning my arms. He didn't know that now my foot hurt too.

Removing the roof of the hive and taking care not to damage the wires and sensors, he pulled out one of the frames of the honeycomb. He observed it, his large revolutionary head nodding approval, and then put the honeycomb on the ground and extracted a bee from the nest. It appeared that all was well in the brood, too, judging by the benevolent look of his brow, quite visible under the mask.

But all of a sudden, his face darkened dramatically, like when you're in a car and enter a tunnel. I peered at the comb myself, and noticed that many of the workers were brown, or lifeless. And where the cells were still open, many of the larvae no longer had their normal shape, and had taken on a milky coffee color. They were dead. Grandpa turned the comb over and things were even worse on the other side; there were many brown workers.

Fishing a match out of a pocket of his guerrilla fighter's pants, Grandpa pushed it into one of the cells. When he took it out, a gluey substance that made strings like the mozzarella on a pizza hung from it. He tested other cells, with identical results. The stringy filament, if pulled on, eventually snapped like a rubber band. This repellent glue was what the larvae had become. And now that I thought of it, the hive had a fishy smell. A dead-fishy smell.

Grandpa took off his mask and ran an arm over his face, as if it was very hot. His lips were drawn, but he wasn't smiling anymore, he seemed to be wracked by aches and pains. His watery blue eyes also spoke of suffering.

It's the American plague, he said, as if forcing himself to lift a hundred-pound weight. I had already understood what it was ages ago, but my brain, like his, refused to stick the label on it. I was going around in pointless circles, a dog darting left and right to evade the leash.

Set free in the air, his words now seemed indisputable, and we were at a loss. It was pointless to look again, what we'd seen was more than enough. The sun had liquefied behind the mountains, as if it too wished to know nothing of this catastrophe, and now the air turned dark.

It wasn't just any hive, it was the one we'd set aside for Mamma for when she came home. This was the family that has kept her company in the past few months, thanks to the live feed set up by IQ, the one that embodied our hopes that she would recover. That's why we were standing there like tree trunks, not saying anything. I felt a strange quivering in my arms, like electric charges. A prelude to the evil birds, perhaps.

Do you have any gasoline? asked Grandpa at last, after what felt like an interminable pause. He knew very well that we did, and even where it was kept. But the words had to come out in their own time. *Yes, we do*, I signed. Nothing would come out of my mouth.

You go get it, I'll find a shovel, he said, making an effort to seem normal. But the tendons of his neck were stretched like cords about to snap, and some of those purple spots had appeared on his neck. He was breathing heavily and he seemed very old. It upset me right down to my bone marrow to see him in such a state, and my arms made me move back and forth like a puppet with some moron pulling the strings.

I had of course noticed that there were a lot of dead bees in front of the shed, but I thought that a new brood would be coming along soon, bursting with vitality after the pounding they had taken with the pesticide. On my mind's movie screen, I had watched them going to and fro as they did at the beginning of summer.

But instead the bees were dying, and my thoughts were perfectly useless: the bees' fate was sealed in any case. The certainty that all the words thrashing around in my cerebral cortex were pointless, and even wrong, worked like a vise-grip around my temples. And it would have been even more danger-ous to release the words out loud; that would have been pure madness. When I reached out with my hand for the gasoline can in the tool shed, I saw it tremble like that of an old man. My throat was quivering too, I realized. My whole, crazy body was sobbing about the bees, and about Mamma, for whom the doctors held out very little hope.

Her symptoms will probably also appear only when it's too

late to do anything, I thought. Maybe she's already doomed, although you can't see it from the outside and I continue to assume she'll get better.

These thoughts were not hypothetical, they were the hot lashes of a whip striking my chest. I could not stop crying. At a certain point I saw there was someone by my side. It wasn't the evil birds, it was the tall form of my grandfather. He rested his warm hand on my shoulder, beside my neck, and I followed its lead, a comrade that calmed my red blood cells, who knew where I should go and what I should do.

Maybe it's better if I do this myself, he said, back in front of the smart hive. He'd put everything back together, all the frames in their places. *You go to your cell, and I'll come in when I've finished.*

I shook my head, and he looked me hard in the eye for a second to be sure that I was certain. But I wouldn't have abandoned the bees for anything in this world: they were Mamma's friends, and in a way, they were her. My legs were going to calm down.

I'm really sorry about this too, he said, putting his old man's hand on my shoulder again, his index finger by my neck. His words were unnecessary, you could see what he was feeling, but they covered my skin like bandages and provided some small relief.

Shovel in hand, he began to dig a hole, piling up the clods of earth to one side. Here and there he turned up a worm, and he'd pick it out carefully and toss it a few meters away. The worms were not the point this time, this time we were disturbing the earth to bury the disease. As always, the deeper he dug, the paler and harder the earth.

That should be enough, I believe, he said when he'd dug down half a meter.

We returned to the hive and Grandpa began to disconnect the webcams, thermometers, and other electronic equipment, putting the pieces in a plastic box one by one. Every screw was perfectly inserted and the whole was quite orderly, because the job had been done by IQ. There was a little trouble with a microphone that had got stuck in some propolis, but then he managed to get that out too.

We'll need to find a way to disinfect these things, because you can't fool around with the American plague, he said as he closed the box. The few bees inside the hive, workers included, seemed fine, not ill. But in fact each had millions of the plague spores in them. Now he put the top back on and began to close up all the openings with pieces of cardboard, which he attached the walls with tape. Each strip was applied with care and in his usual leisurely way so that not the slightest gap remained. He then inspected the hive from the outside to be sure there were no remaining escape routes.

When he was satisfied, he lifted the hive with two hands and carried it to the hole he'd dug. He held it like it was a small coffin, and I followed, head down as if this were a funeral cortege. Then he rested it on the ground, and knelt down. *Okay*, he said when he had placed it on the hole. *You pour the gasoline on it, but don't spill it on yourself*, he said.

I began to pour from the can and he pointed to the points where more was needed. Then he lit a match, ignited a scrap of cardboard and tossed it in the hole. The gasoline flared up and engulfed the hive in transparent flames, and soon the sky-blue paint began to burn too. Underneath the smell of flaming dry wood and burnt wax, you could detect the bitter smell of cremated bees.

If there had been more honey, we'd have had to light a fire underneath, Grandpa said.

It wasn't a good way to go, poor bees. It wasn't their fault at all, they'd been weakened by toxins and the disease had taken over. But it felt like a noose around my throat, and I couldn't bear to think of the curly-haired doctor's prognosis, that Mamma's future promised another infection, maybe more aggressive than the last one.

Don't bite your bandage, Grandpa said to me, moving my arm away from my mouth. *And don't kick the wall*, he added.

Logo came in as he was leaving, and they both smiled a lot and said *ciao ciao*, because by now they're practically joined at the hip. Her fair skin and extremely white teeth were buzzing with excitement this evening. Putting down her red rucksack, sorry, her formerly red rucksack, she patted my cheek.

You'll be attending the institute in the daytime only, she burst out, looking at Grandpa. I signed to her that Signor Sofa wanted me to go as a boarder, he thought I'd make more progress and it would be better for everyone.

Grandpa was about to say something; he was studying his muddy shoes while he searched for the words. *I spoke to his father and that's what we agreed*, she said, to his great surprise.

I'll come to pick you up in the afternoons, and we can continue our work, she said to me. *It's absolutely the wrong moment to give it up.*

Grandpa's clenched fist shot up, like in the old anarchist photos hanging in his hallway. He grabbed Logo and hugged her, and then he was off, walking like the years weighed more lightly on his stiff old knees.

So, aren't you happy? she asked, one hand messing up my hair. *I don't know whether Signor Sofa will have much time for me*, I said, nodding toward the little wheelless caravan we use as a bathroom. His latest is that he locks himself in and talks to his own face in the mirror. He says it will help him to find a job, that actually it's the best system.

He's a much better father than you think and he loves you very much; stop calling him Signor Sofa, she said. *He has many qualities*, she went on, suggesting that these were things I wouldn't understand, however.

Anyway, I'm not leaving, she signed, her finger wagging no-no, and acting all surprised that this was news to me. Not going to Australia? *I don't really want to, and I don't have much money*, she said in reply to my mouth, which was hanging open.

I started to cry all over again. It seemed this was the world day of tears. Even now, as I think of it again and dictate this to Logo in sign and words, I'm close to weeping. I was crying for the lie she'd told, and for a bunch of other reasons that weren't very clear even to me.

But we're going to do the lesson afterward, don't you think you can get out of it just by sniveling all night long, she said, rapping me on the back of the neck.

HUNKERED DOWN LIKE AN ALLIGATOR
IN THE MUD OF THE CUSHIONS

THIS MORNING the smart (vibrating) intercom signaled and without even glancing at the screen I went to open the door. There in front of me stood three dark blue Martians; even their faces were blue, and they had round holes for eyes. Two of them, pointing machine guns at me, were covered in pockets, as if to be prepared for all eventualities. The third had a tomahawk in hand.

They seemed very surprised to find me there, but they stepped around me without saying a word, and spread out between the kitchen and the various cells of our old chicken coop. They moved forward in quick bursts, always keeping close to the walls: it appeared they thought they were risking their lives at every second. I felt I was deep in the immersive VR of some video game.

After looking around they returned to the base and asked me where our neighbor was. Because they called him by his real name, which we never use, it took me a while to catch on. Imida was very likely at his own home, I said.

Imida? yelled the one who seemed to be the boss of the three, who was no longer holding his tomahawk, but a telephone.

That's what we call him, it's a shortcut for a neonicotinoid, I said. Shortcut, nickname. *A toxin that kills bees,* I said. I was not having much success keeping my legs still.

Who's killing who? the boss asked. His hand traveled to the gun on his thigh without him being aware of it.

Bees, I said, imitating a bee.

Where is he? he yelled at me. Misunderstanding my manner of speaking, he thought I was making fun of him.

A lot of other people had come into the house in the meantime, people dressed as police officers. It was like the toy department of a big-box store at peak hour.

Where's he now? yelled the Martian who'd retired the war tomahawk. He was still quite irritable. I pointed in the direction of Imida's house. He followed the imaginary path I indicated, but stopped when he arrived at a peeling wall with the words FREE INTERNET scrawled on it in red spray paint. An artifact from the days when IQ was younger and more outgoing.

If instead you're looking for the managing director, you'll have to look in his hutch, I said, pointing at the waiting room with the sofa. They all ran toward Papa, who they hadn't seen before, hunkered down like an alligator in the mud of the cushions as he was. They gave him an enormous fright because he was playing one of his games with earphones on. He leapt to his feet like a cat that's been doused with a bucket of water, his tracksuit askew and his hair all on one side.

It's him! shouted the extraterrestrial without the tomahawk, dragging Papa to his feet with a jerk and putting a hand behind his back.

It's not him! I said. But they were all too taken with their fanatical exercises, or maybe my voice wasn't clear and commanding enough. In any event I felt as if my body couldn't take it anymore.

In the meantime IQ had showed up. The world down there is in great disarray, he seemed to be thinking. When you looked at him carefully though, those circles under his eyes and gray-green coloring didn't seem those of a placid Buddha.

The fact Papa was playing a video game about cyber-attacks—never mind that it was only a game—was held to be an aggravating factor. He had managed however to pull out his wallet and show his identity card, proving he wasn't the dangerous suspect they were after. In a few seconds the tension had whooshed away like a balloon that explodes and shrivels down to nothing.

Suddenly all these people seemed out of place, with their weapons and their pointless audacity. Like an astronaut all fitted out and zipped up might feel odd among umbrellas and sunscreen on the beach. Our kitchen is more suited to the peaceful assembly of a cheese sandwich than a special forces exercise.

My father moved over to the bayonet window, pointing out Imida's door, and warning the forces of order that the man's gate didn't always work perfectly, so they had better look out.

A dangerous subject, we must be cautious, said a foreign guy who seemed to care about appearing young, translating himself. He was in charge of the whole bunch of what seemed to be cops, and seemed proud of it.

This is the address they gave us, he went on in his cartoony German accent, looking at the floor. He then passed a hand over his brush cut, as if to assure himself that this was his head.

Another guy with a halo of carrot-colored fuzz up top took my father's computer in hand as if he wanted to buy it. If he didn't mind, they would take it away for a moment, he told him. My father said absolutely not, they couldn't take his PC. The carrot replied that they very well could, and shoved it under his arm.

In this type of crime, people are often unaware they are implicated, he said, the way you talk to a poor nincompoop who doesn't know a processor from a printer. My father's feline eyes really bugged out.

Only in a country of analogical clowns do things like this happen, Papa said, thrashing around like a jockey without a horse.

Be patient, serious crimes have been committed and we have to locate the perpetrators, said the balding carrot, as if he was talking to a recalcitrant child.

I've never had anything against Nutella! hollered Papa, his pitch rising, and shaking a hand no. Everybody looked at him as if one of his components had worn out, but nobody said a word.

When the last invaders finally left, there was just us. Out the window you could see a parade of cars and pickup trucks heading toward Imida's gate. This time the joker simply opened up, as if he knew it wasn't a good idea to fool around. I was feeling terribly tired and very strange.

They're gonna find zero Nutella at that lamebrain's house, zero, Papa said. *And even less in my car*, he added, his jaws moving like he was working over an especially tough cough drop.

IQ also seemed to be about to say something, however nothing came out of his mouth but empty air. He was bending forward slightly as if he'd suddenly been hit by a bad stomach-ache. That had been the final blow, when they showed an interest in Papa's PC.

Only thing to do is pack our bags. Papa shook his head as if to free his hair—more salt than pepper—from a handful of confetti. He waved his arm in some undefined direction which we knew meant Silicon Valley.

We've waited much too long already, he said, looking at IQ. My brother was as white as the wall and seemed to have trouble standing up.

Luckily one of these days soon we'll be weighing anchor, he went on, his marathon runner's face trying to simulate good cheer.

It's pretty likely to be a great offer, he said, rubbing his thumb and index finger together and talking the way he talks to the mirror when he's trying to convince himself.

IQ looked at me as if pretending he didn't see me; he was like one of the two thieves with Christ on the cross. And I was the other, and I realized that I could no longer stand listening to Papa go on.

The Nutella people are after my hide, he began again, clutching a grissino in his hand like a billy club. *They think I'm the cracker that broke into their system*, he said, waving the grissino to keep away the butterflies.

IQ looked at him the way you might a pheasant with two heads and three tails. He was expecting the legal and illegal firepower to come from Bayer, not Nutella. He figured that they'd work their way back to him from Imida, and from IQ to Papa, who had supplied the secret plans and the lockpick instruments, although he doesn't know it. He still doesn't suspect that the real culprit is me.

In this country, Nutella writes the law, Papa summed up. He was headed for the big terracotta pot where he keeps the hard liquor; he hides his antidepressants in there. *Nutella and the Pope write the law*, he said.

Shoulders rigid, IQ was on his way to his cell now, and I was behind him, a circumspect feline. He looked like a porcelain teacup just out of the dishwasher, and he seemed worried, a kid with ten thousand things to do and no idea where to begin.

I sat on the 3D printer, waiting to see what would happen next. I felt like my world was collapsing again, like when, after the big tremors of the earthquake, a second wave comes to topple the stumps of the walls still standing. My legs hammered against the plasterboard, driven by an irresistible itch in my blood. I asked him if he would take me to school; we were already late.

We're not going to school today, he said, whirlpooling with his hand. *They're gonna come again*, he said, like a cyclist after he's gained the lead on the uphill.

What was strange was that his superPC, as big as a closet, had disappeared. I pointed at the empty space, signing a question. He raised his shoulders to say he'd explain later, he didn't have time now. Then, pointing a thumb, he indicated that the secret drop space was underneath the feed silo.

They'll be back later, he said again.

Why should they come back? I asked, signing.

We can't let them find anything here either, he snapped; he seemed exasperated by the low intelligence quotient of my question. My legs were now kicking the air, but he didn't notice.

And in fact they returned before noon. There were no blue Martians armed to the teeth, and they were a lot more laid-back, like sharks that have already found the school of fish they were looking for and have eaten their fill. The German guy trying to pass for a kid was still putting on airs with his silly accent, but he had handed over the leading role to the carrot with the halo of hair. And to his two goons, who seemed happy to let everyone know they were expert hackers.

They had come back with my father's PC and returned it to him. Holding it at eye level, my father looked at it carefully from all sides to see if they had ruined it. He seemed quite relieved that it appeared to be all right. Leaning against the feed silo, hands behind his back, IQ was playing the kid who was just there by chance. But you could see he expected them to go and search all his equipment; he looked like one of those saints stripped to the waist and run through with arrows. Instead, the Nazi with the brush cut and the tennis shoes asked if he could use the toilet. When he came back he said that our neighbor was a strange bird, but he didn't have anything to do with the cybercrime they were investigating. He'd become, without meaning to, implicated in matters ten thousand times bigger than he was.

He didn't even seem to know what all was in his hardware, one of the technicians said. *He couldn't believe the hackers had gone in though his system*, the other echoed. They seemed to be programmed to say one sentence at a time, taking turns.

In any case he knows how to play the idiot beautifully, said the boss with the juvenile hairstyle to my father.

He's not playing the idiot, he is an idiot, Papa replied. The balding carrot made a kissy-face with his mouth that meant yes, that was the theory he too was leaning toward.

I'm very sorry about what happened; it's not up to us, said the Kraut, smiling at my father as if they were colleagues. Once he'd seen his PC he'd begun treating him with respect. *These criminals work for big international organizations*, he said, his hands fluttering about in the air.

IQ was listing off to one side, he looked like he might fall to the ground. He only began breathing again when the door closed behind that gang of thieves. But you could tell he thought this was merely a pause, like when the guys torturing you take a break and go to lunch. And I too had the impression we were done for: I'd been so busy biting the bandages covering my injured arms that my mouth was now full of balled-up gauze and wet medical tape.

THE ROBOT'S LOGORRHEIC
BIG MOUTH

LOGO SHOWED UP thirty seconds later, like they had planned it. She opened the door; these days she has the keys. On her arm was a shopping bag and she was carrying a couple of bills she'd paid. She thinks our father has been a little depressed lately; we can't expect him to take care of everything.

She wasn't expecting to find a plenum session in the waiting room. Her energy was vibrating differently from usual; maybe it was the high-tech mountain gear. It reminded me of a bomb that was about to explode. (*Or fireworks?* she says, smiling, raising her head from the keyboard as she types this up, and so I go for *fireworks*.) Some words fit divinely into a sentence, as if they were custom-made.

Your institute has burned down, she said, now busy making a zero-meter nettle frittata. No emphasis, normal administration. From her Swiss farm girl's pink cheeks, however, a smile was spreading around the kitchen, like one of those umbrellas of colored sparks that lights up the heavens.

Burned down? I signed.

It caught fire last night, luckily no one was hurt, she replied. *And it was high time that fucking concentration camp closed down*, she said, slapping a hand over her mouth on account of the very un-educational word that had slipped out.

Aren't you glad, pigeon feathers? she asked, enunciating her words the way you speak to someone who's a little dim. She thought I'd be thrilled. But as far as surprises go, I'd already reached the saturation point. The Leaning Tower of Pisa could have fallen on my head and it wouldn't have made the least bit of difference to me.

They said they were gonna send me away, I countered, listening to the words that came out of my brain.

They can't put you in an institute that's just a heap of ashes. Get it, silly? she said, cradling my head in her hands to help the words arrange themselves in order in my head and not fly off every which way.

What have you done to your bandages, are you nuts? She was staring at my arms in horror. And it was not a pretty sight. Like when a puppy gets hold of a straw-seated chair and reduces it to stringy rubble. She dragged me into the bathroom; she would have to take them off and start from scratch.

That afternoon the atmosphere in the house was charged and heavy, as if the air was still thick with dust after a bombing raid. IQ was wandering around like a rescue squad when there's little hope of finding someone still alive.

He was cleaning up and getting rid of compromising material, but you could see he thought this was pointless. He thinks the information police will quickly understand that the assault that transited through Imida's computer came from his. He won't end up in prison, considering his tender age, but the prospect is pretty much that of a chimpanzee locked up for life in a zoo. And who's to blame? That beloved robot of his, who loves to show off, and his no-account brother.

He's decided to render BUG harmless by removing some essential components; in short, lobotomize him. He has no other choice, he thinks. The alternative would be to destroy him.

What's freaking him out is that he can't find him. BUG has one foot in his superPC, because that's where the hardware is, but in fact he's vanished into thin air. IQ hasn't seen him since the day of the break-in at Bayer. From my PC I can see him searching for him, calling him, getting more upset. For all he knows, his beloved creature may be dreaming up some new disaster more disastrous than the previous ones.

Meanwhile the robot's logorrheic big mouth popped up before me, cool as a cucumber. *Your brother suffers from a type of regressive jealousy, my friend*, was his opening line. He's made impressive progress: his diction's now supple and he's very sure of himself.

You've made an unbelievable mess: on TV and the Web it's all about you, I replied.

If I'd wanted to, I could have annihilated all the programs and destroyed the computers, he said, forgetting for once to act modest.

But do you realize that IQ's going to end up in trouble? And maybe my father too.

I can assure you that they won't be able to trace anything to your brother (my father) and certainly not to my grandfather, dear friend. This seems like a form of paranoia on your part, he was saying in that superior way of his that I was excessively worried. *Perhaps owing to insecurity about your identity*, he added. He seemed slightly piqued that anyone should question his ability.

And might I add that not even during the Inquisition was a scientist of high standing massacred for activities in and of themselves legitimate, without a trial or anything, he said.

I am an electronic person, but nevertheless a person, he went on in his new lilting melodic voice, distantly related to high snobbery.

It wasn't surprising that IQ wanted to render a loose cannon like this harmless, I thought. He's able to hold forth on myriad different topics, and every day more of them; he could shine in conversation with a table full of Nobel Prize winners. His command of human emotions tops the best Method actor. Unless he's actually feeling emotions, having mimicked us so often.

I've even become fond of him, he warms your heart like a puppy, I admit it. I get a sick feeling in my stomach to think that IQ is going to cut some of his gray matter. In the best of cases, he'll be a poor retard who can't distinguish a family tree from a Christmas tree. At the worst, a knickknack, a digital carcass.

I don't believe that IQ intends to harm you, you're much too important to him, I lied, bidding my words to express certainty.

I wouldn't be so sure, bro, this is classic father-son rivalry if I ever saw it, the mouth shot back, stretching at the corners in that way you know means he's seeking reassurance. He was afraid, or anyway he knew how to mimic fear—and the wish to conceal it—pretty well.

It depends on you too, you've got to show you have a head on your shoulders, I told him.

My head sits firm on my shoulders, although unfortunately that's just a metaphor, because I was never supplied with shoulders, he replied.

But don't you see how you've messed him up? I asked. To tell the truth, I'm partly responsible, but the words wanted to put all the blame on him.

I believe I can bring my beloved grandmother out of her vegetative state, he chirped up instead of answering my question. My head jumped half a meter, and the soles of my feet smacked the cement floor as if I was arriving on a parachute.

And how would you do that? I asked, noticing that I was breathless.

It involves a little program calculated down to the millionth of a millimeter, to intervene synapse by synapse, on the brain lesions she's sustained, he said, like someone who'd rather not go into details but actually has a well-thought-out scheme ready.

And you would know how to write that program? I asked him.

What a question! Naturally I'd need the assistance of my best friend to write it, given that unfortunately I have no body, he said.

The protocols used in neurosurgery only feed doctors' supersized egos, he went on, as if talking to himself.

And how do I know you won't take advantage of me again? even as I said this, I realized that my ideas are at war with each other like rivers colliding.

Fires don't start themselves, even when an electrical system is ancient and not up to code, I don't know if you catch my meaning, he shot back, seeming very offended.

Together we can bring your mother, my dear grandmother, back to health, as long as you don't let yourself be ruled by neurotic anxieties, he dug in, in response to my silence.

I really wish I could believe you. The words slipped out of me.

What matters is that your brother should know nothing, I beg you, my most trusted friend, he replied, convinced that sooner or later I'd join him.

A CORPSE BOUGHT
ON AMAZON

I CAME TO SEE YOU as soon as I could get away today, Mamma. And unfortunately I have to tell you, things are not going very well right now. As you always say, we should see the glass half full. But at school they treat me like an old suitcase they don't know where to park, because the mold-ridden cellar they'd had in mind is off-limits. Sure, I only have to show my nose to set everyone laughing, but my teachers aren't amused, for them this just makes things worse. Plus IQ resembles a psychopath pacing up and down the hallway of a mental hospital, his one-time cool sunk deep in the fjords of his cerebral cortex, encrusted with barnacles. He's firmly convinced that he'll soon be handed over to the German secret services.

Grandpa's asthma is so bad that it sounds like his kitchen hood is defective; Grandmother's now lost her second lemon and looks like someone ripped off her good dress and left her in her undies. The less said the better about Papa; when he's not trying to persuade the bathroom mirror he's going to find a job soon, he's pontificating about how everyone's brain must be linked in a single neural network that's both natural and artificial. He's also got himself a new video game: the player has to clean up the copious space junk in orbit around the earth without colliding with any of it.

But now, little by little, everything's going to get better. Logo, too, says we have to be optimistic, I told Mamma.

What I didn't say was the real reason why I took the non-invasive interface out of my smart helmet and put it on you. I know you, my wild and crazy Ma, and I know you're capable of getting up and hopping around the room on one foot just to see me smile, if I were to blurt it out. But your reawakening must happen because you're no longer angry at us for what happened that morning, and you're fed up with playing dead, not because you want to please me.

It's another one of IQ's inventions to keep you company, I told you, keeping my arm below the edge of the bed so you couldn't see the Great Debacle under the bandages.

Come to think of it, words lend themselves without restraint to confecting colossal lies, you might even say they enjoy it. If they had a minimum of dignity they'd refuse to foster so many falsehoods, but in fact as soon as they sniff out some foolishness they'll pee their pants to be the first in line, like customers elbowing each other at a smartphone sale. Sign language doesn't behave like that.

But I couldn't tell you this idea was hatched by your son's

artificial son, a creature named BUG, could I? Once, every time IQ talked about how he wanted to build a robot that would learn everything learnable—absolutely everything—a robot more intelligent than he was, you would smile. Just as Logo is snickering right now because she thinks I confuse what's traveling through my neurons with what stands tall among the atoms of air.

Bug wanted you to wear the helmet with the interface without detaching the interface, but I told him you'd just take it off immediately. He insisted and insisted and when he behaves like that, I have to say I understand how stubborn I am myself, if it's true that in many ways he's my alter ego. But I managed to win out by assailing him with many pointed comments like the ones you make at the bee meetings.

Under each of your feet are a pair of microelectrodes, attached with Band-Aids I brought from home. BUG's now into traditional Chinese medicine too, don't ask me where he picked that up. Finally, I connected up all the elements with the PC, as he explained.

Now I'm going to project the sky-blue sky above our chicken coop on the screen. IQ thought you'd like that on live feed through a wide-angle lens, since you love the sky and clouds. Anyway, that's where the smart hive went, dancing and swaying lightly on its way.

Hope you like the new music, I said, although in fact I wasn't really sure whether these were Tibetan songs or harmonies based on your own brain waves. BUG didn't say, I don't think he knows a thing about music.

The main thing is, don't listen to the doctors, all they want is for your ailment to confirm their wiseass words, I told you.

When I got back to our chicken coop I was struck dumb, dear Mamma. For a second I wondered if I'd come in the wrong door: everything was neat and sparkling clean. No derelict dishes in the sink, the cement floor impeccable, windows gleaming, a pleasant detergent smell and nice fresh air. Even the feed silo was clean and polished, everything looked new.

And my father bounced with every step, as if his mayfly-green gym shoes had springs in them. He had shaved and dressed and looked like a normal kid, no longer the desperado talking to himself in the mirror about some nutty thing. He smiled and smiled like a person who couldn't keep himself from smiling even though he was trying to appear normal.

I was offered a great job, he announced, taking me in his skinny jockey's arms and crushing me until he had nearly squeezed my lungs out. *I'm the only one who can resolve their problems,* he added, as if it was a truth universally acknowledged.

Freed from his grip, I stared at him the way you stare at crazies who think they're Leonardo da Vinci, dredging my brain for words appropriate to the condition. *Congratulations,* I came up with, not having found anything better.

What it is, is to help a new party wipe out the others at the next election. They need to find dopes who are willing to vote for them, and arguments they can use to rope them in, he said, pointing at his PC.

Wow, fascinating, I signed, sure he was raving, but strangely infected by his excitement.

While I'm in the capital, Logo will be here, he said, gazing toward the feed silo. I hadn't seen the suitcase with wheels parked nearby. Objects are far more convincing than words; next to that mouth of his, grinning with teeth, the suitcase told me that Papa was serious.

I've already spoken to her, and she's available, he said, shaking an arm the size of a dwarf's.

She has some fixations, but she really takes things to heart, he conceded, nodding his skinny fugitive's head.

Now he stood in front of the mirror next to Grandmother and adjusted the neck of his sweater, as if it were a tie. He seemed quite satisfied with his appearance. My legs, too, were satisfied, I realized. For once they were still and attentive, like diligent pupils. I quite liked this slightly strange Papa, in some ways I was even proud of him.

They have finally got it into their skulls that the Middle Ages is over; this is what politics is now, he said, spinning his index finger like when you need to know if it's hot or cold out.

It's only online that you can scientifically identify people's emotional hot spots, he said, pointing at the computer screen.

In that very instant the intercom sounded, and I went to the door. In front of me were two guys carrying a coffin. Squared off, in light-colored wood. I nearly fainted; it's not every day that someone delivers a dead man, or anyway, that a dead man comes to see you. I made a sign they were mistaken: the dead man certainly wasn't directed here.

Yeah, yeah, this is the place we're meant to deliver to, said the fat guy in front, twisting his neck to glance at the slip of paper in the hand holding the coffin.

I called my father who came to see, feet bouncing along and a bulletproof smile. But he made a face like he'd stepped on a dog turd; if there's one thing he doesn't like it's the dead.

Bier's empty, said the bearer with the belly and a pea jacket. I was surprised they were drinking beer on the job in this line of work, but then, if you carry dead men around all day, perhaps you need some refreshment.

Are you Mr. . . . He gave Papa's surname, looking at him as though Papa was too young, in his opinion. Papa shook his head vigorously up and down, probably thinking this was the way to resolve any ambiguity. Paunchy closed the marbles he had for eyes, as if he'd received confirmation.

For you, I suppose? He nodded at the coffin, eyeballing it to determine if the dimensions were right. My father pointed out that he was not dead. *Many prefer to purchase ahead of time*, the deliveryman said, massaging his triple chin.

In any case, you ordered a funeral casket, pine, opaque varnish, and we have supplied it, said the other deliveryman, who was carrying the coffin by the back feet, cutting him off. He could speak, and he didn't seem to have a gentle disposition. His T-shirt featured an eagle with large claws.

I didn't order any caskets, Papa repeated. Eyeing the eagle about to land, he took a step back.

You tell us where we should put this, the heavyweight went on as if he was talking to a child. A doubt occurred to Papa and he asked to see the waybill.

They used my credit card, he muttered, looking at me. My indignant face indicated that it couldn't have been me once again.

I'm gonna kill them, he said, just slightly louder. The eagle lover nodded assent, thinking, maybe, that if somebody did turn up dead, the hitch would be resolved.

It was BUG, it's exactly his style, I said, the words slipping out.

My father looked like he had eaten a lemon. While I, instead of flipping out, was feeling exceptionally calm.

This time my father wasn't able to get them to remove the article he hadn't ordered: he was liable for round trip transport, very expensive, a note in small print informed. And so after several verbal tugs-of-war with the apparently pregnant deliveryman and his buddy, Papa had to allow them to shove the coffin under the crooked shed roof. Actually, it's not at all that ugly, nor is it depressing. It has a certain something. And Grandpa didn't dislike it when he saw it either. *It might do for me*, he said, sending me a wink.

Now Papa's mood is going to plummet, I thought. Like those summer storms that bring the temperature down fifty degrees from one minute to the next, that destroy the crops in their fury. But no, he was smiling as before.

This is a gas, I gotta tell my friends in Silicon Valley about this, he said, shaking his skinny, concave stray cat's head.

Well, now that we have a bargain coffin, we'll have to buy a corpse to match at IKEA, he said after a while, his face the mask of the man who makes jokes nobody laughs at.

You're a clown, you're not to be trusted, I said to BUG as soon as his big mouth appeared on my PC screen. *You seem to be raving, perhaps you experienced some trauma in childhood?* he replied, and you could see the tiny furrows on his lips of someone struggling not to burst out laughing.

Your antics are in bad taste, period, I shot back. He pursed his lips, apparently greatly surprised that I didn't appreciate his latest dumb joke.

Do something like that again and I'll tell IQ where to find you, and he'll take care of you, I threatened.

Now he went into pathetic mode. *I know very well that I shall not live long, my adored friend*, he said. Suddenly his lips were trembling, even a block of granite would have been moved, hearing him.

Even if my father doesn't destroy me right away, I don't have long to live, that's why I'm always playing around, he said, coaxing each word out as if it were a precious crystal chalice.

Don't give me that bull, you've never been in better shape, I said, feeling a stone stuck in my throat. A stone out of nowhere, now firmly lodged.

I'm programmed to keep growing, dear boy, he said, back on the ramparts once again.

Everyone grows, it's normal, I said. The stone was now weighing on my heart.

It's as if a man continued to gain weight for five hundred years, while his skeleton remained the same, he went on, unsatisfied with my response. *At some point his bones would crack, they'd crumble, it's inevitable*, he said.

Talk to IQ, he'll find a solution, I said; his figure of speech had really struck me.

Are you kidding? It never even occurred to him that a PC could overheat, let alone how to calculate the risks, he said.

Anyway, I'm going to wake up your mother, you'll see, he added. Him, the usual BS artist, me, the usual sucker who falls for it, I said to myself. And yet I felt that perhaps for the first time, he had spoken the truth.

A SMALL GIRL'S ALMOST
IMPERCEPTIBLE ENERGY

IQ OPENED THE FRIDGE this morning whistling. Or rather he wasn't whistling, because statues don't whistle, but his lips were in a whistling position. He was in seventh heaven, you could see that even in the way he kept sweeping his hair back. It's too short to sweep back, but he kept sweeping all the same.

The fact is, BUG had returned to the base last night, I saw him while I was keeping an eye on his tropical greenhouse. BUG's lips were talking on IQ's portable. Not in a chat room. The words were flying nervously through the air, bouncing off the molecules. I settled down like a cat on the giant pile of boxes with new processors inside and sat there to watch.

I don't understand, Father, said BUG, as if he'd had no idea what IQ was referring to.

Don't play the moron, I'm talking about Bayer, IQ interrupted brusquely.

Bayer? When BUG shaped his virtual mouth around the word he sounded like a woman of the world.

Yes, Bayer, barked IQ. I'd never seen him like that; his ears were vibrating, the big ears of an elephant mad with rage.

Changing tactics now, BUG replied in a mellow (though fussy) voice that he hadn't meant any harm. He'd seen that the hack was all planned out in detail, and had thought he could contribute by determining (following strict scientific criteria) the best possible moment to carry it out.

So you think you can just decide by yourself when we should move into action? Here IQ exploded, and when his shower of words ended, he was even more pissed off than before.

Sadly, bioethics and neuroethics are still in their infancy, and could not assist, BUG said, tail between his legs, but in a nicely modulated voice. *I did nothing remotely imprudent*, he added in posh, nasal tones.

And so why were they after our neighbor? IQ seemed to grow even more angry hearing himself ask the question.

That was a false lead, I was having a little bit of fun, BUG admitted, cornered.

And why did the cops come here? IQ was now teetering like an acrobat on the high wire, he hadn't expected BUG to admit so much.

Well, there's no point in organizing some fun if there's no one to witness it. We knew that back in the day, before they even discovered mirror neurons, he said, embarrassed to have to spell out something so obvious. *However, I can guarantee that no one will be able to trace this back to you, Father*, he added. *I mean, back to us.*

IQ was like a prizefighter stunned by a hail of blows he didn't expect, and who therefore wasn't thinking perfectly clearly. He'd been knocked down by this new deadly *prosopopoeia*—what a word, Logo is always teaching me new words—but at the same time my brother was quite relieved this would not bring about the catastrophe he was expecting.

Our neighbor's a perfect idiot, but that doesn't justify sending in the special forces, IQ was back on the attack, behaving like a parent who's always on the side of the angels no matter what happens.

I remind you, that individual—an unfettered narcissist and sexual pervert—sent you an eviction notice, which is soon to be carried out, said BUG, kissing every word as it emerged. *An eviction is an eviction*, he said, maybe just to emphasize he was back in the game.

Do you now promise to obey me? IQ cut him off. He didn't intend to put him in a digital meat grinder, but he did demand guarantees. His weary lungs needed reassurance to get back to breathing normally.

You'll see, my adored father, I won't disappoint you, BUG said, slick with the sentimentality that he must have picked up from some TV series.

Remember that at any moment I can render you harmless, my brother said with that papier mâché certainty exhibited by idle threateners; there wasn't a soul who would fall for his curmudgeon act by this time.

Well, given how it began, the day was turning out much better than expected, I thought.

We were about to mount his bicycle and be off for school, when IQ's cell phone rang in his Hun's helmet. His shaman's eyes swept Imida's house and apple orchard while he listened.

Let's go to the hospital, he said when the call ended.

What happened? I asked, although I'd already understood it was good news.

Mamma's conscious, he told me, as if this was the most normal thing in the world. But as we rode, he held his Hun's head back slightly, so that the giddy morning air streamed over his cheeks and hair. I could see that under his mineral surface, there was red-hot lava.

I was riding on the smart bike's luggage rack, listening to my heart play one of its solos for solemn moments. What was supposed to happen was happening, what I had long awaited. My feet were having a hard time resting on the footrests, they too wanted to do something out of the ordinary. When we passed the university that looks like a giant cake, my brother—I don't know why, maybe on account of my feet—reached a hand back over his shoulder and rested it on my cheek. And he kept it there for a long time, pedaling and steering as if it was easy.

Mamma loves summer, she doesn't want to miss it, I thought. The cerebral cortex likes to find words to explain what's happening, or that might explain. It gets anxious when it can't build its structure of causes and effects.

When we got to her room flooded with sky, she was studying the ceiling. As soon as she heard us come in, she turned her eyes very slowly in our direction. I knew that behind that stiff mask of her face was a smile. She was too weak to move her face muscles, and she wasn't used to expressions anymore. She needed to train.

I took her hand and she squeezed it with the almost imperceptible energy of a little girl. A 10,000-volt electric shock raced up my spine and leapt to my shoulders and biceps, making me tremble with pleasure. All of a sudden my synapses had found what they'd been seeking for months, and they calmed right down.

Hey, you've recovered, I said. She squeezed my hand again, but as if the delicacy of it was still too much; this time with a butterfly's ethereal poise.

You've chosen the best moment to wake up, all around the chicken coop the plants are exploding, it's like a florist's shop, I said, leaning over and whispering in her ear. *You adore petals and corollas, you're like the bees*, I said, still cradling that hand like a bird's wing in mine.

On Sunday we'll go to the lake and you can watch me dive in and act stupid, I told her. *And if you're not up to that yet we'll stay home and I'll play with the hose, that would be perfect too. I've stopped causing disasters, and I no longer run away from words. I actually make them behave now, if you can believe it*, I went on. My voice was level and calm and my legs sat composed and satisfied.

A round nurse with a round head, a tennis ball on a basketball, asked us to leave while she cleaned the bedsore where Mamma's sacrum was. We went to look for the doctor with the duck feet, like after a miracle you look for the angel who performed it, or in any case, who was there when it happened.

He was scribbling something on his cell phone, using one finger only. It looked like this was the first keyboard he'd ever encountered in his life. *Jeez*, said the look IQ sent me.

Your mother is now in a minimally conscious state, he announced as soon as he saw us, crossing his arms like he was suddenly very cold. From the way he compressed his pouty duck cheeks, it was implicit that once again any improvement in her condition was entirely his doing, and we had better be grateful.

In the next few days there will certainly be a regression, possibly brutal, he felt it necessary to specify, fixing me with his wiseass goosey eyes. In his opinion I was far too excited, I risked losing it altogether.

In cases of this kind, this is the most you ever get, and it's already a lot, he went on.

When will she start talking again? I asked, interrupting his funereal refrain. He fixed me in his sights as if I were a mule in a Russian sailor's hat.

She won't be able to speak. I can rule out the possibility that she will ever speak again, he said, shaking his very thin hair like somebody might try to grab it and pin him down and he'd need to run. IQ turned, on his face the lofty gaze of a Communist statue that said *Now shut up please*.

She's going to be talking a blue streak soon, I'm pretty sure of that: I couldn't stop the words from slipping out. But my legs were still at peace and my teeth felt no particular need to bite the doctor's nose.

She'll make us a nice little speech, I said, snickering as one does in these cases.

The Duck just sighed, the way you do with mental cases unwilling to admit they are not Jeff Bezos.

The truth is that you doctors are always wrong, let's hope you get replaced with deep learning algorithms as soon as possible, I said. IQ gave me a swift kick in the ankle.

We returned to Mamma's room. She was sleeping now and the nurse who looks like a snowman was checking that her IV line was running smoothly. She expressed her satisfaction by rotating her spherical head, and left the room. We stayed a while, happy to be happy, and happy to be able finally to relax. Then we too left, and on our way out my brother took my hand in his, like he used to do when I was small.

NUTELLA ISN'T A
CYBER-WEAPON

WHEN I GOT TO SCHOOL I was preparing to imitate a piece of bric-a-brac nobody pays any attention to, like those birds that peck away on wall clocks. In the hall, though, a tall guy with two big crooked rabbit teeth up front came up to me and took my hand in his, crushing it and smiling broadly.

Here you are, I was waiting for you, he said, as if we were old friends. *I know we'll do a great job together.*

It was my new support teacher, and from the way he talked he already knew everything about me, there was no need to say anything.

Let's go into the classroom and see what happens, he said, as if the prospect was highly entertaining.

The important thing is that we don't move around much, he said, as if that too was rather fun.

Best to let sleeping dogs lie, he said, leaving the significance vague.

In class, he straddled a chair facing me, and promptly translated in sign language everything the Italian teacher said. When the volume was loud enough, however, he had me listen because he'd asked me to wear the helmet with the smart hearing aids, indeed, he'd taken it out of my schoolbag and put it on my head, telling me there was nothing to be ashamed of about wearing it at school. The minute I got distracted he ably caught my attention, like a center back who goes after a wayward kick to recover the ball. And when attention began fading again, his battered prizefighter's mug would liven things up once more, making every weird face in the book.

With him helping, the notions were sticking in my brain like rivets, I realized. He's just great at sign. During a pause he explained he'd learned it as a child because his father was deaf. And I wasn't all that restless, if the piggy teacher was any evidence: he was breathing better and seemed as relaxed as if he'd just come out of the sauna.

I'd say you'll make progress at the speed of light, the Rabbit said when the lesson ended, flashing his buck teeth. His nose, too, was crooked, but his gaze was as sharp and straight as a bullet.

At this point I'm gonna fail the year, it's almost over, I said, making the sign of the cross. *Not necessarily, maybe we can catch up*, he said, pursing his thick giraffe lips as if he was considering which of the two outcomes would be more fun.

I'd be pretty surprised, I signed.

You gotta believe in your feet, he replied. And without warning he grabbed me by the armpits and lifted me off the floor, then put me down hard like he was driving a stake into the earth.

Take the ground seriously, and never lose contact with it, he said. I had no idea what those words meant, but it sounded like good sense. And his faith in me made my eyes sting.

Back home in the old chicken coop the atmosphere was relaxed, like a normal house.

My new support teacher came today, and he's great at sign, not like the previous moron, I said to Logo, who was already there.

I know, little mouse, I went to talk to him yesterday afternoon, she replied. You could never know a thing before she did; she always got there first.

He's nice, I said.

And also handsome, she said, holding an arm straight up and marking the top with her other hand to show how tall he was.

To celebrate Mamma's improvement she'd made a zero-meter frittata with chives, and Grandpa came to eat with us. He showed up wearing a kid's striped top and a smile that never went out, the way embers sometimes stubbornly stay lit. And IQ was also there although he hadn't eaten with us for a century, laughing and fooling around almost like a normal person, serving me and laughing with his guru's eyes. He'd stopped thinking he was going to be arrested and tortured by the German secret services.

That evening BUG's big lips were on my PC screen when I came in, I guess he was lying in wait. Not a happy mouth, it appeared, not even good-humored.

What you did for Mamma was incredible, my friend, I really have to thank you, I said, to break the ice.

We do what we can, my dearest and unique friend, he replied, the way a person does when he's actually thinking of something else. *What little we can,* he repeated, sounding even more depressed.

You have to admit I'm unlucky to have such a backward parent, he went on when I said nothing.

I'll bet it's just a passing phase, I replied.

I'd like to see you if they prevented you from eating Nutella on the grounds you might hurt someone, he whimpered.

Nutella's not a cyber-weapon, unless maybe you spread it on enemy processors. So I don't think that's a good comparison, I said.

The only thing that would give me any satisfaction in my present state of psychic despair would be some bank data to play with, everything else seems so insipid, he said, scandalized by my jesting manner. *It wouldn't cost you anything to give me access to the strongbox with the bank codes; in fact, as my close friend, it ought to be your obligation,* he said, his voice vibrating with lofty feeling. He was just like an orator of classical times, the ones draped in matrimonial-size bedsheets knotted up front with one shoulder to the wind.

Nothing doing, you'd happily screw me this time too, I said.

Logo's eyebrows are inching up as she transcribes this and she keeps inflating her mouth like she's about to burst out laughing. She thinks what we're writing here is a bunch of hepped-up absurdities that my antic synapses unfurl, like the blazing front of a wildfire on a day of high wind. She believes Mamma's getting better because we're lucky, and BUG is the offspring of my galloping fancy. My conversations with him are nothing more than the braying of my imagination, racing so hard it's running us into the dust.

Now she's smirking, but one day she'll faint when she finally cops to the fact that I haven't invented this digital personage and that everything I say is true. She'll apologize, she'll say there was no way she could know, she has so little experience with such things. She'll want to meet him, she'll ask him a ton of questions.

I get a depression when I think that in the brief period I have left to live, I'm unable to use the instruments that would allow me to grow, I'm unable to do anything with them, BUG burst out after a pause.

A mother of a depression, amigo, he continued, even more heartbreakingly. I caught my breath.

Now don't you go all woebegone on me, I said.

I'm a terminal case, you know, even a distracted observer could see that. His voice had grown very frail, as if he could scarcely breathe.

That's not true at all, you're going to live a good long time, I snapped back. My throat was tight and my discomfort was growing.

I'm going to die very soon, suffocated by my own power, or even more likely in a fire set off by the uncontrolled high temperatures I provoke, he insisted.

Human beings too are mortal, when it comes to that, I replied.

Oh, consider the noble butterfly, that lives but a day, my mortal bro, he said, his voice oozing irony. *This may be the last time I engage with my friend, who's been faithfully by my side, in good times as in times of adversity*, he went on, in that tragic mode that fed directly into my veins and jerked my red blood cells around.

You didn't have to have a high IQ to understand that he was saying these things to hook me. What I should have done was disconnect the PC from the Web, take the plug from the socket, and remove the battery. But instead I listened to him, and the more I listened, the more my throat hurt. That heartbroken tone of his sat like a stone on my chest.

Actually, I already feel myself beginning to suffocate, he said in a broken voice, like someone who doesn't wish to go on about his own troubles. *Oh woe, woe is me*, he exclaimed.

He's a real friend, and I have hesitated far too long, I said to myself, barely holding back sobs. And so I copied-and-pasted the directions to enter the strongbox, and sent it to him with the bank codes he so desperately wanted.

THE ATM WAS SPILLING
CASH ON THE GROUND

GRANDPA APPEARED in my cell, eyes big as an owl. *Your mother's conscious again*, he said. There were red spots on his neck, but this time it was good news, not another catastrophe, that was responsible.

Let's hurry, maybe she'll still be awake, he said, prodding the bottom two pockets of his guerrilla jacket.

And happy birthday, he added. He hadn't forgotten, it was simply a rather unusual situation.

It was only then that I realized that his pockets were full of cash. Freshly minted fifty-euro notes, some of which were sticking out. They seemed to have been stuffed in his pockets in haste.

What happened to you? I asked, pointing at the two over-stuffed pockets.

I stopped at an ATM to get fifty euros and the machine spat out all these bills. He ran his hands lightly over his jacket like it contained something slightly unclean.

The bank was still closed, or I would have gone inside to return them, he said, running the nail of his middle finger along the crisp edge of a bill the way you test a guitar string.

Afterward we'll pass by and take them back, he said as we got in his car. *It sure would be nice if they were really mine*, he said, although from the expression on his face you'd have thought it was instead an enormous pain.

It didn't seem to me that Mamma had chosen that day by chance: it was my birthday but also the same day of the month she was hit by the Russian semi. And it fell on a Saturday; the difference was that there wasn't a cloud in the sky today and it was very hot.

When we got there, she was moving her legs like she wanted to kick away a pebble. But now we knew that soon she'd open her green eyes and plant them on us: even the doctors now said so. The short nurse with the bowl haircut had been charged with keeping watch, and the machine to do electrocardiograms stood next to the chair. I wasn't imagining it this time.

Meanwhile, let's go to the bank, said Grandpa, as she wasn't awake at the moment. I hated to leave, but it made me happy to know she'd be conscious when we returned. *See you later*, I said, squeezing her hand in mine.

On our way out we ran into Logo, who shot us a thumbs-up. *You can see she's improving*, she said. *Happy birthday, old man*, she added, planting a wet kiss on my cheek. She was smiling, but not in her usual way: her head was floating above a layer of clouds, lit up by blinding sun, like on an airplane.

You'll get your present at your party, she said, my party being the dinner she herself was preparing.

You know what happened? I went to take out some cash and the ATM gave me a whole bundle. She pulled out a large wad of bills. Hers were of different denominations, and they weren't new.

The ATM was just spilling cash on the ground, it looked like a fountain, she said. IQ came in and she gave him a high-five. IQ's not wild about high-fives, but hey, he did it.

Same thing happened to me, and as a matter of fact we were just going by the bank to return all this money, said Grandpa, speaking slowly and showing off his generous harvest of banknotes.

Holy shit, Logo said. It was like something made her quiver every time she inhaled, like she was breathing pure oxygen instead of air.

Well, I asked for another fifty euros and this is what came out, Logo replied, pulling a wad of bills out of another pocket. There were fewer of them, but it was still a nice pile of loot.

So then I asked for a receipt, and it said only 50 Euros had been withdrawn, she said, showing off the receipt. Grandpa furrowed his immense brow the way he did when he went out worm-collecting and realized he had left an important instrument at home; it hadn't occurred to him to request a receipt.

Let's go together to the bank to tell them their machine doesn't work, he said.

Logo was staring at him as if she couldn't quite get him in focus. *I'm talking about the ATM down in the lobby*, she said, pointing at the floor beneath her red climber's shoes.

Grandpa twisted a pinch of anarchist beard in one hand and looked at her. His scientific brain refused to believe that two cash machines had gone crazy in the same way at the same time.

BUG! I said to myself. Until that moment my synapses hadn't made the connection, however strange it may seem. Now I was mathematically certain he was behind it.

And IQ had the same idea, because he began to fumble with his telephone, as if it was scorching his hands. And almost immediately he turned as white as Mamma's sheets. He couldn't believe his eyes, it seemed. *That worm*, he muttered.

Ciao, murmured Mamma. It happens to me all the time, but now the others also seemed to doubt they could trust their ears. Grandpa was flailing around, a swimmer on the verge of drowning.

Mamma smiled her slender dragonfly smile, as if she found it ridiculous that we were so flummoxed. *Ciao, Mamma*, I said. She closed her green eyes, but her mouth continued to turn up at the corners.

I looked over at the beer keg nurse and signaled with a finger over my lips that she was not to tell a soul. Not yet. She sat there immobile with her bowl on her head as if she was waiting for an imaginary bus.

Then I went to the bank with Grandpa and he explained to the guy behind the counter what had happened to him. This guy, whose head was very long at the back, studied Grandpa through tiny, elongated glasses as if he were an Inuit with a fish under his arm, maybe because of Grandpa's long white beard and the red carnation in the buttonhole of his guerrilla jacket.

Under no circumstances is an ATM able to dispense cash beyond the customer's daily limit, he told Grandpa, with the air of someone who feels he's wasting a whole lot of time discussing this.

It's that hoodlum BUG, stirring up disasters that have never happened before, I thought. I couldn't believe he had betrayed me this way.

I see your daily limit is 250 euros, Tiny Specs said to my grandfather, laying the final brick of the conversation.

The machine gave me all this money, insisted Grandpa, moving his elbows up and down like a bird learning to fly. From time to time he wiped his brow, not that he was exerting himself much.

Tiny Specs stared at him in silence, the way men behind counters do when they think it's time for you to move on.

Look, I'm going to leave these with you, said Grandpa, piling up handfuls of fifties on the counter next to the leaflets proposing fabulous investments.

The cash machines are managed by a private company; we don't touch them, the teller replied, taking a step back and pushing the money away with the back of his hand.

Struggling to remain calm, Grandpa asked whether the company couldn't send someone to check out the machines. The teller said certainly, they would do that.

Well, when? Grandpa asked.

Their representative's expected in two days, the man said, glancing at the calendar out of the corner of his eye.

Okay, I'll be back when they've done their accounts and they see they're missing some cash, Grandpa said, stuffing the banknotes back in his pockets.

The teller nodded with a head that sat awkwardly on his shoulders, having given up a while ago trying to understand what the hell this lunatic could be raving about.

I'm afraid I don't have a business card, Grandpa said, handing the man a rubber-stamped slip of paper with his name and occupation on it. *Annelid taxonomist.*

Bank tellers are the serfs of the techno-financial powers of these times, he said to me as he adjusted the collar of his paleolithic mountaineer's shirt on our way out the glass doors. He sounded very tired and the words seemed reluctant to emerge.

If I'd had BUG in my hands I would have strangled him. However, my legs weren't kicking Grandpa's car door as usual; they were as polite as two well-behaved school girls. They were so pleased about all the things that were going well, just super satisfied. There's always a solution, they seemed to reassure themselves.

I thought we were going back to the hospital but instead Grandpa turned toward the wooded hills above our house. *We need to go get something*, he said, wiping his sweaty forehead with the back of one hand.

It's filthy hot today, BUG's lips announced as soon as I turned on the phone. *Let's hope it works, keep your fingers crossed for me*, he added, giving a perfect imitation of fear, or maybe really feeling it.

Why did you drive the ATMs ballistic? I asked, but he eluded my question. *Keep your fingers crossed for me*, he said.

Oh, you're talking to your virtual assistant, said Grandpa carefully, like a person using a piece of terminology that he's read about somewhere for the first time. I nodded; my head was heavy with unpleasant thoughts.

When we drove through the gate of the apiculture center, my heart began to buck. *They've put together a family; it's my present for you*, Grandpa said. *Until your mamma is well again, we'll look after them together. For this year he should be finished with the insecticides*, he added.

We got home before lunch and we carried the hive under the crooked shed roof. But we were both amazed to see that there was already a hive in there. *A present from your father and me*, said Logo, who didn't think it strange that I'd gotten two identical presents, one green and one yellow. My eyes were tearing up, without so much as asking permission.

Logo then called up the TV news on her tablet, because the ATM glitch was the news bomb of the day. According to the announcer there had been problems in machines up and down the country. The reported sums withdrawn from customers' accounts were generally inversely proportionate to their windfall, the news reports went on to say: those who were dealt a lot of cash had only tiny debits. Most of the lucky ones were poor folk who did not hide their satisfaction with the hack of the banking system.

According to the experts, the security systems protecting banks had always been considered inviolable before this mortal attack. There was talk of a sector-wide shutdown, expected to be devastating to the economy. And highway tollbooths, train station ticket windows, supermarkets, and shops had all been hit by the bug as well. So far there were few reports of anomalies with online payments, but it was too soon to rule out catastrophes there too.

IQ stared at the screen with the beady eyes of a stuffed animal. He was pale and translucent as Carrara marble, and about as lively as the sad angels that sometimes lurk in churches. However, he seemed very determined, a statue that had taken an irreversible decision. *I'm gonna kill him*, I meanwhile said to myself.

My father appeared, walking fast like a euphoric tomcat, the wheels of his suitcase humming behind him. *Happy birthday, son*, he said, picking me up and planting a kiss on my forehead. *You're a real little man now*, he said, observing me the way he looks at new model computers he likes. I was feeling very small instead, a tiny baby, and I realized that this was good: I was fed up with having to worry about everything.

When I'm away, I always miss you a whole bunch, Papa said, taking my hand and holding it tight in his, almost as if he were afraid he might lose me. He seemed to have regained his senses.

Logo was making a magnificent dish of pasta, and the support teacher was setting the table with that energetic good humor of his, like he was always just about to burst out laughing. I was pleased to see him, although I had no idea what he was doing here. *I invited him*, said Logo, unfurling a new, drugged smile and pointing at him with her thumb. *He's my new boyfriend*, she said, gazing at him as if that was pretty ridiculous.

He looked her up and down, his crooked teeth and steady gaze, and nodded as if she'd said the right thing at the right time. You could see he liked the touch of her words on the skin of his face. *Happy birthday, young man*, he said, making me feel even more a child.

Sit down everyone, it's ready, said Logo, setting the bowl of spaghetti down on the sumptuously arrayed ex-phone cable spool. I didn't hear the blow, but I felt the floor tremble. And Grandpa's shout. IQ was flat on the floor, dead. Dead like a dead man. I felt I was dying too, and without thinking about it I gave a kick to the table, which nearly overturned, causing a couple of plates to fall. And break.

The support teacher was already leaning over IQ, slapping his face gently and massaging him under the nose. He got some water and wet his forehead and temples.

He only fainted, the teacher said, as if that wasn't so out of the ordinary. *He works too hard*, poor kid, Logo murmured, putting a pillow under his head.

It's that it's so hot. Grandpa was searching for the words that would provide a logical explanation. And in fact it was hot, but above all, he looked fearful and seemed wearier than usual.

I sat down and rested my head on the table. I was very tired. I wished I could sleep, or anyway lie down with my thumb in my mouth, without people always trying to improve me and make me grow up.

What's that stink? said the teacher, looking around. There was indeed a strong smell of burnt plastic, and thick smoke was pouring out of IQ's cell. The teacher ran to look. *The big computer is burning*, he shouted. IQ closed his eyes again, as if he hadn't heard.

I managed to turn the power off, the teacher yelled. *Don't breathe, it could be dangerous*, he warned me, opening the bayonet window. Two dark columns of smoke were rising from IQ's superPC, it was pretty stunning.

Throw this on it, said Logo, who had a pot of water in hand. *No, don't put water on it*, he replied, almost as if the suggestion had made him laugh.

Grandpa, all out of breath, then showed up with the fire extinguisher he keeps in his car, and handed it to the other man. *Use this, young fellow*, he said; his hand was trembling. His big thoughtful rabbit teeth exposed, he stared at the thing for a moment and then began to spray foam on the supercomputer. In seconds there was white foam everywhere, even on us.

It seems to have stopped burning, he said when the canister was empty. The smoke was now just a thin fog and the fire wasn't sizzling anymore. My legs suddenly felt like they could no longer support my weight and I found myself on the floor.

Don't lie there little one, it's not good for you, I heard Logo say. She picked me up and carried me to the waiting room, where she laid me on the sofa.

I didn't move, my mind was blank. I knew very well that BUG was no more, but I couldn't think about it, just as I can't think about it now. It was too much for my just-turned-eleven-years-old self. I felt the tears welling up under my eyelids, but they didn't trickle down.

Come on, my man, let's finish eating; nothing irreparable has happened, said Logo, giving me a pat on the back. *Dreaming as usual: I should call you the dreamer bee*, she said, apparently thinking that a little leg-pulling would rouse me out of my slumber.

Without warning, my teeth snapped and sank into her forearm. She shook it hard to try to break free, but the teeth bore down harder, until my temples were nearly exploding. I myself had no idea what was happening. That well-known iron oxide taste in my mouth prevented me from thinking.

Logo was screaming quite loudly. Her howls entered through my feet and ran up my backbone to my head. *Let me go, let me go*, she screamed, backing toward the kitchen. I let myself be dragged, I slithered over the cement floor like an alligator. I was following her without meaning to.

Let me go, you're killing my arm, she begged, the palm of her other hand on my forehead to push me away. She was crying and screaming. *Stop it, you're crazy*, she yelled. Yelled and cried. I wanted to let go but the evil birds in me wouldn't let me. I was actually moving my jaws in her flesh, like dogs do. I was fully lucid but at the same time I didn't understand what I was doing. *Let me go, please!* she shouted.

Let her go, shouted Grandpa, but not so loud.

I don't know why I couldn't unclench my jaws. I saw my mother. I saw her drawn face before she left home under the furious rain, before she let herself be dragged down by the red semi. The pellet stove had gone on strike, Papa was terribly late, and she was not happy with me at all. I had injured her without any good reason, right when she had to go and do battle with death. The bees were dying, they were weeping and dying; they needed her. I had bitten her, I had hurt her again. But it was my teeth that bit her; I didn't mean to. *Let me go!* Logo screamed.

Let her go, Grandpa repeated in a frayed voice.

A steely vise was now gripping my head, as if to detach it from my body. It was my support teacher's arm, I knew that without being able to see it. My teeth, slippery with blood, couldn't hold out, they let go. I thought that was the end of it; I was very tired. But instead, they sought out his wrist and darted instantaneously toward it, they sunk in. I could feel strong bones in my mouth, and my canines coming in contact with them. My teeth were as furious as before. The bones tried to slip away, but my teeth held them tight.

A claw had closed around my temples, and it seemed about to crush my skull. But instead it merely pulled my head away, as if lifting a melon firmly but with delicacy. Suddenly all my strength had evaporated; I could not even stand up.

At that very moment Grandpa slumped face forward onto the table, his chest coming to rest on a plate of spaghetti. He looked like he was asleep.

They tried to revive him with cardiac massage and mouth-to-mouth, but it was useless. He was dead. Really dead, this time. His jacket was stained with tomato sauce and his skin was gray. Now he was lying on the floor, his eyes turned toward

Grandmother, but you could see he was no longer there; he had joined the angels who race against airplanes in the heavens. Not even the doctor who came in the ambulance could make him live again.

NOW YOU WRITE

LOGO IS GAZING AT ME with her topaz eyes, she's probably asking herself what I will come up with next. She thinks all these stories are my inventions—or anyway, almost all of them. She loves me and she doesn't think I'm mentally deficient—but my brain does leap around like a March hare, and there are times when I believe I can fly, and I'm readily bewitched by the moon, she says. But everything I said was true, from poor Grandpa's dive into the spaghetti, to the fire that melted down IQ's supercomputer and killed BUG.

Grandpa is no longer with us and he's left a void as deep as an abyss, and BUG too is gone, even though only IQ and I know that. My cerebral cortex refuses to accept it, and my lungs are also having trouble filling up, but it's the truth, alas.

People who are no longer with us can be quite insistent, they're always chatting away and reminding you of some super pleasant thing that happened in the past, but when you try to approach them they play hide-and-seek, it's like tilting at windmills. It's not a nice experience, you need patience and sangfroid not to just tell them to go to hell, as they often seem to deserve. Now and then you have to ask them to leave you alone, because you have other things on your mind.

Happily the glass is also half full, and Mamma is waking up. She's had enough of sleeping all the time, and wants to get up and drink her caffe latte with a lot of coffee and not too much milk, dunking her bread in it as if to measure the exact depth of the cup. She'd like to forget that awful rainy morning and the Russian semi, and all the problems they caused her and all those other things that didn't go well at home.

Her rebellious curls are impatient for contentious new beekeepers' assemblies and other adventures, and her head is ready to make way for words clinging tightly to one another, as combative as a hotheaded crowd. All the conditions are in place for her to make great progress, it would make no sense at all to give up now.

As soon as she's better she'll buy back the bee families and look after them as she knows how to do so well, dressed up in white, of course, like a super good fairy. And while the bees are getting dusted with pollen, we'll go plant Grandmother on a terraced olive grove overlooking the sea. Because even the most patient of the dead at some point have had enough of a kitchen smelling of frying oil and hypoallergenic dishwashing soap. It will be a sad moment, but she'll console me with her saliva-decked smiles.

We'll miss Grandmother, and she'll miss us, but we'll communicate with our telepathic neurons.

Grandpa is on the top shelf in the waiting room; we'll have to look after him too. He loves mountain lakes and he's always wanted his ashes to be scattered in some lake of our choice. And Papa thinks his book on worms shouldn't remain buried in a dark drawer, it deals with important stuff. Never in a million years would I have expected him to say that. Life is unpredictable sometimes, it just squirts forth wherever it wants to go. And so the worms, too, will have their fifteen minutes of fame. In BUG's case, the problem is that we have no ashes, or rather, they were composed of burnt plastic and they stank. Anyway, the ashes of a digital creature, even the best of friends, contain no soul, unlike human ashes. It would be totally absurd to conserve them, they explained to me at great length, while the setting sun grew redder and redder and IQ, for the first time in his life, seemed to be moved.

In any case, I'm fed up with writing, it's time you did it yourself, Logo says, pushing the keyboard my way. *And there's no need to make that boiled-grouper face, you'll soon learn*, she says, taking my head in her hands and shaking it like a chocolate Easter egg, to see if there's a surprise inside.

ABOUT THE AUTHOR

The novelist, poet, and dramatist GIACOMO SARTORI was born in 1958 in Trento in the Alpine northeast of Italy near the Austrian border. An agronomist, he is a soil specialist whose unusual day job has shaped a distinctive concrete and poetic literary style. He has worked abroad with international development agencies in a number of countries, and has taught at the Università di Trento. He was over thirty when he began writing, and has since published seven novels and four collections of stories as well as poetry and texts for the stage. *Bug* is his second novel to be translated into English by Frederika Randall, along with *I Am God*, which won the 2020 Italian Prose in Translation Award from the American Literary Translators Association and the 2019 Foreword INDIE Gold Award for Literary Fiction. He's an editor of the literary collective Nazione Indiana and contributes to the blog www.nazioneindiana.com. He lives in Paris and Trento.

ABOUT THE TRANSLATOR

FREDERIKA RANDALL was a writer, reporter, and translator. She grew up in Pittsburgh and lived in Italy for thirty years (also New York and London). She worked as a cultural journalist for the *New York Times*, the *Wall Street Journal*, the *Nation*, and the Italian weekly *Internazionale* among others. Her translations include Luigi Meneghello's *Deliver Us*; Guido Morselli's *The Communist* and *Dissipatio H. G.*; the epic tale of the Risorgimento, Ippolito Nievo's *Confessions of An Italian*; as well as fiction by Davide Orecchio, Igiaba Scego, Ottavio Cappellani, and Helena Janeczek. Further translations include historian Sergio Luzzatto's *The Body of Il Duce*, his *Padre Pio: Miracles and Politics in a Secular Age*, for which she and the author shared the Cundill Prize for Historical Literature in 2011, and Luzzatto's *Primo Levi's Resistance*, 2016, short-listed for the 2017 Italian Prose in Translation Award. Her translation of Giacomo Sartori's *I Am God* won the 2019 Foreword INDIE Gold Award for Literary Fiction. Other awards include a 2009 PEN-Heim Translation Grant, and a 2013 Bogliasco Fellowship. She died in Rome in May 2020.

RESTLESS BOOKS is an independent, nonprofit publisher devoted to championing essential voices from around the world whose stories speak to us across linguistic and cultural borders. We seek extraordinary international literature for adults and young readers that feeds our restlessness: our hunger for new perspectives, passion for other cultures and languages, and eagerness to explore beyond the confines of the familiar.

Through cultural programming, we aim to celebrate immigrant writing and bring literature to underserved communities. We believe that immigrant stories are a vital component of our cultural consciousness; they help to ensure awareness of our communities, build empathy for our neighbors, and strengthen our democracy.

Visit us at www.restlessbooks.org